THE INDIANS WARNED
THAT NO ONE RETURNED ALIVE
FROM DEVIL'S MOUTH . . .

Alexander wrapped the tapers and flint in several layers of oilcloth and tied the package tightly around his chest. The tidy bundle wouldn't interfere with his dive.

He clutched a boulder to aid him in his descent and plunged feet first into the bubbling spring water. He sank rapidly.

Sooner than he had expected, he saw the gaping entrance to Devil's Mouth and squeezed through the opening into a narrow passageway.

Suddenly his face was above water. He struggled upward until he could stand. Water swirled about his feet and ankles. The air in the musty chamber reeked of an odor like rotten eggs.

A man could stay alive here. But for how long?

"Claude!" he shouted. The walls echoed the name of his friend.

Alexander undid the bundle tied to his chest and lighted one of the tapers. There was an acrid puff of yellow smoke. Gradually, his eyes adjusted to the eerie, amber light and he looked around him.

Across the ceiling of the tunnel he saw long streaks of dried blood. On the rocks below lay the bones of fingers broken by Indians who'd tried desperately to claw through solid rock.

"Claude, Claude," he whispered.

"*Mon ami*, we are lost," a voice replied.

ALEXANDER MACKENZIE

LONE COURAGE

ALEXANDER MACKENZIE

LONE COURAGE

Published by
Banbury Books, Inc.
37 West Avenue
Wayne, Pennsylvania 19087

Copyright © 1982 by Guy Forvé

Guy Forvé

All rights reserved. No part of this book may be reproduced or transmitted in any form or by any means, electronic or mechanical, including photocopying, recording, or by any information storage and retrieval system, without the written permission of the Publisher, except where permitted by law.

Dell ® TM 681510, Dell Publishing Co., Inc.

A Dell/Banbury Book

First printing—May 1982

Published by
Banbury Books, Inc.
37 West Avenue
Wayne, Pennsylvania 19087

Dell ® TM 681510, Dell Publishing Co., Inc.

ISBN: 0-440-00066-1

Printed in the United States of America

First printing—May 1983

Explorations of
*Alexander
Mackenzie*
1784~1793

Hudson
Bay

N O R T H W E S T

Montreal

Atlantic
Ocean

········ ROUTE TO
THE ARCTIC
------- ROUTE TO
THE PACIFIC

Chapter 1

He'd been staring at people for so long that he decided to rest his eyes by lifting them upward. It was a trick he'd learned in the old country. How strange to think that—the old country. He felt the muscles loosen in his neck, as if they'd been the ones he'd been using to stare with.

His eyes caught glimpses of the morning sun as it penetrated cracks in the large wooden rafters of the ceiling. The rays of sunlight mingled and crossed one another to produce a spider web of light above the crowd. He followed one particular ray downward past the long timbers that framed the massive hall. Down through the beams, the errant ray of sunlight settled on one of the two huge banners that had been strung across the entire room. Both proclaimed welcome, one in English and the other in French. Such, thought Alexander, were the wonders of the New World, his new world. He felt a trickle of excitement run through him once more.

The hall itself was more massive than any he'd ever seen in Dundee, or in Glasgow itself, for that matter. In fact, he assured himself, a structure this size couldn't be found anywhere in all of Scotland.

It was the Central Marketplace. Not the only marketplace, he reminded himself, but the central one. Here merchants operated stalls to sell wares of every description to everyone in Montreal and the outlying districts—pots, pans, fish of all kinds, clothing, scarves, even fur pelts. Every order of things known to man, it seemed, was for sale. One entire section of the marketplace had livestock on display, and if someone had the money, need and inclination, he could buy a cow, a goat or a horse on the spot. There was nothing he could think of that couldn't be bought and there wasn't a single stall without at least one customer.

Today an area of the market floor had been cleared to greet the new settlers who'd arrived on the two ships from the Old World. The arrival of both ships had been anticipated for weeks and an anxious community celebrated now that families were safely united after so treacherous a journey. In honor of the occasion they'd festooned the hall and piled a table high with food and drink. An itinerant fiddler provided music.

When the ships were unloaded the passengers were told that their baggage couldn't possibly be on shore until the next morning and to return at that time. Until then, they were told, they would be welcome at the market on St. Paul's Street. Alexander stifled his impatience at the delay in getting his trunks and allowed himself the opportunity to see a part of the New World.

There had been times during the past seventy-two days when he'd thought he would never see Montreal. The crossing had been far rougher than he'd ever anticipated. The ship that had looked so mighty, so overwhelming in Glasgow harbor, seemed a small craft indeed, once it had put to sea. The waves buffeted it, swept down its decks with a stinging spray of sea water.

And when the ship tossed and pitched, spun and heaved during an angry storm, Alexander felt certain his time had come. He vowed that if they crossed safely, he would never sail the ocean again.

He'd thought himself an experienced sailor, as at home on the lochs and bay waters of his county as he was in his room. He'd navigated through many a white water lashing, but never, never had he experienced so difficult a time on the water as he had these past seventy-two days. It was with great satisfaction and even greater relief that he first caught sight of the harbor of Montreal.

The idea of participating in festivities at first didn't appeal to him. He was anxious to be about his business immediately. But when he realized he had nowhere to go until his trunks were unloaded, he more willingly joined the welcoming party. After his first plate of prairie chicken and a cold glass of cider, he was more than happy that he had. He relaxed and became his old curious self.

He noted that the crowd of welcomers and new arrivals had separated into two distinct groups, one French and the other English. Each group stayed under the banner that welcomed the arrivals in their native language, as if the signs were boundaries beyond which no foreigners could pass. Except for their language, however, the newcomers in each group were indistinguishable. Shabbily dressed, most of them had slept in the clothes they'd worn the night before. Dresses on some of the women sagged no matter how valiantly they tried to pin them and men's coats were seas of wrinkles. Colors had no rhyme or reason to them.

Those welcoming the weary travelers looked more prosperous. Many of them even sported beaver hats and beaver collars, which were the very latest fashion in all of Europe. In eager groups, they descended on a new arrival and stormed him with a barrage of questions. They wanted to know where he and his family came from—not the country, but the county, the village, the grange. And if they were from such and such a place, did they know so and so? Or if they were from north of there, had they ever heard of such and such a family?

At various times from different parts of the party, happy shouts of recognition rose above the general chatter. People were hastily called to join the group, and strangers of five minutes earlier turned out to be long-lost cousins or friends of friends someone had left behind in the Old World years before.

Watching them, hearing them, seeing their excitement at news of loved ones or beloved places, Alexander suddenly realized how lonely the lives of these settlers, so hungry for the most meager report from their old homeland, must be. He determined then and there never to let this happen to him. He wouldn't ever allow his past to get in the way of all that he dreamt of achieving in this new world. He had too much to see and more to do. With a swift surge of Scottish resourcefulness, he summoned his courage and put the heather and purple hills of his native land out of his mind. But like the burr that was in his speech, so was Scotland and all that was Scottish locked in his heart.

When he'd decided to set sail for Montreal, he'd realized he'd be leaving behind him every family comfort, every kindness and every gibe of the quirky villagers, every familiar smell, taste and sight his young life had known. He'd been willing to trade it all for the unknown. Thirsting for adventure, he'd sought a new horizon beyond his native mountains and the sea.

Now he had to reckon with his new world. It's people swept through the marketplace in an array of clothing he wouldn't have seen in Glasgow town in a year of Sundays. Some were no more than ragamuffins with their leather trousers pulled in every direction under their greatcoats of beaver and muskrat. Others strode resplendent in starched collars and long ash-grey morning coats, they held their arms high and at the proper angle as they escorted their wives and families about the hall. No one seemed to mind the incongruities of dress. And when a fur-covered ruffian stood in the path of a finely tailored gentleman, Alexander noticed the ruffian was not obligated to give way. He noted, too, that he would have to learn more of the manners and ways of Montreal, if he were to succeed.

Success was the reason he'd traveled so far. Success at something he hadn't been able, for some while, to put into words. That the New World held many opportunities for an ambitious lad of good character and love of hard work, Alexander was sure. He knew it. He felt it. But he needed a sounder reason to act upon it. He could not, as his townspeople would say, follow any flutter in his heart. No, like any good Scotsman, he had to have a practical purpose too, in leaving the land of his youth. That he found in the fur trade.

Booming and growing with each passing year, the fur trade had created the greatest demand for any one single item that the world had ever known. For one hundred and fifty years, the public demand that no manufacturer could meet was for beaver—beaver for hats, beaver for collars, beaver for trimmings on coats of any fashionable design. No proper gentleman would ever appear in public without his beaver hat, and in the year Alexander sailed to Canada, the Hudson's Bay

Company alone exported to England enough beaver fur to make over half a million hats. And that was just for England.

Furthermore, the most insatiable demand for beaver was creating a demand for furs such as marten, fox and otter as well. All of them were found in great abundance in North America, where many men were getting rich beyond their wildest dreams. Success stories were endless, and even the tallest of invented tales had a hard time matching the true ones. Alexander read everything he could find on the flourishing commerce in furs and the fortunes to be made, for he'd found his reason. He resolved to sail for Canada.

The final and most convincing argument for Alexander's resolution was his discovery that in eleven months of trapping beaver a man could earn upwards of five hundred dollars. It seemed incredible to him that a trapper could earn so much while his father, a skilled carpenter, worked eleven hours a day, six days a week, and earned ten times less, a mere dollar fifty a week.

His mind was set. He wouldn't become a trapper, but he would find work in the fur trade. For, he reasoned, if the lowest man on the ladder commanded such a wage, those who traded in the skins must earn considerably more. He wrote to Joseph McGill, a Scotsman who operated a fur trading business in the recently conquered British territory called Canada. Beyond this simple information, he knew nothing else. A year and one week later he heard from McGill. The message was terse and to the point. "Come to Fort Montreal, an island on the shores of the St. Lawrence River. Present this letter and you will be given suitable employment." That was it. No more, no less. But it was enough to change completely the course of Alexander's life. It took him two years more to save enough money for the passage. And every night for two years he fell asleep with the same dream—a dream of the New World, of Canada, and fur.

Alexander stood apart now at the party, but he was hardly unnoticed. He was, as a matter of fact, the object of many whispered conversations. Any unattached young men were highly prized in this young town, and because of his good Scots looks, Alexander attracted more than one long, lingering stare. He stood well over six feet tall, but his big frame, his broad sweeping back and muscular shoulders made him seem even taller, more imposing. Brawny and well-built, lean and sinewy, he exuded virility, good ruddy health and indomitable power. His legs were long, and his expansive chest narrowed into a trim, well-defined waist.

His hair, thick and heavy, flowed back from a wide brow in hues of tan and blond as variegated as a sandy beach. Deeply set under his highly arched brows, his eyes were as blue as a sunlit northern sea. But they flashed with fire when he was angry and turned a tragic grey when his Scottish soul fell melancholy. Both demon and angel danced in those eyes as he'd been told many a time when he was a boy in Glasgow.

Although his complexion was fair, his high cheekbones held a tinge of ruddiness that came from his long exposure to the sea and the wind. His nose was straight and his chin cleft. When he laughed, which was often, dimples appeared on his cheeks and his face became vital and animated.

Yet it wasn't his handsome good looks, his laughing face or bright flashing smile that set Alexander apart from most of the other men. An easy charm, apparent wit and a spirit that was constantly enchanted by life combined to give Alexander a self-confidence that so many other men his age lacked.

Nor was Alexander unaware of the whispers and stares. At first he thought it might be his clothes, but he reassured himself, he was no more outlandishly clothed than anyone else. Then he thought it might be his manner. He had a habit of drifting away from a place into a daydream or pensive trance. Only today he was attentive to every detail, every activity and enterprise of his bustling new land. Confused by the scrutiny of strangers, Alexander couldn't fathom its cause. More embarrassingly, he didn't know how to react to it all. Occasionally he would try to catch and hold the stare of some woman's eyes, but he was always seconds too late. The woman would quickly avert her gaze.

Then, one woman did not. Her candid eyes held him fast when he turned his own to meet them. They were beautiful eyes, alive with wonder and surprise, and as luminous as the early autumn sunlight that haloed her soft, lovely face.

She was French. Of that he was certain. He'd read of the French, and he'd heard stories in his town of merchants who traveled to the French cities of commerce. The French, he'd concluded, were more open, friendlier than the Scots, and the young ladies more exquisitely feminine. Yet this was no typical colonist's daughter, protected and demure, as far as he could see. Her candor and the independence of spirit in her gaze arrested him, while something more indefinable fired his imagination and took his breath as he looked at her.

Her face was a perfect oval with high cheekbones, a straight and narrow nose, and a mouth that curved delicately into a dimpled smile. Her rouged lips, he thought, held the promise of both sweetness and

8

innocence when she let her eyes, as bright and green as emeralds, fall from him. A widow's peak dramatically set off the golden brown arcs of her eyebrows and accented her flawless Gallic complexion. She was petite and young, but it was apparent that she would grow into a tall and slender woman of remarkable beauty. Alexander noticed the swell of tender breasts and rounding hips under her fashionable dress.

He could not quite believe that here and now, on the first day of his arrival in Montreal, he was in the middle of an adventure with of all people, a beautiful French girl. Her aristocratic good breeding and refinement impressed him, but her boldness and openness did take him aback somewhat. Nevertheless, he felt that since he had been so forward as to hold her gaze, he must be the gentleman and approach her properly. Above all, he reminded himself, he must be a gentleman.

Her bonnet, Alexander noted, was trimmed with beaver. So was her taffeta dress. Taffeta was a fabric he knew well, as he had often helped his mother unroll yards and yards of it whenever she started a new outfit for one of her shop's customers. Its drape and perfect fall down to her ankles told him it was expensive taffeta at that. The wide border of pleated ruffles around the hem was raised slightly in front to show off her white kid boots. Around her shoulders she wore a shawl, its color the same pale pink as her dress. It reminded him of the delicate pink found inside the seashells on the beaches near his home.

As their eyes met Alexander opened his mouth to speak, but she'd already prepared what to say.

"Everyone else is staring at you, so I decided to see you up close. For myself." She was smiling, for she had gracefully covered her boldness with a joke.

Beautiful, beautiful indeed, thought Alexander. He had been right, too, about her being French, for her accent proved it.

"Do I frighten you?" he asked.

"No. Should you, sir?" Delight more than laughter was trapped in her playful words, for she'd heard a wondrous sound. That accent of song, Alexander's lilt so musical and so foreign to her ear, composed a moment she knew she would never forget. She almost blushed at her warm response to it.

"And . . . ?" he asked with a smile of his own.

She turned to him slowly, hoping he wouldn't notice how flushed she was sure her face was. "And what, monsieur?" she asked.

"Was I worth your staring?"

"I do not know . . ." she began as if she were going to tease him, but she was interrupted suddenly.

"Juliette! What are you up to?" A square, small man, not much older than she or Alexander, grabbed her tightly by the arm.

Alexander started forward as if to protect her, but then realized this dull, rather unpleasant man must be in some way related to her.

"I've come to fetch you," he continued.

"Oh, Marcel. I'm perfectly fine without your concern." Alexander was relieved that he'd taken no steps toward the interloper, for it was obvious from her tone that he was a brother or cousin. Their manners, however, were so contrary that any family resemblance was not apparent unless one looked closely, for she was slender and playful, whereas this Marcel seemed bovine and sly. It would not be hard to dislike this person, thought Alexander. As soon as he thought it, he as quickly resolved, for the hundredth time, not to be hasty in judgment.

"It's Mama who is concerned, not I," Marcel singsonged in a childish manner that made him all the more unappealing, and Alexander felt compelled to speak up.

"We were merely joking with one another. No harm was intended." Alexander's own words made him angry with himself. For no reason at all, he had put himself on the defensive and he deserved whatever happened.

"No harm? Of course, no harm was intended. I am aware of that, even knowing you are not French, monsieur," Marcel replied haughtily.

"There are those of us who are less than fortunate." Alexander swallowed his pride in an effort to be gracious. His determination to be the gentleman overcame his infamous fiery Scottish temper. Nor did he want to spoil his entry into this new world. And he was much taken with Juliette. As he watched a sly smile appear on Marcel's lips, Alexander decided to do what was only proper.

He introduced himself. "I, sir, am Alexander Mackenzie from Dundee, Scotland."

"And, I, monsieur, am Marcel Dentere. I believe you have already had the privilege of speaking with my sister, Juliette Dentere."

"Monsieur," said Juliette as she curtseyed.

"Milord. Milady." Alexander acknowledged each of them with a slight bow from the waist.

"And now," said Marcel, "now that we are properly introduced, allow me—"

Before Marcel could finish his sentence, Juliette

broke in. "Oh, Marcel, you are so, so like an old man."

"Juliette, I am going right now to tell Mama how you're acting. Showing off this way in front of a stranger, making—"

"Excuse me, sir," said Alexander very calmly. The relationship between this brother and sister, who acted with each other as if they were still small children, baffled Alexander. He could excuse Juliette, but Marcel's behavior hardly befitted a man. "Perhaps we can all go over to your mother and father." Although he didn't want to stop talking to Juliette, Alexander could think of no other way to rid themselves of her brother.

As they crossed the great floor, Juliette held Alexander back a moment. "Please," she whispered to him. "Overlook my brother's zeal. He means well, but for him there are only two kinds of people in Montreal. In Canada, I should say. There are those who are French and those who are not."

"And what of you, Juliette?" shot back Alexander. "Do you think there are only two kinds of people in Montreal?"

"No," she replied. "Now I think there are three."

"Three?"

"Yes, three. The French, the not French, and the Scotlanders."

They laughed together. So it was that Alexander met Juliette's parents with a smile in his eyes and laughter on his lips.

Alexander knew in an instant that Papa Louis and Mama Marie were as charming as their son Marcel was boorish. Their warmth and good nature put him at ease long before any words were spoken.

When Marcel had finished with the introductions, Juliette added, "You forgot, Marcel, to tell them that Alexander is not French." Her quip prompted a round of genial laughter that didn't please Marcel.

Most of the good-natured banter that followed was lost on Juliette. She was not so intent on what Alexander was saying as she was entranced by how he was saying it. The timbre of his voice, the slow pitch of his rolling r's and flattened vowels mesmerized her. His face, too, its handsome features and strong, decisive lines, captured her attention. She read a powerful will, determination and redoubtable spirit in those lines, and she tried as best she could not to be too obvious in her admiration of this remarkable Scotlander.

Her behavior was not lost upon her father, however. "Were both of you a little older," he said, referring to Alexander and Juliette, "we would be asking you your intentions with our little Juliette."

Juliette flushed and Alexander reddened. "Is this a custom of the New World?" stammered Alexander.

"No, no," boomed Papa Louis. "It is the practicality of a French father who has a beautiful daughter."

"You must forgive me, sir, if I seem rude, but I have just arrived this morning. My ship has docked only now." Alexander was at a total loss for words.

"Then you have not yet had an opportunity to see our beautiful Montreal Island?" asked Juliette's mother, coming to his rescue. Her question told Alexander that he had no need to apologize, and that he was most welcome to her and her family. More important, it told him that she liked him.

"Of course, he has not, Mama," replied Papa Louis. And to Alexander he added, "Don't think all of

Montreal is what you've seen of St. Paul's Street. There is much, much more.''

"That's the street you took from the docks to here," explained Juliette.

"I assume, monsieur, you will be looking for work?" asked Papa Louis. He was a giant of a man, imposing, and he twisted his long handlebar mustache at every opportunity. Most likely, thought Alexander, he spent a good part of each morning waxing it.

"I've already found my work, sir," answered Alexander. "I sailed under the sponsorship of Mr. Joseph McGill and as of now I am in his employ."

"McGill has taken to that, has he?" Papa Louis asked the question of no one in particular. "I told you, Mama, they would bring their own kind in, didn't I? They must have found new territory. Fertile new territory. More than we expected." Fiercely twisting and tweaking his mustache, Papa spoke as if Alexander weren't there. Then he asked Alexander, "Were there many of you on the ship?"

"No others I'm aware of, sir. Are you also in the fur trade?" Alexander inquired.

They all laughed. Again Alexander reddened, but his embarrassment quickly turned to anger. This family is too quick to laugh, he told himself. Aloud he said, "You mustn't laugh, I've told you I've newly arrived and know nothing of your land or yourselves."

"We're not laughing at you, Alexander. We're happy you've made Papa a little humbler than he was this morning," said Mama Marie.

Papa Louis wasn't merely in the fur trade, Alexander discovered, but was indeed almost half of it. He and Alexander's employer, McGill, between them owned and controlled the vast Canadian fur-trading empire.

14

Their rivalry in the search for new territories, new grounds, new sources of beaver, fox and marten to meet the ever-increasing demands, was as fierce as it was legendary.

Papa Louis was the managing director of the Hudson's Bay Company, a company fabled even in Alexander's native Dundee. The very ring of its name opened bank vaults as easily as it did new trading outposts. This company dispatched fearless men thousands of miles into unknown terrains, across uncharted rivers and over unheard-of mountains to have them return laden with the bounty of fur pelts, with reports of natural phenomena too beautiful to describe, with stories of mysterious regions too frightening to explore and with bleak tales of greed and revenge.

The Hudson's Bay Company was the adventurer's mecca. To the young man impatient for wealth and success, it was the door to golden opportunity. One nod of the head of one director could make that man rich beyond his needs forever.

And here was Alexander talking with the director of all directors, the man who could offer any courageous, young adventurer new worlds to conquer.

" 'Tis I who am humbled, sir," stuttered Alexander. "I did not mean any disrespect."

Juliette felt tears rush to her eyes as she witnessed her proud Scotsman's helpless bewilderment. She wanted so much to run to him, to reassure him, to tell him that Papa was after all, only Papa and not to worry. At the same time, she also felt that she'd been privy to a glimpse of her father's world, a hard world of hard men doing hard things. She wanted Alexander to be strong enough to withstand its rigors and her father's. Holding her breath, she tried to will all of her strength into him.

Marcel, too, noticed the effect of his father's disclosure on Alexander. "Perhaps you would prefer to do as many of your English compatriots are now doing. You could apply to Papa for a job," he gibed.

"I have an agreement already with Mr. McGill." Alexander was almost whispering. He was exhausted and had suddenly begun to feel the toll of the difficult ocean voyage.

"So many of your English cousins have been coming north since the American revolutionaries drove them out. Our office must have need of an English-speaking clerk. No, Papa?" Marcel was enjoying keeping Alexander frazzled.

The insult of considering Alexander for clerical work found its mark. His face fell. He was, however, in no position to argue with the director of the Hudson's Bay Company or with his pouty son. "If you would excuse me," he began.

Juliette whirled on Marcel with sibling hatred in her eyes. "Marcel, you are very rude!"

Weary and distracted, Alexander lamented his unfortunate entry into this new world. The family of the most powerful man in the territory was squabbling because of him, his ignorance and ineptitude. He told himself that he was serving no useful purpose in being there and that he had to get out of the hall and into his lodgings at once.

But Alexander misjudged the largess of Papa Louis, especially toward a man who had caught his daughter's fancy. He liked Alexander, and at that moment he may have even liked him a little more than his own son.

"Clerk? Clerk!" boomed the bass voice of Papa Louis. After a loud laugh, he continued, "You say clerk, my son? Why, I think with the proper schooling

16

in the matter, Monsieur Alexander could lead a rendez-vous for me with great ease." He paused for full dramatic effect. "What do you think about that, my son?"

Marcel drew in his breath. Contradicted by his father before everyone, he retreated and hid behind a look of smug disbelief. "I don't believe it. How about that?"

Juliette and her mother, on the other hand, seemed most pleased and quite surprised by Papa Louis' dictum.

Alexander had understood little that had been said.

Juliette took her father's rebuke of Marcel and praise of Alexander as a personal triumph. She knew already that her interest in Alexander was not simply a momentary curiosity and she read the promise of future in Alexander's generous smile. Her father's implicit approval of the Scotsman bolstered her own feelings about him. For hadn't Papa told her since the time she sat on his knee that he and he alone was the true judge of men and horses? Associates, friends, friends of friends and distant relations traveled miles to seek his opinion of a new mare as often as they did to learn what he thought of a prospective son-in-law.

Alexander remained silent. Juliette knew that Papa being Papa expected some acknowledgment of his compliment from Alexander. So she dropped both her gloves and her shawl onto the dirt floor. It was a remarkable ploy, but somehow she managed it. As she and Alexander both stooped to gather them up, she whispered to him, "Tell Papa thank you."

As Alexander handed her the gloves and shawl, Juliette reinforced her cue by saying sweetly, "*Merci, monsieur.*"

"You are most welcome," Alexander replied to

Juliette. "And sir," he said to Papa Louis, "you are most kind to say these things about me."

Papa Louis accepted his awkward expression of gratitude with a large smile that made Alexander wonder all the more what in thunderation everyone was so happy about. The nature and extent of the compliment still eluded him.

Mama Marie at that point changed the subject in the simplest of fashions. "Are you pleasantly surprised by our warm weather for this time of year, monsieur?" she asked him.

"It's a kind of warmth I am not at all familiar with," answered Alexander, relieved to be on more certain ground.

"That's because we're surrounded by water," explained Mama. "The water in the air makes the heat cling to you. I rather like it myself."

"And yet," Alexander responded, "I notice shawls and scarves on most everyone. That seems peculiar to me."

"That, my lad," stepped in Papa Louis, "is because our weather is only as constant as a young girl's heart. It changes by the minute and sometimes twice within one beat of the heart." He chuckled at his analogy.

Papa Louis' remark bothered Juliette, who worried it might be a reference to her. Papa, however didn't pursue it. "Are you up for a bit of a tour?" he asked.

"Papa, he's just now arrived. Let's save the tour for another time, after he's had a chance to rest."

"Nonsense, Mama. When I came here, I walked almost thirty miles no sooner than my ship had anchored."

"I would like a tour," answered Alexander heartily.

"Well, Marcel here is a bit of a teacher and guide."

Papa Louis turned to his son and asked, "Marcel, why don't you take Alexander for a small look at the town? And you can show him our new home while you're at it."

"May I go too, Papa?" Juliette asked so rapidly that she even surprised herself.

"What if the weather turns colder, Juliette? You're not at all prepared," warned her mother.

"Go, my Juliette. Go. Enjoy Marcel's chatter. But two things. If you see it's going to storm, I expect you home immediately and not driving us half-crazy with worry like the last time. And keep these two rascals off the river. It's not the time for sailing."

"Do you tell that kind of thing to your trappers?" asked Marcel.

"I tell them to behave or . . ." Papa Louis made a thrashing gesture with his hand and began to laugh. Soon everyone was laughing as well.

Amid bows, handshakes, adieus and good-byes, the trio set out on their tour of Montreal. Marcel, a rather unhappy guide, led the way.

Chapter 2

Marcel turned out to be a man of many answers. Eager for information about the town, the fort, the harbor, Alexander asked question after question. The one he did not ask, however, concerned the meaning of the compliment paid him by Papa Louis. Although it still baffled him, he resolved to be patient and to question Marcel or Juliette about it at a more opportune moment later on.

Marcel was at first reluctant to talk of Montreal. As they walked in the warm September sun, though, Marcel's love of his city warmed him into conversation. He pointed out Mt. Royal, the mountain which gave the city its name. Although it had been discovered by the proud Frenchman Jacques Cartier over two hundred fifty years earlier, the region was left unexplored, Marcel told him, until Samuel Champlain reached the area a century later. The original settlement was called Fort Montreal. As it grew, the Fort was dropped and Island was added.

"You can still tell the oldest families," Marcel clued Alexander, "by what they call our city. The old guard still calls it Montreal Island." For Montreal was an island surrounded by two rivers, the quiet Quebec and the treacherous St. Lawrence, a waterway often as wild as the ocean and running, at times, almost ninety miles wide with a fierce current to the Atlantic. It was two islands, in fact, for the settlement of Fort Montreal had spread northward to include Market Gate Island as well. Marcel promised Alexander a short sail to Market Gate that very afternoon.

The street they were walking on, St. Paul's, had first been no more than a dusty trail, but it had soon become the busiest street in the thriving village. Marcel pointed out the stone walls and pillars that had once held giant gates. The settlers had erected the barricades to protect themselves from the hostile Hocheloga Indians, who, like the friendlier Iroquois and Huron, were native to the area. The walls, however, did little to prevent the American colonial army from occupying Montreal during the revolutionary war against England. When the American troops departed after three long years, they left behind them the remarkable invention that Marcel now pointed out to Alexander. It was the printing press that had been brought to Montreal and erected there by Benjamin Franklin, the American colonial statesman and scientist.

Alexander was all eyes and ears. Never in his wildest fancies had he imagined he would see the sights he saw that day. Indians with feathers in their hair and paint on their bodies strode through the city streets. Men in fur caps and greatcoats looked less like men than giant bears. Carriages larger than some cottages he knew glittered in the autumn sun. And everywhere he turned, he saw things for sale, from pots and pans and straw bonnets to a huge orange food that men thumped and women prodded. Fresh fish swam in great barrels of water, while others were strung out to be smoked or fired. Had his life depended upon it, he couldn't have identified half of what he saw, heard or smelled. To Alexander, Montreal represented everything and more that he'd dreamt the New World would be. He had dreamt, and now he had arrived at the very center of the great northern fur trade.

As they continued up St. Paul's Street, they entered a more genteel, sophisticated part of the city. The limestone houses of wealthy fur merchants lined both sides of the broad street. Marcel pointed out the mansion of one merchant who'd been a water carrier when he first arrived in Montreal. Alexander could only try to envision the lavish interior Marcel described, its plush furnishings and velvet drapery and black walnut floors that servants had to wax every day. Marcel added that he, of course, had been a guest there on many occasions.

Alexander eyed the bookstores. He found their presence incredible for books, a rare and priceless commodity in Dundee, were a luxury he couldn't believe anyone could afford. They passed a theater. Alexander had no idea what a theater was and he listened red-faced as Juliette and Marcel shocked him with details of its libertine entertainments and rowdy clientele.

Alexander's responses to the novelties of Montreal fascinated Juliette. If he had at first seemed to her a man of unbounded experience and worldliness, she now saw that he was also a country boy, naive in many ways and unfamiliar with city life. She admired him all the more, because he admitted his ignorance and strove to overcome it at every step with unceasing questions.

Marcel managed to shock Alexander again when he steered their party into a small shop that Alexander at first took to be a tavern. Although Alexander was by now very hungry, he was more concerned for Juliette. No self-respecting young lady he'd ever known would dare set foot in a tavern, let alone sit down in one with two men to have drink and food. This was one custom of the New World he would choose not to accept, he told himself.

His fears, however, proved to be unfounded, for several other women sat at the neatly laid tables and the shop served only tea and cake.

"Didn't you eat at the marketplace?" asked Juliette.

"I'm afraid I don't remember. I think not."

"If you're hungry, you should speak up. I would have taken you to a shop that served more substantial food," said Marcel, surprisingly civil.

The teahouse suited Alexander fine. It was another first, but he did not tell Juliette and her brother that. "Do you believe," asked Alexander, more relaxed, "that this is my first day? My very first day in the New World and here I am sitting in a proper teahouse with two friends showing me my new home. If you believe it, convince me, as I still cannot."

"But, my friend," Marcel rolled the r in "friend" in an attempt to imitate Alexander, "it will be ending soon. But end it we will on a high note, for I will now take you upriver to Isle d'Normandin. It's a place, I assure you, like nothing you've ever seen before or will ever see again. An entire island of traders—fur traders, Indian traders, merchants and madmen. So finish your cake and tea and we'll hire a ketch and hoist a sail."

"Marcel," interjected Juliette, "we promised Papa we wouldn't sail the river. It's much too treacherous now. Don't you remember?"

"Oh, Juliette, if we only did everything we promised Mama and Papa . . ." He ended his argument with a conspiratorial wink that he hoped would silence any further protests from his sister. "Besides, there's something there I have to do for myself."

"But, Marcel . . ." persisted Juliette. She felt herself on the brink of yet another heated argument with her brother. Quarrelsome words were common enough between her and Marcel, but she wanted to avoid them in Alexander's presence.

"If you are frightened, you child you, stay here. We men will be back within the hour, just enough time for you to have another pot of tea. Unless you, too, are frightened, Alexander?"

"Of a river crossing? No. But if Juliette thinks it dangerous, you mustn't risk anything on my accord." He looked at her for a long time, then smiled.

From that moment on, there was nowhere Juliette would not go for Alexander.

"I am making too big of something we do very very often." She spoke softly, but Alexander heard more than acquiescence in her voice and saw something more wondrous than the New World in her eyes.

Marcel laughed. "But you must tell me," Alexander pressed him, "is it truly dangerous?"

Annoyed and flustered, Marcel insisted both of them accompany him outside. "Look. Look at the sky," he demanded. "Tell me, do you see storm clouds? Do you see any cloud? *Mon Dieu*! If you children wish to stay home, I repeat, I will return within the hour."

"We'll come with you, Marcel. I want to see and do as much as I can in this new land of mine."

"*Your* new land, hey? *Yourrs*? Well, you do move fast, Scottie. Let's go then, before all the boats are let."

By midafternoon of his first day on land after more

than ten weeks at sea, Alexander found himself once again on water. Sitting peacefully in the bow of a sailboat, he surveyed the city of Montreal and drifted into his dreams.

He'd come to Canada for the riches to be gained in the fur trade, or so he'd told his family and the villagers when he'd decided to leave the farms and beaches of his home. Wealth was a reason, but not truly his dream. His real dream he hardly dared admit to himself. For he dreamt of discovery, of exploring new lands, of charting the first routes into vast territories and opening up an unknown world for all who dared to follow. He would return to Dundee with his name on a river, a mountain, perhaps an entire territory. In the New World, the name Mackenzie would never die. Immortality, not riches, was his unspoken dream. And he couldn't believe but that it would come true.

A soft wave ripped through the river. It lifted the boat, then dropped it with a loud wet splash that wakened Alexander from his reverie.

"We are some tour guides, my brother and I, to have put you to sleep." Juliette slipped into the seat beside him.

She'd been studying Alexander's face while he daydreamed. At first stern and filled with misgivings, it had by degrees become soft and tender, and loving she thought. To the young girl she was, loving was still without passion or driving needs. It meant openhearted affection, innocent laughter and touching.

Yet some half-fear that he may be committed to someone back in Scotland, wherever that was, troubled her. Her girlish imagination had been captured by this man-boy, for he was as much a man of boundless resources as he was a schoolboy embarrassed in situa-

26

tions beyond his experience. Mostly, though, she was happy that they'd met and had had the afternoon together. She had only to share him with Marcel, and he didn't count. Still, she dreaded the moment when Alexander would tell her of some lovely girl waiting for him on his native shore.

"I wasn't sleeping," answered Alexander. "I was counting my blessings."

Before Juliette could comment, Marcel interrupted. "Better start counting something else, because look what's headed our way."

Both Juliette and Alexander looked up at the sky. It was terrifying. Though bright blue sky spread behind them, leaden grey clouds rolled into an inky black menace directly in front of them. It meant one thing only—storm.

"How far is this island?" shouted Alexander.

"I overshot it because I was looking to spot a friend's boat. So now we have to double back and it will take a good forty minutes."

"Can we get back to shore any sooner?" asked Alexander. He was beginning to take charge.

Marcel tested Alexander. "Out of the question. Do you have an aversion to getting wet?"

"Then I think we'll be getting wet," replied Alexander, giving no indication he'd heard Marcel's taunt.

"I hope that's all!" shouted back Marcel with as much derision as before.

"I'm frightened. Don't joke, Marcel, please," pleaded Juliette.

"No need, Juliette. You're acting like a child. We've been through storms far worse," Marcel tried to calm his sister.

"Besides," chimed in Alexander, trying to lighten

the mood, "nothing can happen to me on the first day of my new life."

Juliette smiled and Alexander offered her his hand. She clasped it tightly, but nevertheless she was still afraid.

"Do you see land? Any land will do. A shore?" Alexander yelled to Marcel.

"No. Nothing." Marcel's voice was strained, irritated. Alexander feared Marcel was starting to panic.

Alexander knew what had to be done and searched the ketch for lines and floats. The river had begun to swell, its waves rolling deep blue, then purple, then black. Battling the rising wind and the pitch of the boat on the ebony waves, Alexander crawled along the deck.

"We have to lower our cloths!" he shouted to Marcel. Marcel, however, was frozen in fright. His arms wrapped tightly around his legs, he'd curled himself into a ball of helpless manhood.

Lowering the sails was a two-man job. No matter how strong Alexander was, he needed help. Juliette stood ready, but the driving rain and spray had soaked her dress so thoroughly that she could hardly move under its cumbersome weight.

The waves were pounding the sides of the boat at heights of almost twenty feet. They flooded the deck as they tossed the boat headlong into the raging storm. Slowly, Alexander worked his way toward the immobile Juliette. With no time to spare for modesty or decorum, he began tearing at the heavy, drenched taffeta. For a moment, Juliette thought Alexander had lost his senses. She looked at him in horror and uttered a little gasp. When she realized his purpose, however, she overcame her modesty and assisted him in loosening the unwieldy dress.

To be heard over the howling winds, Alexander had to press his face to hers. "Do you know how to uncloth a mast?"

"Uncloth? What does that mean?"

"This. This is a cloth." Alexander seized the sail to illustrate. "We have to pull it down from this pole or else we'll capsize."

"I know nothing of boats. Marcel . . ." Her voice trailed off.

Marcel was incapable of doing anything. He'd vomited and his skin had gone as white as the breaking water. He tried to move, but then, weak and shivering, he returned to his crouching position. That fool, that fop, thought Alexander.

Shouting instructions to Juliette, Alexander struggled to lower the sail inch by torturous inch from the mast. When he had worked it more than halfway down, a blast of wind assaulted the boat and cut the sail into hundreds of ribbons.

Alexander fought to control the wheel against the rising wind. He'd lashed it as best he could when wells of water surged over the bow and thundered over him and the valiant Juliette.

"We're being pulled into the rapids!" she cried.

The boat swirled in the river's treacherous currents. It shot up thirty feet, then crashed down into the white water. Then up, again, ever higher and back down. Everything loose aboard it flew over the side. The three passengers clung to the mast and each other for their lives.

The storm had darkened the day pitch-black. The winds, increasingly intense, ripped through the waves and flattened their plumes so that the river seemed to have swelled high beyond its normal level. The boat rose even higher than before. For a split second, it sat perched on a mountainous wave. Then, in a furious blast, the wind struck. The boat careened toward the frothy water. Flat on its side, it landed in the fierce current of the river.

All three of them clung desperately to the sides of the boat. Marcel's face was pale with terror. Alexander looked over to Juliette and she gave him a small, wan smile. He was very proud of her, very proud.

Like a wounded sea lion, the boat slowly began to right itself. Marcel managed to clamber aboard while Alexander hoisted Juliette back to the relative safety of the upright deck.

The three of them lay sprawled across the floor of the boat as it coursed wildly downriver. Borne on the crest of wave after wave, it slammed down to meet the river harder and harder each time.

Juliette and Alexander watched in horror as Marcel rolled twice across the flooded deck. The boat dived and the next thing they saw was Marcel treading the river's water as furiously as he could. Juliette moaned in despair for her brother.

Alexander raced to secure a line around his waist, then made a turn with it around the mast. He timed his leap overboard almost perfectly, but not perfectly enough. Although he cleared the boat, he struck a barrel floating in the river with such force that he felt his chest collapse.

He was seized by a spasm of coughing. A violent pain cut through his stomach and lungs. Within minutes he was spitting and coughing up blood. The icy river water numbed him. Desperately he tried to catch his breath and to spot Marcel as he treaded the turbulent water.

Marcel clung to a loose timber. He was yelling to Alexander, but the wind and the pounding water drowned his cries for help.

Slowly, painfully, Alexander worked his way to Marcel. Then he dived underwater. He managed to avoid Marcel's thrashing legs and to tie a line under his shoulders. Alexander kicked his way clear of Marcel, who in his panic might have sunk them both.

Somehow he had to signal Juliette to pull on the line encircling the mast. Any instructions he would shout to her, if he had the strength to shout, would be lost in the wind. Nor was there any certainty that she would have the stamina to pull Marcel in. For the moment, he could only hope to keep Marcel from floating too far from the boat. Ideally, Marcel would pull himself along the taut line back to the boat, but fear had paralyzed him.

The pain in his chest, the bitter wind and rough water were taking their full toll on Alexander. Summoning up the last of his strength, Alexander lifted himself out of the water onto the bow of the ketch. A crashing wave propelled him aboard and he landed face down on the deck.

He couldn't move. He tried to raise his head and fell into another fit of coughing. His blood speckled the deck floor.

"Alexander," Juliette called to him. "Alexander." Desolate, she moaned. *"Mon Dieu*, Alexander, *mon Dieu.* Is Marcel lost to us?" She was inconsolable and great sobs came wrenching from her. In her despair she failed to notice how extreme Alexander's injuries were.

Alexander raised himself to one knee. He pointed to the line, still secure around the mast. "We must pull,'' he said. But it took him such an effort to speak that he wondered how he possibly could.

He and Juliette pulled together, hand over hand over hand. Whether the current was with them or Marcel was swimming with the line, they were able, finally, to pull Marcel to the boat. With fierce determination and the last of their strength, they yanked Marcel onto the deck. He was water-logged, cold, exhausted, barely conscious and numb.

Alexander lashed Marcel to the deck. He still had to secure a line around Juliette. Trying to ignore the excruciating pain in his chest, he inched his way toward her.

The storm battered their powerless craft with fury and rage. Jagged streaks of lightning rent the black sky and thunder roared off the horizon. Rain pelted his face and body. The wind screeched and ripped at his clothes. Pain tortured his every movement, each one sending a stab more acute and fierce than the last coursing through his chest and brain. But he had to reach Juliette.

''I'm so scared.'' She could barely whisper and had to struggle for breath. ''We're going to be pulled to the ocean and die.''

''We don't have time to be scared, my bonnie lass.'' Alexander held her in his arms as he fitted the line over her hips. ''You've been wonderful, an inspiration. You are my strength. And we are miles away from the ocean.''

Juliette started to giggle. She was becoming hysterical. Alexander held her at arm's length, then slapped her across the face as hard as his own pain would allow. His action brought on a spasm of coughing he couldn't control. He coughed and spat blood until he was nearly doubled over with pain. He had to fight for his breath.

Juliette snapped to attention. "Alexander, don't die. Don't die. For if you do, we are all surely doomed."

"I'll not die, my Juliette. Not today, not on my first day. Not on my first day." He repeated the words over and over as he fastened the life line around Juliette's waist.

The three of them now secured, Alexander sank wearily to the deck. At the same moment, the swollen tide swept their craft to its most towering height and a furious blast of wind spun it completely free of the water.

"God save us, we're flying like birds!" screamed Marcel.

The boat crashed down with a roar. At every seam, every joint, it broke apart. In minutes their sailboat was shattered beyond recognition.

They clung to fragments of the riven deck. Alexander offered Juliette an outstretched hand. She clasped it tightly and together they were carried down the stormy river. Propelled by the current, Marcel might have passed them and been lost, but his line snagged on Alexander's decking. They were still three, but now they were all three in the hands of Providence.

Alexander could do no more. The water, ice cold and swirling, kept him from screaming out his pain. It had become an intolerable weight on his chest and he had to battle it for every breath. He could hear Juliette moaning, but he could do nothing to comfort her. The storm continued to rage, and he thought he heard Marcel, terrified, pray.

Then he sensed a modulation in the roll of the waves. They rose more gently and the winds began to slacken. He didn't want to allow himself the luxury of hope but it seemed the storm had passed. Their make-shift raft, three fragments of decking joined by their hands, seemed to have settled into a milder rocking movement. It was over, he told himself, and had he had the strength, he would have given a triumphant shout at having withstood this nightmare of nature. As it was, he could only manage a smile. Every muscle in his body relaxed and he gave in to his own need at last. He fell asleep.

Several hours later the squawks of ducks flying directly overhead awakened him. His head cleared instantly, but his body wouldn't react to its commands. He couldn't move for the sharp daggers of pain that pierced his entire frame. His arms and hands were numb, for he'd fallen asleep with both arms outstretched and his hands clasping those of his companions. As he loosened his grip, he awakened both Marcel and Juliette.

Alexander tried to speak, but from his lips, swollen and flecked with dried blood, came only a crackling sound. Again he tried to ask Marcel and Juliette if they could see a shoreline. Again his utterance was incomprehensible. Nor could Marcel and Juliette make sense of each other. Instead, the three of them joined their hands and laid their heads as close as possible to the wood of their makeshift raft.

For the entire morning they didn't lift a hand or head, as they bobbed along the gentle, nickel-colored river. Had it not been for a small hunting party of Hurons, they might have drifted into oblivion.

The storm had propelled them forty miles down the St. Lawrence almost to Quebec. It had been no fiercer or more disastrous than any of the dozen or so storms that struck the river that autumn, as they do in the fall of every year.

Three days later, after being dragged, carried and carted through thickets, brush, beach and village streets, the three survivors, more dead than alive, were delivered to the Dentere mansion.

Chapter 3

When Papa Louis met the Indian party and saw the wretched condition of his children, he acted with all the decisiveness that had made him director of the Hudson's Bay Company. He thanked God for returning his children to him from heaven and dispatched servants on his swiftest horses to Au Claire Hospital. Within the hour a team of surgeons had arrived at the Dentere house.

Upon examination the doctors determined that the young Scots friend of the Denteres had suffered the gravest injuries of the three. His entire rib cage had been crushed and several ribs were broken. One bone had pierced through the skin. Another had punctured a lung, which, if their diagnosis was correct, had collapsed.

When the Huron had first found Alexander, he was scarcely breathing. His skin was cold and clammy and almost as blue as the sky. No matter how many blankets the Huron had wrapped around him, they hadn't been able to warm him. Then their village medicine man had strapped him to three poles to keep him immobile and he applied a poultice of herbs and roots on his chest. After that he'd wrapped Alexander tightly in deerskins.

The Huron medicine man had probably saved Alexander's life. But he still needed expert medical attention quickly.

While the doctors conferred, Mama Dentere prepared a room for Alexander. She chose the upstairs sitting room. The vaulted ceiling of this vast, square room was lavishly decorated with white plaster cornices, moldings, and panels inset with ovate plaques and cherubs. From its center hung a magnificent, shimmering crystal chandelier. Tall and majestic windows stretched from the floor upward. Their drapery matched the pale, sea-foam green of the walls. A huge fireplace, its grand mantel and carved columns cut from white and grey marble, dominated one entire wall of the beautiful room. A fire burned constantly in its hearth. The rugs on the wide-planked walnut floor were a dark forest green. Mama Dentere had a giant bed placed directly in its center for the courageous Scotsman who'd saved the lives of her children.

Marcel could not, would not speak. He stared blankly into space for hours, first in one direction, then another. He suffered from exposure and lacerations. The life line that Alexander had fastened to him had left a deep rope burn around his waist.

"A small price to pay for life so sweet," Papa Louis kept repeating. When he thought of what the consequences would have been had Marcel had no line, he would look to the sky and cross himself urgently.

Juliette was the first to show signs of recovery. Although she would rather not have been confined to her bed, she was happy simply to be home and, indeed, to be alive. Her eyes shone. Through lips that were cracked and swollen to almost twice their normal size, she made joyful sounds. With chapped and swollen hands, she applauded the attentions of her doctors and nurses, her family and friends.

It was decided that Alexander needed an operation. Although the procedure was dangerous, Alexander could not be moved to the hospital because of the nature of his injuries. Especially critical was the rib that had broken inward and pierced his lung, collapsing it. The surgeons would first have to slice into the rib cage, then cut off the rib and lift it out of the lung. Once they had patched both the lung and chest, they could only hope that nature would take its course and heal the vital tissue. They would also have to work very rapidly because Alexander could not sustain a great loss of blood.

The Dentere household, which had already been mobilized to take care of the three survivors, now took on the appearance of Au Claire Hospital. Extra help was hired to assure Alexander full care during his operation and recovery. The doctors worked quickly and silently over the high bed in the grand upstairs sitting room, and when they had completed the difficult surgery, their message was terse but sweet. Alexander survived the operation.

Within days of each other, both Marcel and Juliette were eating solid foods and able to walk about. Alexander, however, remained unconscious. No one could say definitely whether his ribs had begun to knit properly or if they were still splintered. All anyone could do was continue to apply compresses. His condition continued to be of great concern to the entire Dentere household.

Both Marcel and Juliette spoke in detail of their adventure. From their accounts, it was clear that Alexander was the sole reason they were still alive. As the picture of his deeds emerged, growing more and more heroic, Marcel became more and more sullen. Alexander's strength and bravery only called more attention to Marcel's own inabilities, his helplessness and terror in the face of danger. Marcel began to resent Alexander and soon he truly disliked him. He convinced himself that had he and Juliette been alone on that boat, he would have acted as quickly and performed as resourcefully. He would have saved the life of Juliette and reaped the honors that now went to Alexander.

For almost a full week, Alexander showed no signs of improvement. Although his color was less ashen and his raw, burned skin had started to heal, his breathing hadn't improved at all. Nor had he awakened from his deep sleep.

Papa Louis' concern grew more intense daily. He decided to send a wagon far to the East, almost to Quebec for a specialist in these matters. The wagon returned without the doctor. He felt he could do nothing more than had been reported to him. He offered no other advice but to be patient, because for nature one had to wait.

And they did. Juliette did more than wait. She sat by his bed all day every day. She changed his compresses and arranged to have a barber shave him. She watched. She prayed.

And then Alexander opened his eyes. He focused with difficulty, but no matter how hard he tried, he couldn't determine where he was. When he tried to move, he couldn't. He was paralyzed.

A cold sweat enveloped his body. He couldn't move and all his dreams seemed to die in that awful moment. He could feel his body, but he couldn't make it work. When he tried to call out, his throat and tongue and lips resisted his brain's command. He tried to touch his mouth, but he couldn't raise his hand.

Then, suddenly, a seizure gripped him. Nervous spasms tormented his entire body. Minutes later his eyes closed tightly and he drifted back into a feverish sleep.

No one was there the first time Alexander awoke from his coma. The second time, though, Juliette sat by his side. As soon as he was able to adjust his eyes to the light, he saw her lovely face. He thought he must still be dreaming, but this was an enchanted dream with her luminous beauty at the center of it.

"Alexander, Alexander. You're awake! Blessed Virgin, Mother of God. *Mon Dieu*!" She was ecstatic. As quickly as her warm tears fell on his face, her fluttering soft hands dried them. "Mama. Fetch Mama, Mariou. Alexander has opened his eyes."

He thought he was smiling from ear to ear, but the happy grin he felt was no more than a wry twitch. He tried to speak, but again he couldn't. Nor could he raise his hand to her face.

Juliette saw the panic in his eyes and felt the tension in the muscles he strove to command.

"Try not to exert yourself. Don't move, Alexander. They've put straps on you, all over you, so you wouldn't hurt yourself," Juliette tried to assure him, but the words were lost on him.

Soon, Alexander felt a cool cloth being pressed upon his mouth, around his lips and his gums. He welcomed its relief.

Once again, he tried to speak, but he was capable only of an incomprehensible gurgle. He fell back exhausted. He surrendered once more to sleep. For the rest of the day and night, he slept.

41

Rough hands awakened him. They were pulling at his face, then moving his slack jaw up and down, gyrating it, flexing it. His throat seemed less parched and his mouth less swollen than the last time he'd awakened, but still he couldn't move. He seemed to remember a last time, although he had no real recollection of time.

"Where is this place, please?" Alexander surprised himself with the sound and ease of his speech.

"You're in the home of Monsieur Louis Dentere." After a long pause, the voice added, "In Montreal." In another long pause the stranger continued to massage Alexander's throat and chest. "In Canada." Then the strange voice asked, "Do you understand? *Comprenez vous?*" The voice was taking no chances with language.

"Yes," crackled Alexander.

"I'm Dr. LuClerc. You have had a bad experience. You are better, no?"

"Juliette?"

"Fine."

"Marcel?"

"Fine, too."

"Will I be able to move again?"

Dr. LuClerc was confused. "What do you mean, move again? Of course, you will move again. Don't you want to move again?"

"Why can't I move now?" groaned Alexander.

"Of course, now, you cannot move. You've been strapped to the bed."

Alexander strained his neck to get a glimpse of the wound, white sheets that bound him to the bed. He heaved a sigh of relief and felt his muscles relax.

"Can you take them off, please?" asked a jubilant Alexander.

"We put them there for a very specific reason. It might be dangerous to remove them so soon." The doctor had started to waver.

"Off! Take them off, please," demanded Alexander.

LuClerc did as he was asked. Alexander slowly and deliberately moved each of his limbs in turn. With more strenuous effort, he shifted his entire body upward. He waited for the pain, the intolerable pain in his lungs and chest. But it didn't come. He was sore and weak, but the pain that had plunged him into his long, feverish sleep had disappeared.

It was another two weeks before he took his first steps away from what everyone had feared would be his deathbed. Too slowly for Alexander came the day that he was able to leave his room and take his first brief walk with his beautiful Juliette. When they reached the foot of the staircase, he could not contain his excitement at the prospect of walking the grounds of the Dentere mansion. Juliette, however, insisted they save an outdoor adventure for another day.

About that same time, Papa Louis himself visited Alexander. He thanked him profusely for saving the lives of his children and offered him his hospitality for as long as Alexander wished, certainly for as long as it took him to recuperate. Furthermore, Papa Louis promised Alexander he would help Alexander in any endeavor he chose to pursue. Alexander did admit to Papa Louis one all-consuming fear.

"Don't worry about McGill. His offer was only one of many jobs available."

"I had my heart set on it. It was all I hoped for, for three long years now."

Papa Louis strode around the bed like a bull. He wanted this exceptional young Scotsman to realize fully the extent of his gratitude, so he shouted. "Whatever position you were to be offered with Northwest, I assure you Hudson's Bay will match in service and in salary."

Alexander was taken aback by the kindness of this powerful man.

"You're most generous, sir. I assure you I will earn every—"

"Of course you will, of course you will," interrupted a calmer Papa Louis. "But you, too, are a benefactor indeed. You've given me my children's lives, and for this I cannot thank you enough."

The first walks outdoors were short. Alexander and Juliette would stroll to the end of the lane that swept up to the grand Dentere house and then come back again. When the days began getting shorter and the weather brisker, their walks got longer. They spent more and more time together.

He and Juliette gathered blueberries by the fistful and he grew fond of blueberry everything. He savored the rich smell of the plump, ripe apples in the Dentere orchards and the scent of maple leaves thick upon the ground.

Smooth, round chestnuts that crackled and popped when they were roasted over an open fire fascinated him. He tasted freshly made cider, pumpkin pie, corn pudding and fresh trout.

With Juliette as his guide, Alexander explored every foot of the Dentere estate. Here was a mighty chunk of Canada, larger, thought Alexander, than his entire home town. Neither of them ever tired of the vistas that stretched out before them. Dusk filled the vast and awesome sky with every color on an artist's palette and fell over the wide expanse of deep green woods as overwhelming in their majesty as in their mystery.

Winter came with a long, silent snowstorm.

"Early," said Papa Louis.

"Late," said the groundskeeper.

"Right to the minute," said the groundskeeper's grandson.

Juliette and Alexander didn't debate its timing. They reveled in its effects. Knee-deep in snow, with drifts coming up to their hips, they walked far into the wilderness. They found an old sleigh and took turns pulling each other along forest paths and across frozen ponds. They sleighed down hills. They laughed. And they talked.

Incessantly, they talked. Old tales, village gossip, any sudden memory or thought they shared with each other. Alexander learned more about the fur business from Juliette. She'd listened well to her father's stories. She repeated, too, the lessons in the fur trade that her father was teaching Marcel. It was Juliette who explained the compliment that her father had paid Alexander and that even now he didn't understand.

"How could you understand? You didn't know what a rendezvous was."

Juliette explained how each year, in order to keep in touch with the trappers spread out over the territory, trading companies like her father's would meet or rendezvous at a prearranged place, usually at the fork of two giant rivers or at a waterfall or large natural clearing. From far and wide, the trappers would gather at this landmark sometime in midsummer, when the trapping naturally came to a halt. The rendezvous saved the trappers a great amount of time because they didn't

have to move out of their general locale. Nor did they
have to face a torturous trip back into the wilderness
laden with a year's weight of supplies.

For the trading companies came not only to meet
the trappers and buy their pelts, but also to provide
them with food, guns, whiskey, ammunition and any
other staples necessary for their survival in the wilds.

At first the rendezvous served mainly to bring
together two different breeds of men in the wilderness.
It was a crude meeting between the trappers who didn't
want to return to civilization and the trading companies
which had moved their headquarters out of the wilderness. As trapping and trading in furs became more and
more lucrative, the rendezvous became more refined.
Companies like Northwest, Hudson's Bay and Lisa sent
regular caravans of wagons to carry to the trappers their
necessary supplies and to carry back all the fur pelts for
which the goods had been traded. The rendezvous had
grown to become not only the trading event of the year
but also, for the trappers, its social event of the year.

So, when Papa Louis had said that Alexander could
easily lead a rendezvous, he'd been acknowledging in
him the many traits and skills required to lead so important a venture. More than at any time before, Alexander
longed for the opportunity to prove that Papa Louis'
faith in him truly was justified.

Juliette fired Alexander's imagination further with
the tales that trappers had to tell. More than one of them
had been left to die after a vicious grizzly bear attack,
but nevertheless had crawled ten miles to an Indian
camp where he was nursed back to health. Then he
had tracked down the ferocious bear and killed it. All
these proud and weather-beaten men in her father's

employ had extraordinary stories to tell, for they had battled nature, sometimes tamed it, and survived.

When the gentle snows of early winter gave way to raging blizzards and shrieking arctic winds, Alexander and Juliette were forced inside. As much as the doctors wanted Alexander to walk, they feared consumption even more. A congestion in his lungs and one fit of heavy coughing would undo in minutes what nature had accomplished in the long months of healing.

In a wing off the main house, Juliette and Alexander sat in front of the roaring flames in a fireplace that stretched from the planked floor to the high ceiling. They drank tea spiked with cinnamon bark and ate overstuffed sandwiches, while outside the winter raged in a frenzy of wind and ice and snow. And they continued their unending conversation.

Alexander described for Juliette the sweeping landscapes of Scotland, the heaths and hills of heather. He recounted childhood tales of ghosts and eerie spirits that roamed the land. He told her, too, of restless kings and brokenhearted queens who wandered forever through the highlands because they'd found so little peace in the world.

Then he spoke to her of the New World, of strange and wondrous things even she had never heard of. He knew of Indians in the hinterlands who practiced strange rites and unutterable customs. For hours he described to her mountains of clear salt or of crystal, cliffs imbedded with jewels, villages where gold nuggets lay on the ground like fallen chestnuts. He'd heard of the Fountain of Youth and of California Island, a vast, green land of tropical fruits and eternal warmth that rose out of the Pacific Ocean. He told her of unicorns, elephants covered in wool and beavers seven feet long. Marvelous were the tales of this New World.

As the days passed into weeks, the two of them stirred each other's imaginations and fed each other's dreams. They wanted to discover these lands, these Indians, these animals for themselves. They believed they would, if only spring would hurry.

Juliette recounted her father's stories of great mountain men who'd become legends in their time. She spoke of the almost immortal Champlain who opened more trails and discovered more trapping grounds than any man who ever lived.

They sat together every day and entertained each other with stories of people and reports of worlds beyond the mountains of Montreal. Every day, too, without either of them realizing it, each became more and more woven into the fabric of the other's life.

When they joined the family for dinner each night, they were equally inseparable. Often Papa Louis would chastise them for whispering or for exchanging a secret smile or a knowing look. Marcel contended that they acted like schoolchildren and should stop being so silly.

Nevertheless, Juliette seemed to have worked magic on Alexander. He had recovered his strength with extraordinary speed and he became more limber and more spirited every day.

Juliette had fallen in love. Alexander had become her reason for being. She had only one concern that fall and winter, and that was to be with him, to take care of him. What had begun as an obligation, "After all, Mama, he saved my life," had turned into an unashamed passion.

Toward the end of the coldest days, when the sun

had started to linger a little longer, Papa Louis surprised Alexander at dinner one night.

"You're feeling much better now, Alexander? I can tell." He didn't wait for an answer. Alexander had learned that when Papa Louis made a statement in the form of a question, he didn't expect an answer. "The color has come back to your face. You move with ease. In a month or two, perhaps you'll be better than when we found you."

"Will you throw him back then, Papa? He's eating us out of house and home!" complained Marcel.

"Marcel!" reprimanded Mama, shocked. No one at the table knew how to react.

"I'm joking, Mama. A jest. You know that, Alexander, no?"

Alexander nodded yes.

"How sensitive we all are. He won't break, you know."

"Marcel, you are a better trader than jester."

"Thank you, Papa." He singsonged his answer. Then shaking his head back and forth, he resumed eating.

"When I first met you," Papa Louis continued as if there had been no interruption, "I told you that with the proper training you could lead a rendezvous."

"I remember, Papa," Juliette put in quickly, for she sensed that something very good was going to come of this conversation.

Everyone smiled. Alexander put down his spoon. He was eager to hear every word his benefactor was about to say, for it might alter the course of his entire life.

"In a few months from now, our company will be leaving for a major rendezvous with several hundred of our trappers and anybody else out in the woods who wants to do business with us. It will be a very important rendezvous for us, because this season we have new and powerful competition." He was savoring the undivided attention he was receiving from everyone at the table, although Marcel tried to feign nonchalance.

"Although the rendezvous is several months away, we must begin making our plans now. That is what I want to discuss with you this evening."

"I feel honored, sir." Alexander had learned the courtesies of the household well.

"But first, I must have more soup. Mariou, this soup is delicious, like your mother's. One more bowlful, *s'il vous plaît.*"

"Oh, Papa, proceed please," said Mama impatiently. She voiced the sentiments of everyone except, of course, Marcel.

"The simple point of the matter is, I've decided to take Alexander along on this very important rendezvous."

"Instead of Marcel!" blurted Juliette.

"Together with Marcel," corrected Papa.

Juliette's remark went unnoted by everyone but Marcel, and everyone but Marcel virtually cheered. Even Mariou smiled and patted Alexander on the back as she passed by him.

"Sir, I don't know how to thank you for this opportunity." He felt his life had now begun. It had been launched in a most spectacular way that leapt over years of apprenticeship in the McGill or any other organization.

"No, no thanks are necessary. It's a small price to repay . . ." He let the sentence drift, as anyone in his household would know how to finish it. "There'll be a lot to learn."

"I'll do it, sir."

"I know you will. Marcel has offered to teach you as much as possible in the weeks that are coming. It's most generous of him, no?"

"It is indeed. I thank you for that offer, Marcel."

Marcel remained silent. He merely smiled slightly and raised his wineglass in a vague sort of salute.

"And I can help too," said Juliette, already feeling cut off.

"You've helped more than enough already by bringing him back to health."

"If there's a way to be of more help, my Juliette will find it, I'm sure," added Mama.

Did she know, wondered Juliette. Does it show so much, my love for Alexander? "Thank you, Mama," replied Juliette softly.

A fire seemed to have been lit in Alexander, for he felt a glow from within him spread upward and outward until his entire body was tingling from it. If man had been meant to fly, at this moment he would be soaring far above the Dentere home, over Montreal, over all of Canada.

He was going on a rendezvous. He was going to be a part of something most men only read or dream about. He would journey to enchanted lands and travel over legendary places. Maybe he would stumble upon the city where gold lay glittering in the streets. He would see amazing plants and fabulous animals. But, most of all, he would be in the world of the trapper.

There would be no sleep tonight, he knew that.

What faith Papa must have in him to offer him such an opportunity. Perhaps, if he learned his lessons well, he would be leading the next rendezvous just as Papa had predicted.

"Alexander. Alexander. Are you so excited you cannot eat?"

He turned to face Juliette. "Yes, Juliette?"

"I've been calling you, but you've been off somewhere."

"He's on a rendezvous," laughed Marcel as he arose and left the table.

So, too, were the other Denteres leaving. "There's nothing wrong with being excited, Alexander," Papa said. "I would be disappointed if you were not." With that he disappeared into his study. Mama followed closely behind him.

Juliette stayed with Alexander at the table. He poked at what food was left on his plate. A hundred questions darted through his mind, yet he couldn't form one to ask. With a deep breath, he tried to calm his churning insides.

"I've never seen you like this."

"I . . . My apologies, Juliette. This is an opportunity beyond my belief that your father has given me."

"Only three short months ago, you knew nothing about rendezvous, and now, now it's so important to you?"

"Of course, Juliette. Of course, I knew nothing of it. It isn't something you read about in books. It's something you live, something you learn about by training and working in a business. Your father is taking a chance to bring me along. I must be worthy of his faith in me."

"You're making something so big out of this rendezvous. I thought Papa had other things in mind tonight."

"Juliette, you're changing your tune. Only a while

back you told me how big a compliment your father paid—"

"I changed my mind, Alexander," she interrupted him. "Isn't that permissible with you?"

"I don't want to let him down, or myself." He added, "Do you think Marcel truly will help me?"

"Of course, he will. Why shouldn't he?" She seemed continually more irritated by their conversation.

"Because," confessed Alexander, "I don't think Marcel likes me at all."

"Oh, Alexander, what do you say? He owes his life to you. That's just his manner, you'll see. He'll help you. Marcel isn't at all a mean person. He may act silly sometimes, but he isn't mean. Of course, he likes you."

Juliette's defense of Marcel made Alexander feel that he'd struck a very sensitive area. It seemed to prove to him that she knew Marcel didn't like him. Before he could press the matter further, she changed the subject.

"You'll have so many difficult things to learn," she remarked.

"I must read all about Indians. The ones you can trust and the ones you can't."

"I'll help you," she offered contritely.

"And plants. Which are poisonous and which are not. There will be no doctor in the caravan, will there?"

"I'm not sure, Alexander."

"Mechanics. I must learn how to fix a wagon when it breaks down. That will be expected of me, won't it?"

"I don't know that either."

"Aiee! I'm forgetting the most important thing. I

must learn about furs. That's why we're going, isn't it?''

"I'm sorry, Alexander, I can't answer you.''

"Juliette! You told me you would help me and now you know nothing?''

She was silent and almost as panicked as Alexander. Both of them thought the priceless opportunity her father had given Alexander was slipping through his fingers.

Juliette began to cry quietly.

He began to pace. "Perhaps I should admit that it's too much too soon for me.''

Again there was a long silence.

"My mistake is that I haven't strayed from this house in all the time I've been in Canada. I should have been out to see the world for myself.''

"No, Alexander. Don't say these things.'' She was patting her face dry.

"In all the time I've been in Canada, I've been only to two places, the marketplace and here. How can anyone expect—''

"Juliette! Alexander! What's wrong?'' Mama had left the study and discovered the two of them anxious and tense. "Have you two been fighting?'' You're getting more like brother and sister every day. What's wrong? Answer!''

"I . . . I'm afraid the opportunity I've been given . . .'' Alexander couldn't find the proper way to begin.

"Alexander thinks he cannot learn enough in so short a time to be of help on the rendezvous,'' Juliette said all in one breath.

"Yes. That's it,'' he confirmed.

"Nonsense,'' Mama rebuked him. "You'll learn

more than enough to be helpful to Papa, you mark my words well. Marcel will show you everything. He's very clever, your brother, Juliette."

"Are you certain, Mama . . ."

Again she interrupted. "Now you're asking silly questions. Stop this ridiculous worry and learn a little every day. It's not as hard as you imagine."

Alexander was right about one thing, however. That night he got no sleep.

Chapter 4

During the ensuing weeks, Alexander realized that his apprehensions were far out of proportion to the actual demands of the situation. By no means did he have to learn all that he'd cut out for himself, everything from covering a wagon to trading at the rendezvous. He also realized even more fully what an enviable opportunity Papa Louis' offer was. It would give him a firsthand look at life in the raw, untamed wilderness. Furthermore, he would be able to study it from the protection of a wagon caravan filled with any provisions he might need. Most important, he would be surrounded by men with experience, men from whom he would learn what books could never teach him.

This particular rendezvous, Papa Louis had told Alexander, would be the most ambitious the Hudson's Bay Company had ever attempted. Marcel took time out from his day to tell him why.

A bold, new venture, this rendezvous would be the first in an area called the Great Northwest Territory. The supply of prime furs in this territory was reported to be as bountiful as the pelts were fabulous. Trappers who were unafraid to try new lands had pushed into this vast region in their constant search for new trapping grounds. Although they guarded their finds with their lives, others had followed and the network of trappers had expanded.

So it was that the Hudson's Bay Company would not be the only one at this rendezvous. It would be competing with the Northwest Trading Company of that Scotsman McGill, with Lisa Furs, which was owned by a Spaniard, and with an American firm called Astor Furs. Along with these four established companies would be numerous independent agents and Indian traders.

This particular rendezvous would differ from all others, too, in that its distance from Montreal was far greater than any before. To compensate for the time it would take to get there and back, the actual trading time would be shortened by one entire week. Also, as many extra men as possible were being hired so that work shifts could be cut. Alexander was not pleased by these irregularities. He would have preferred a normal rendezvous with which to begin his career.

At first, Juliette resented Marcel for taking up the time she ordinarily would have been spending with Alexander. When she finally realized that Marcel was only doing what Papa had asked him to do, she resigned herself to the situation. She saw Alexander only briefly at dinner. Occasionally more lucky, she might have an hour alone with him afterward.

No matter how much she missed Alexander, she couldn't but admire the changes in him. He was more alert, quicker than ever before. Bursting with the events of the day, he was eager to share them all with her. She enjoyed listening to every detail of his daily work and training. As his excitement over his prospects grew, so did hers. Her regrets were twofold. She couldn't supplement what Marcel was teaching him and she would be unable to accompany Alexander on this grand adventure. She constantly threatened, in a joking way, to hide behind a sack of potatoes and come out only when it was too late to turn back.

Juliette and Alexander devised a more feasible plan by which she could follow him on every step of his journey. He would keep a journal.

Each night after the rendezvous wagons had made their circle for the camp and before he went to sleep, Alexander was to write in his journal everything he saw and did that day. If he found a strange and exotic plant, he was to press it between the leaves and preserve it for her. If he encountered a strange beast, whether awesome or harmlessly small, he must sketch it for her. He would catalog every detail of the landscape and record every event along the way. When she read it, she would take his journey with him.

Yet, for all his outpourings, Alexander kept one thing from Juliette. He withheld a major disappointment, which was the job he had been assigned on the caravan. Juliette often asked him about his specific duties on the rendezvous, and when he could dodge her questions no longer, he made his responsibilities sound a bit more important, slightly more grand than they actually were. He could only hope that Marcel wouldn't explain to her exactly what he would be doing on the caravan.

He was being trained to grade pelts. Although he obviously lacked the experience to work as a master furrier, he did feel he might be employed on a less rudimentary level. No experienced trapper would damage the pelt of an animal when capturing and skinning it. If he did, he would be cutting his profits considerably. A pelt marred by buckshot holes or a knife slash was next to worthless.

The experienced trapper would wade into the icy water of a river, pond or swamp until he found the water deep enough to be effective. There he would set the only trap knowledgeable trappers used, a Newhouse trap. The Newhouse was so designed that when an animal stepped on a disk in the center of the trap, steel jaws snapped shut and springs on both sides of them flew up to lock the jaws in place. The jaws were smooth so as not to pierce the animal's skin in any way and the trap held the animal underwater until it drowned. Once his traps were set, all the trapper had to do was check on them every few days, recover a forty or fifty-pound beaver and then repeat the process. The trapper might, however, find only a bloody paw in his trap, for the one drawback to the Newhouse was that it allowed animals with a strong instinct for survival to gnaw off an imprisoned foot and escape.

When the trapper brought his pelts to the rendez-vous, he would spread them out for Alexander's inspection. As a grader, Alexander would report which of them had cuts, holes or even bruises, imperfections of any kind. Once Alexander had graded and separated a trapper's pile of furs, Marcel, Papa or any one of the other directors would set a proper price for each of the pelts.

That wasn't all, however, that Alexander had to learn in order to grade furs. For no matter how perfectly a trapper captured his animal, he might damage the pelt in other ways. To finish his pelts, the trapper had to attach the skin to four pieces of strong wood and then stretch it as far as he could. After stretching it, he had to scrape it with a rough stone and at the same time allow no twist or bend to mark the nap of the fur itself. If a trapper was careless, tired or drunk, he might stretch the pelt too far or scrape it too hard and thus decrease the value of the fur.

Detecting any blemishes in the hide or fur and discerning which pelts had been thinned out too much was a tedious and exhausting job. Just when a grader felt he could easily spot the bad skins from the good, he might misjudge an entire lot. "Be careful, Alexander. Learn this part well. These men would sooner shoot and skin *you* if they thought you were cheating them out of money," Marcel warned.

As Alexander became immersed in the process of grading furs, he began to doubt his early dismissal of it as a simple duty that could easily be performed by anyone else. What he was learning, it seemed to him, was often complicated and certainly essential. After all, he reasoned, his judgment ultimately would affect the profit the company would be making on the furs. He finally came to the conclusion that his assignment was hardly a mindless job. And the more seriously he considered it, the greater seemed its demands, its challenge and opportunity. After he'd lived with his conclusion for a while, he told Juliette.

Spring came suddenly. For Alexander, more invigorating than the season, more thrilling than budding dogwood trees and forsythia, were the preparations for rendezvous. For Juliette, though, every day of that glorious spring brought her one day closer to the sad day when Alexander would leave for the northland and she would have to say good-bye.

The wagons for the caravan were being assembled in a clearing behind the main offices of the Hudson's Bay Company. A thick rope strung to four sturdy poles

squared off the entire huge area. The size and number
of the wagons surprised Alexander. He'd never imagined
they would be so massive or grand. Without their white
canvas coverings, their hoops of steel arching high
above the buckboard bottoms, the wagons reminded
Alexander of the skeletons of mythological beasts that
had made their way to a sacred and secret burial ground.

Guards were posted night and day around the square.
Only upon recognition was anyone allowed to pass
under the rope and approach the wagons.

Alexander was introduced to several of the sentries, all of whom carried long guns. They studied
Alexander's face and walk. They instructed him not to
try to pass by any sentry who didn't know him because
he easily could be fired upon.

This was the second time Alexander had been
warned he might be shot. Whether it was a bullet from
the gun of a trapper who felt he was being cheated or
one from the rifle of a guard who failed to recognize
him, he didn't like it at all. The Hudson's Bay Company certainly had its share of quick-triggered adventur-
ers to contend with. Maybe, he thought, that's what
made the fur trade so exciting.

As he walked with Marcel past each wagon, Marcel told him what supplies each wagon would carry to
the rendezvous and what stock it was expected to carry
back. Marcel informed him, too, which men would
handle what cargo, which blacksmith would attend to a
particular team of horses, even which horses were assigned to which wagon and why.

Marcel's store of information reminded Alexander
that he himself was a mere beginner and it made him
feel like a simpleton. Although Marcel wasn't much
older than he, and an oaf in many ways, Marcel was

very much further ahead of him in the business of furs. Alexander could see now why Papa Louis suffered Marcel's lapses in good taste and humor. He suffered them gladly because he relied so heavily on his son's knowledge and acumen.

Alexander viewed Marcel with new eyes. Certainly he'd saved Marcel's life, but here was Marcel offering him a wealth of learning and information so that he could pursue his goals and dreams. And he had had the nerve to think that Marcel resented him, his abilities. What abilities? How blind and ridiculous he'd been. Marcel knew more and could do more in this business than he could hope to learn in ten years. His chances for success and those imagined millions suddenly dwindled in his mind.

"Aren't you feeling well?" asked Marcel. He noticed that Alexander had flushed.

"I'll be all right, good friend. But perhaps I could be alone for a while, to sort some matters out."

"Certainly, good friend! Ha, ha," laughed Marcel. "Scottie, you're full of surprises. Now I'm your good friend." He turned at the next wagon, before Alexander could reply. It was just as well.

Alexander stayed away from the dinner table that night. When a servant came to fetch him, he dismissed him courteously but firmly. He had to come to terms with himself, his prospects and inadequacies, and with Marcel and the world. Reality that afternoon had shattered his dream.

For three whole days Alexander avoided the company of everyone. He could confess his doubts in himself to no one. Nor could he untie the knots in his stomach. At night he would awaken suddenly from a fitful sleep. He'd thought he had so much to give and nothing to learn. Blindly he'd followed that flutter in his heart, only to discover his own futility. Unless he could overcome his shortcomings, he, like so many others before him, would fail in this challenging new world.

Then he remembered a childhood verse he'd learned in school. It would serve him until he regained his faith and control, until he was certain again of his direction and goals. He could almost hear his Latin teacher reciting it from Martial, "Live each day as if it were your last and learn as if you would live forever." He would, because he couldn't stay in his room forever.

Juliette was waiting for him when he finally opened the door of his room. As she walked with him down the long, carpeted corridor to the stairs, neither of them spoke or even acknowledged each other. When they began to descend, she stopped, turned to him and said, "I've missed you, Alexander."

"I'm sorry, my Juliette, but I needed to be alone."

"Has Marcel frightened you so much about the trip? What's expected of you? What—"

He held up his hand to silence her. He was hurt, he was angry. Her mistaken assumption that he had been scared by mere stories rankled and offended him and he struck back.

"Juliette! You're such a child! Marcel was right. You're just a silly child." He spat it out. He spoke with all the fury he could muster and Juliette turned swiftly on her heels and rushed into her room. He could hear her crying.

Early the next morning, long before anyone else had risen, Alexander slipped out of the house. He wakened Joseph, the blacksmith, to take him to the wagons. As they neared the large, roped-off square, Alexander didn't even wait for the carriage to stop. Instead, he leapt off it and approached one of the sentries to whom he had been introduced.

Recognized and admitted, Alexander walked the campground slowly. He peered into each wagon to determine what cargo it carried. He was often surprised. One wagon was filled with locks and flints, powder, lead and long .60-caliber rifles. He picked one up gingerly. He studied the tooling and inscription along the stock. "Made by hand, in St. Louis, America," it read, and farther down, "by the Hawken Brothers." It was a heavy weapon. He returned it to its open case.

"I know what you're thinking. Yes, they came all the way from St. Louis, America." Marcel startled him, for he had slipped out of nowhere and then read his very thought. "For this rifle," continued Marcel, as if nothing extraordinary had happened, "a mountain man will trade fifty, maybe sixty prime skins."

Alexander remained silent. He was still recovering from Marcel's sudden appearance.

"Making up for your little holiday, *mon ami*?"

Still Alexander said nothing. He had barely moved a muscle since Marcel had encountered him.

"The Hawken Brothers rifle is both accurate and powerful. They claim that it can shoot a grizzly bear at two hundred yards. Are you familiar with it?"

Why must he mock me, thought Alexander. "No, I'm not," he said offhandedly, as if he had fired countless other makes of rifles.

"Neither am I. Perhaps some night on the trail, when we have nothing better to do, we'll teach each other how to fire one."

In a pig's behind we will, thought Alexander. "Why not?" is what he answered, however.

"This is a very important wagon for us. We can't afford to lose it or cut it loose if it's struck. Next to the Indian girls and whiskey, rifles are the first thing our trappers want.

"And this is perhaps the most important weapon. Without it we had better not begin our trip." Marcel pulled back the end flap of another wagon and revealed oak barrel upon oak barrel of whiskey.

"The rest of the wagons are also practical," he said as he dropped the flap. They walked down the long line of perhaps forty wagons. One was filled with tea, Hudson's Bay's own brand in green tins. Chewing tobacco and beef jerky were in another. Some wagons were loaded with canoes, both dugouts and birch-barks. There were snowshoes and traps in one, new oilcloth trousers and boots in another, calico and beads and trinkets for trading with the Indians in still another. One wagon contained patent medicines of every description, for trappers were a sickly lot. They were afflicted by rheumatism from constantly working in freezing water and by dysentery from eating so steady a diet of fatty meat. They also suffered from snake bites and poisonous plants and berries.

Alexander fought not to let the lists of goods overwhelm him. His job was to understand furs, he knew that. What he was trying to do now was to acquire a broader knowledge of the caravan and rendezvous.

He asked only one question. It had been nagging at him ever since he had peered into the first wagon. "How do you know how much of each to bring?"

Marcel looked at him with a smirk. "You don't know, you guess."

"And if you guess wrong?"

"Then some poor devil has to wait until the next rendezvous for what he needs or make do with two of something he didn't need in the first place." Marcel laughed.

Alexander wasn't sure he understood the answer.

Juliette was disturbed. As the day she dreaded, the caravan's departure day, was drawing nearer and nearer, she and Alexander seemed to be drifting farther and farther apart. They rarely spoke. Alexander left the house before dawn. When he returned with Marcel long after dark, he was often too tired even to eat and no longer sought her out for one of their talks. She was convinced he hated her now and had forgotten his promise to share his experiences with her in a journal. She resolved to mention this to him at the first opportunity.

Juliette couldn't understand Alexander's total absorption in activities of the caravan that didn't even concern him. His own assignments had been made clear to him and she was sure that by now he had mastered his duties thoroughly. Still, for some reason, he continued to go daily to the wagons. Had he found some Indian girl, perhaps? No, not her Alexander. That, she decided, had to be impossible.

She also decided several nights later that she had to talk with him. After a swift and unceremonious dinner, for now the entire household was fraught with the tensions and excitement of the upcoming departure day, she cornered Alexander and wouldn't let him pass. She was very bold. She confronted him with all the demons that had been plaguing her the past few weeks.

"I'm determined to learn as much as I can about the fur-trading business and I won't learn it if I stay in this house by a fire." He spoke to her so softly that she knew he must have understood her pain.

"Still, you can find some time in your day for me. Papa does for Mama," she protested.

"My life's work is calling me, Juliette. It's not easy to answer to so many masters."

"We've made plans, Alexander." Her eyes were growing darker and beginning to glisten with tears. "We've made many plans and provisions, Alexander, that in your travels I would be forever with you."

She was right, he thought. They had made plans. Without hurting her, he had to convince her that he thought no less of her. He had to explain that if he neglected his calling, he would be doing both of them a disservice.

As they talked, Alexander realized that Juliette was concerned about more than the journal he had promised to keep. The journal was mostly an excuse and he began to understand this friend, this frightened beauty who thought she was going to lose him to the wilderness of the great Northwest.

He silently rehearsed his response to her. He would have to be both cautious and tender with her, but firm too. Don't worry, he would tell her, for the two of them would always have dreams to share and a future to plan. But right now he had to do what he'd been waiting so long to do. Until he did, he could commit himself to nothing else.

Alexander was gentle with her. He spoke softly, and his words were not without comfort for her. Then they planned to spend the day after the next with each other.

That day was as glorious as any in Montreal in the late spring. The sky might have been painted by a blue jay's wing and speckles of sunlight filtered through the budding chestnut trees. Birds were everywhere whistling and jabbering to each other. The young green of the season had begun to appear on paths, up trellises and on silver-branched birch trees that had been planted long before Alexander and Juliette were born.

Juliette and Alexander ambled down the familiar walkways where he'd limped so painfully months before. They held hands or locked arms, whichever happened to be more comfortable at the moment, but what mattered to Juliette was that they were touching.

"In two days, Juliette, I'll begin a dream we've shared for a long time," he told her.

"You'll take care, Alexander."

"If I don't who will come back to tell you of all the wonders the lands beyond the last horizon hold? Tell me that."

Juliette sighed. "You'll remember me, Alexander? You will?" As soon as she'd spoken, she felt foolish.

"Sh. Sh," he soothed her. "I'll be gone only a short time, my Juliette, a shorter time than it took to come from Scotland. And no, I'll not forget you. Will you forget me?" She shook her head emphatically.

"Every night. Every single night," he went on, "I'll write my day down for you as completely as I can remember it. It will be for you and we'll live my first rendezvous together from the moment I return."

"Oh, Alexander," she was becoming heady, "I thought you were keeping busy so you could leave without seeing me and that you never would come back to me."

"We Mackenzies are of more contant stock than you give us credit, my Juliette. How can I forget you? Put that silly thought out of your head."

She gazed steadily into his eyes and raised her face as close to his as possible. They'd stopped walking and now he led her slowly to a small clearing in a brace of trees.

They sat silently in the warm sun. Then Alexander lay back on the surprisingly dry grass and Juliette rested her gloved hand on his broad chest.

"There's something else I've been waiting to share with you, Juliette, for a long time. There's something I want you to have without misleading you as to my intentions. It's for you as a remembrance, nothing more and nothing less."

"You cannot possibly mislead me, *mon chéri.*"

He looked surprised at her use of the endearment, but let it pass. Then he handed her a small, flat enameled box about the size of her outstretched palm. He'd pulled it from the inside pocket in which he'd been carrying it all the time he'd been in Canada.

"What is it, Alexander?" When he said nothing, she pressed a worn corner of the box and the lid lifted slowly by itself. Inside it lay three unset diamonds. They glistened like blue fire in the bright day and it seemed as if she had harvested sunlight and held it in her hand. They were flawless and beautiful gems. She picked each one up and carefully examined it, then as gingerly she set it back in the case.

Alexander pointed into the box. For a brief second Juliette was flustered, then she noticed there was one thing more. She hadn't seen the small, very thin gold cross. It was pale and much worn, but it hadn't lost its elegance. Studying it closely, she tried to read the engraving on the back. Its lettering, however, was too faded and indistinct no matter which way she twisted or turned it. Finally, she asked him what it said.

"It was my grandmother's, my mother's mother's. It was a gift to her from my grandfather." He answered her in this way to keep her from asking any further questions.

He stood up and she took that to be a signal for her to rise as well. They were facing one another when he said, "They're yours to have and to hold from your dearest friend."

"Oh, Alexander. I don't know what to say, how to thank you except that I . . ."

Her sentence remained unfinished as he took her in his arms. He held her tightly. She clung to him and the moment. His heart beat as furiously as hers. She wanted to stay like that forever.

But he pulled away from her.

Although she wasn't sure if she'd imagined it or not, later on, alone, she swore to herself that his lips had kissed her hair.

Chapter 5

Departure day arrived. The sun was high, the sky bright and the compound that had been so carefully guarded day and night now took on a festive air. Wives and children of the men who were traveling with the caravan had turned out in their fanciest. Dogs ran underfoot. A picnic basket weighed down many an arm. All that was missing was a brass band.

Papa Louis and Mama walked arm in arm through the encampment. They greeted everyone and called to most of them by name.

Even Marcel made a perfunctory appearance, but he was there to work, not to be sociable. He hopped from wagon to wagon amid the bustling onlookers and wagoners. Alexander envied Marcel's long, whispered conversations with Papa Louis. They would eventually nod their heads in agreement and then Marcel would walk resolutely off to settle a problem.

The conferences, Marcel's orders to drivers and stockmen and their quick responses only served to remind Alexander how far he was from the men in charge of the rendezvous. Although he kept telling himself he was lucky just to be on the rendezvous, he still felt small. He felt even smaller in the eyes of Juliette, who, he reckoned, must realize his insignificant position.

Nevertheless, dozens of men in the festive crowd would have traded places not only with him but even with one of the horses. Had he not met the Denteres, he might now be a clerk in one of McGill's offices and this rendezvous only a dream. Live each day as if it were your last, he repeated to himself over and over again.

The caravan started to roll. His face flushed with excitement, Alexander leapt onto his assigned wagon to begin the most thrilling journey of his life. He turned for one last look at Juliette. He flashed at her and Mama and Mariou the widest smile they'd seen on his face ever, for he was bound north by northwest on his great adventure.

Lumbering down St. Paul's Street, the caravan pulled out of Montreal slowly. Alexander sat impatiently beside his skillful driver, a squat, smelly man named Chubb. Their wagon was traveling third in the second file of forty-six. When Alexander stood on the buckboard's shelf to look behind him at the caravan, however, he didn't see a long, unbroken line of wagons. He saw chaos.

Wagons were scattered everywhere. Some were headed in the wrong direction. Others had broken axles and men were furiously unloading them to repair the damage. Men on horseback and boys on mules rode willy-nilly among the wagons and a rabble of curious spectators. Indians were hawking blankets, chickens, corn and skins of wine. This was no caravan; it was a carnival.

"Sorry you looked, *mon ami*?" asked Chubb critically.

"This is madness," said Alexander in awe. Huge

clouds of dust billowed over the crowd and caravan. Men were shouting conflicting orders. Dogs were yapping and horses reared. Women ran with their children between the wagons calling to their husbands for a last good-bye.

"No. No madness. Start of the caravan. You never see this before?" asked Chubb.

"No, I've never seen anything like it. They can't all start this way?" reasoned Alexander.

"Ten years ago, maybe no. Then it was one or two wagons go out to meet trappers for a month, maybe two. Like everything in this world, it got bigger and bigger. You get used to it." He spat out a long stream of tobacco juice.

Alexander became silent. The utter confusion bewildered him. He valued order, and if this is how the twig is bent, he wondered, how will grow the tree.

"There was a wagon going the wrong way," he told Chubb, as if to explain his dour mien.

"Little boy driving that one. Probably lied to get the job. You see how long it takes to find out?" Chubb smirked and let fly another river of tobacco.

"There was another with an axle out and we've only begun to move."

"They load too heavy. All the wagons get too heavy and it takes long to go to the mountains. But the good part is, it takes a short time coming home. You like tea?" asked Chubb, trying to lighten up his companion's mood.

"Of course," he answered as he remembered his mother's strong, black tea.

"Well, that's good. We have whole wagon full of it. Soon we get to be popular fellas." He made a grand circle with his free hand and added, "Everybody love tea."

"You know the rendezvous well?" Alexander was beginning to feel inadequate again, the more so for having to ask leading questions of a simple wagoner.

"Been on many a year. They get to be one like the other. You'll see."

"What's it like where we're going? What's the land like, the people . . ." He stopped himself. He was behaving like a nervous schoolboy. To cover his chagrin, he stood again and surveyed the scene behind them. Chaos still prevailed.

"Better to save your looks behind until we come to the edge of the Blue Mountains. You get too jittery, *mon ami*." Chubb knew the feeling. He'd seen the same distress in the eyes of dozens of others who'd sat beside him on his wagon. To set out on a journey hundreds of miles into nowhere in such a riot of disorder seemed to augur poorly for the entire enterprise.

"You see all of them get in one beautiful line very soon. Monsieur Marcel, he know his work."

The sting of Chubb's leather whip would have startled Alexander less than his comment about Marcel. His absorption in all the business of the departure had blinded him to more pertinent observations. He sought Papa Louis among the leaders of the caravan, although by then he didn't really expect to find him. In vain, he scrutinized every rider who galloped past. Twice he saw Marcel and both times he waved to him, only to be ignored. But he didn't see Papa anywhere.

"I don't see Monsieur Dentere anywhere," he remarked to Chubb. "Could it be he's riding a wagon and not a horse tonight?"

"Monsieur Dentere? Louis Dentere? You expect

him to come on a rendezvous? He's too big a shot for that.'' Chubb shook his head good-naturedly.

''If Monsieur Dentere isn't in charge, my good friend, then who is?''

''In charge? The boss, you mean? Who else?'' asked Chubb with a tug on his reins. ''Monsieur Dentere. Marcel, of course.''

Alexander looked at Chubb for a long time, then he stared straight ahead at the horses' heads bobbing in response to Chubb's steady command.

This was news he hadn't expected. Marcel was in charge. The man he and Juliette had mocked at dinner so many nights, the man who'd cowered in fear on the deck of their crippled ship, was in charge of the largest caravan ever to be sent from Montreal. He tried to convince himself that had he not known Marcel, he would have faith in his knowledge, skills and leadership. Try as he might, he couldn't. For he did know Marcel and the Marcel he knew was a sly, cunning person in charge of this caravan only because his father was the managing director of the company.

Again Alexander resolved to seize every advantage this opportunity afforded him. He would observe, he would learn and he would prove Papa Louis' prediction true. One day he, not Marcel, would be leading a rendezvous.

One question, however, continued to nag at him. Why hadn't anyone told him Papa wasn't accompanying them? He'd been treated like a member of the family by practically everyone and yet this secret, if a secret it was, had been withheld from him. Whatever the answer, it would bother Alexander for the entire trip.

*   *   *

Chubb, it turned out, was right. Alexander should have waited until they'd traveled the afternoon before turning to view the wagons behind him.

The sun had begun to set when the Blue Mountains loomed up before them. Tall, slender spruce trees threw long shadows across their path. Seated high above Chubb's team of horses, Alexander savored the serenity of the woods. And when he stood to view the caravan, he saw what he'd often envisioned. A long, unbroken line of wagons, their white canvas tops like a string of beads, stretched out behind him as far as he could see.

The Indian merchants and rowdy camp followers had disappeared. The caravan now traveled alone. It would blaze a trail into an untamed land far to the north. Alexander would be among the first men ever to tread through virgin forests, to discover wild rivers and vast blue lakes, to know the fabulous unknown. His spirits soared even higher than his expectations.

That night, after they'd set up camp, Alexander discovered something else. All the disorder that had so confounded him at the outset of their journey, all those men on horseback and boys on mules and persistent Indians, had been serving, too, a practical purpose. They'd been selling food and drink.

The caravan, Alexander learned, carried neither a cook nor food. He'd imagined that after they'd driven the wagons into three giant circles for their nightly camp, they would light roaring campfires and then all the wagoners would line up for their grub. He'd imagined wrong. Every man had to provide for himself. Rather than bemoaning the disruptive boys and Indians, he should have been bartering with them.

"They would even sell you their sisters for the trip."

"What would that cost?" Alexander watched Chubb eat. Between mouthfuls, Chubb explained to him how necessities were obtained.

"Not much. Some lead, powder maybe and a couple dozen strands of beads. They don't think much of women, those dogs don't."

"And the Indian girl is yours?" asked Alexander incredulous.

"For as long as you want her. Here, look down the row. See, there's one feeding her man."

"And he bought her?"

"Next encounter, I think I buy you one."

"Not me," objected Alexander rising rapidly. "Not on your life, Chubb."

He didn't mind Cubb's laughter as he walked away. Alexander liked Chubb, respected his know-how and common sense. He went to sleep hungry that night as he wondered at a people who would trade a wife or sister for a few strings of beads.

The next morning for breakfast, he and Chubb pried loose a green tin of the Hudson's Bay tea from the stockpile in their wagon. Chubb had also been right about tea. No sooner had they brewed a pot of it than they were surrounded by eager wagoners, all of them with empty cups. The pot was drained before he and Chubb had finished their one cup of company tea.

Refreshed, Alexander wanted to write his first entry in the journal that Juliette had given him. His duties, however, allowed him no time until the wagon train was again on its way. Then he could barely keep himself in the seat of the bouncing lorry, let alone balance an inkhorn and journal on his knees. As Alexander leafed through the clean white pages of the journal, he noticed to his surprise an inscription on its cover. "Each night as you take down this book, think of me. My love, Juliette.'' Surreptitiously he kissed her graceful script and remembered her delicate hand. With some reluctance, he stowed the book in his pack. He would write in it that evening.

They left the Blue Mountains behind them. Rolling hills and verdant meadows rose and fell before them. The motion of the wagon steadied. The morning was quiet. Alexander drifted in and out of a light sleep.

He welcomed any diversion. Small bands of Indians occasionally came out to greet them. He recognized the Huron immediately and familiarized himself with the Iroquois and Attawandronk, three of the friendly tribes that had helped the British fight the American colonists. When one of the wagons became mired in a riverbed, Alexander leapt to the task of wrenching it out of the deep mud. No matter how strenuous, the physical activity invigorated him.

They passed tobacco fields that recently had been planted by a tribe of Iroquois and many of the wagoners exchanged beads and trinkets for sacks of the dried, cured leaves. As they approached the Iroquois village, Alexander expected to see deerskin tepees. He was surprised to find long houses sturdily built of unbarked saplings and large enough for several Indian families. Fascinated by the village and its people, Alexander had to be reminded by Chubb that they needed food. They bartered for freshly caught trout and got free turnips in the bargain.

Chubb and Alexander smoked the trout for their meal that night. Later, Alexander took his ink, quill and journal from his pack, and wrote to Juliette.

* * *

The thaw preceded the caravan in its journey north. Melting snow swelled the rivers, lakes and streams. The woods were newly green and wildflowers grew in soggy patches of the forest floor.

Occasionally they passed the abandoned outpost of a trapper. Once a sanctuary, his small, fortified camp now stood overgrown and silent. The search for new trapping grounds was taking men farther and farther north.

The days grew longer. The terrain became flatter and unfamiliar even to the veterans of the caravan. When Alexander stood on the wagon seat he saw only vast green fields, flat and unwooded. Trees were rare. He couldn't see the herds of wild bison, but he could hear their hooves thundering far away over the prairie. In this strange land known only to a handful of guides and scouts, Alexander felt that at last the adventure truly had begun.

The Indian tribes were also strange to him. The men seemed especially fierce, for they painted their faces and swarthy, smooth skin. They were Sioux and Algonquin. They were excellent horsemen too and Marcel decided to stop the caravan there for several days so as to provide the horses some proper care and rest.

The Sioux took to the task easily and freely. They tethered each team of horses and led them to fertile pastures. Alexander, meanwhile, seized this opportunity to explore new land and ride free of the wagon train. He borrowed the horse of a young brave and rode the prairie as hard and long as he could. Then, no less exhilarated than he was exhausted, Alexander stretched out at the edge of the copse of cypress trees and slept.

The wild whoops and hollers of Sioux braves awakened him. In the distance several braves were riding in circles, while others rode back and forth in arcs. Long streamers flew from the sharp heads of their feathered lances.

Fearful that these young Sioux might be torturing one of the wagoners, Alexander climbed a small bluff in order to determine a plan of rescue. He was relieved to discover that these were no warriors but a hunting party and that they had besieged not a helpless white man but a giant bison. They'd isolated the mammoth animal from its herd and Alexander watched fascinated as the unflagging braves made ready for the kill.

The bison was fighting for its life ferociously. It charged and bucked and whirled at the braves encircling it. When one of the braves would try to divert its attention by whooping and brandishing his lance, the bison would appear unaware of an attack from the rear. But at the very moment a young brave would raise his lance to plunge it in the animal, the bison suddenly would reverse and charge at the attacker. Again and again the bison charged and the braves attacked. Finally one lance found its mark. Then two, then four. The bison fell.

The braves cheered their victory. With a whoop of his own, so did Alexander. The Sioux broke their revelry instantly. In a silent circle they stationed themselves around the thrashing animal, which, despite its mortal wound, had not yet succumbed. Coldly they eyed this white man who had suddenly appeared to claim, they thought, the prize of their difficult kill.

As Alexander strode up to congratulate the braves, he didn't read distrust or suspicion in their eyes. He was grinning broadly and had spread his arms wide to indicate his appreciation of the bison's gigantic size, when two of the braves leapt at him. They threw him to the ground. Gesturing wildly at the dying animal, they shouted at him. Pinned down and stunned, Alexander smiled to show them he was friendly and shook his head in an attempt to tell them he didn't understand. He tried in vain. A third brave straddled him and slowly ran the sharp head of an arrow across Alexander's neck. It nicked his skin. Alexander paled when he felt the pressure of the arrowhead at his throat.

The ground trembled. Men were shouting in the distance. Horses' hooves beat the earth. The Sioux braves yelled excitedly to Alexander's tormentors. Gunpowder exploded in the air. Fifty men with long rifles were riding in, no doubt to rescue the white man. The young braves released Alexander and mounted their ponies. The entire hunting party had disappeared in a cloud of dust before Alexander had struggled to his feet.

He turned his gaze from the empty plain and found himself face to face with Marcel.

"You, perhaps, are wise in the ways of the sea," Marcel choked, "but here you are stupid! An oaf!" Red with anger, Marcel berated him in front of six wagoners.

"You disobeyed a direct order. If this were our army, you would have been saved only to be shot in front of the entire company. As it is, you should be flogged and sent back to Montreal on foot. Do you understand the harm you may have caused? Do you know what balance you may have upset between our traders and these tribes?" Marcel allowed Alexander no explanations, no defense. Nor could Alexander have offered any, for Marcel spoke the truth.

"This will not, cannot, be overlooked, Monsieur. You may have caused us more trouble than Father thinks you're worth. Now, help drag that carcass back to our camp. We must invite every Indian within fifty miles to come join our feast tonight.''

Alexander and one of the wagoners, a burly Frenchman named Claude, tied saddle ropes around two thousand pounds of dead beast. Claude fastened the other end of his line to his saddle horn. As Alexander had ridden bareback, he had to hold his line in his bare hand. They began the long haul several miles back to camp.

Claude stared straight ahead as they rode. Nor did he look at Alexander when he spoke in a brusque, melancholy voice. ''You're lucky we arrived when we did,'' he told him.

''Do you think they would have run me through?'' Alexander asked with real concern.

''No question, monsieur. You were a threat to their sacred animal.''

''A threat? I was no threat.''

''Apparently, *mon ami*, they thought differently.'' Claude's heavy French accent warped his every word. ''They were going to kill you to protect their find. To them the beast is everything. It's their food. Its skin is their clothes and from its bones came the very arrow that today would have pierced your throat.''

What impressed Alexander more than Claude's words was Marcel's decision to share the bison they had so unexpectedly acquired with the ruffled Sioux. Marcel's diplomacy somewhat lessened Alexander's shame, but it didn't alleviate the raw pain in his hand. The rope had begun to cut into his flesh. Without a word Claude tossed him a pair of leather gloves.

Back at the camp, the huge bison was roasted over a pit and served to a hundred and twenty Hudson's Bay men and almost as many Sioux. After the feast the

Sioux circled the pit and performed a ritualistic dance of thanksgiving. They celebrated the gods who'd provided them with an entire herd of bison to meet their needs for the coming winter. Among them danced the three braves who had attacked Alexander that afternoon.

Alexander paid little attention to the revelry. He would willingly have celebrated Marcel's success had he not learned that Marcel had invited the Indians to this feast at the suggestion of the old wagoner who had ridden beside him and whispered counsel in his ear. Nevertheless, Marcel had rescued him from the three Sioux braves. In the firelight the Indians danced to praise their gods, while Alexander searched for the proper words to thank the man who had saved his life.

Chapter 6

Days passed into weeks. The caravan continued its trek north by northwest to the rendezvous. The prairie was far behind them and dense forests and wild rivers slowed the progress of the wagons. Tree stumps broke their axles and snarled roots wrenched off their wheels. It took days to make the necessary repairs.

No one in the caravan knew this territory, its rough terrain and hidden hazards. The rules that no wagon break the line and that no man leave camp were strictly enforced by Marcel.

Each night in his journal Alexander not only recorded the rigors of their journey but also described vistas more spectacular than any he had ever seen. The sun set in a breathtaking array of pinks and lavender over the stately pine forests before it surrendered to the glory of cold, northern starlight. Fox and beaver were plentiful and Alexander wondered why the trapper's had abandoned this region rich in bounty. He wrote, too, of the Indians, the Athapascan and Yellowknife, who hunted caribou and rabbit, fished for salmon and willingly shared their catches with the wagoners. And each night when he'd finished with his journal, Alexander fell asleep to the distant baying of timber wolves.

The caravan arrived at one village where the Yellowknife were much less friendly to the white men who'd penetrated their territory. No one could explain why. Then on a fishing expedition Claude, Chubb and Alexander came upon a strange sight that puzzled them even more.

As they were leaving the lake shore they suddenly spied a young Indian girl like no Indian girl any of them had seen before. Tall and slender and bronze, she looked perhaps fourteen. Her face was a perfect oval. Though almond-shaped, her eyes were pale. Her nose was small and her mouth formed a delicate bow. She stood naked in the sunlight. But what amazed the three of them was her hair. It was the color of straw.

Captivated by her presence, they watched her. When she detected them a faint blush accented her high cheekbones. At the same moment, a long-legged Indian woman in a brightly beaded deerskin appeared and pulled the young girl roughly back into the woods. In seconds, without a trace, the two had disappeared.

Claude insisted they had seen a specter. Chubb half agreed. Alexander found his companions fanciful and they told him he lacked romance. Yet all three men had been strangely affected by the scene. None of them could deny its mystery. It bound them in an unspoken intimacy and they shared the secret with none of the other wagoners.

Alexander did, however, write of the two women in his journal that night. Their enigmatic appearance had aroused in him a painful longing for Juliette, her voice, her touch, her scent. When he slept, she invaded his dreams in brightly beaded deerskin.

Lone Courage

*   *   *

Excitement ran high the next few days. Rumors that they would soon reach the point of rendezvous ran through the caravan. But as the wagons traveled through yet another narrow pass in the towering bluffs, the wagoners received no official word about the rendezvous. The men's spirits flagged further when they, along with bands of Yellowknife, were pressed into hauling and pushing the wagons through rocky passages barely the width of an axle.

Whiskey was fast becoming a popular cure for exhaustion and frustration. One afternoon, two men were found drunk and asleep in their wagon. In camp that evening Marcel gathered the wagoners into a circle and then hotly berated the two culprits. Afterward he warned all the men that any further drunkenness would not be tolerated and would meet with punishment considerably more severe.

Three days later one of the drivers, blind drunk, obliviously tried to ford a stream the wrong way. That night, in front of every member of the caravan as well as every Indian in the camp, the man was flogged. Each time the whip slashed into the man's taut flesh the chief of the Yellowknife winced. As the punishment continued, the old chief began wailing aloud. Flogging was alien to him and his people. A Yellowknife would never strike another in his tribe, not even to discipline a troublesome child.

Intrigued by this revelation, Claude asked the chief if unruly behavior among his people would go unpunished.

"No," said the chief, "it would not be tolerated. "But we would never flog the wrongdoer."

"What would you do, Chief?" asked Claude.

The chief's answer was chilling. "We would simply kill him."

The wagons continued northward. They entered the land of the Kutenai, or "easy fishermen" as they were known, for this was a land of brilliant, blue-green lakes and sparkling rivers. These Indians, too, met them on the trail and traded with the wagoners. Then they disappeared. The Kutenai seemed to have no villages.

Nowhere along their trail could Alexander, Chubb or Claude find a tepee, long house, cave or camp. With no success, they searched the riverbanks for a Kutenai settlement. Then, one night Claude decided to follow a band of the Kutenai when it left the wagoners' camp.

The Indians rode quietly through the dark pine woods. Claude stole behind them on foot, for he feared the sound of a pony would give him away. He followed them as swiftly as he could and as closely as he dared along their circuitous route. Their direction seemed aimless, they seemed constantly to be changing their paths. The Kutenai quickened their pace and Claude was running when, abruptly, they stopped.

Certain he'd been detected, Claude held his breath. The Indians dismounted and began milling about a grove of pines. Three braves led their ponies into the woods. Then, all of the Kutenai men fell to their knees. Claude froze. He feared he'd stumbled upon a secret religious rite and he knew he'd be tortured were he discovered.

What he saw, however, startled him more than any arcane rite. The men were lifting up large slabs of earth. They were hinged, like gates, and once opened, eerie yellow light poured out of each passageway. The men climbed down into the earth. One by one, each slab closed and each light went out. Claude stood staring at an empty, moonlit grave of pines.

"*Sacre bleu*," he muttered to himself. "These creatures live under the ground, like the mole. No wonder we could not find their village. We were walking over it."

"Are you so surprised we live like this?" The soft, almost womanly voice of the young brave unnerved and dumbfounded Claude. He hadn't heard even one of the brave's footsteps behind him.

"Monsieur, forgive me. I was curious . . ." Claude could only babble, for in this brave he saw his end.

"I mean you no harm." The voice was softer than before. "There's no reason to hide. You are welcome in our homes."

"You surprised me so. *Mon Dieu*, I'm still shaking."

The boy laughed and sat down in front of Claude. His easy manner belied any threat and Claude managed to regain some of his Gallic composure.

"Where did you learn to speak English so well?" he asked the boy.

"I was raised by an English trapper. Perhaps you know him. Lucas Whitestone. Knew him, I should say. He took in me and my mother one very bad winter and we stayed on for years. Would that I know the language of my own people as well."

They'd been speaking a long while when the boy reached into his britches and pulled out a stone. Deep green and luminous, it glowed like a hard, green fire in the darkness of the night. At first Claude thought himself the victim of some deception. Then he held it in his hand and he coveted its magnificent green flame.

"We call this grass fire. It's very valuable to my

people. For your people, too? There aren't many in this world.''

"Fortunes could be made with stones like these, fortunes vaster than with furs.''

"I know the place where the grass fire grows. The stones are many, but only the bravest men deserve them.''

"*Comment!* What do you mean?'' Claude feared he would have to undergo some bitter ordeal to gain access to the invaluable stones.

Claude spent the entire night talking with the young brave and plotting.

When Claude returned to camp, Alexander and Chubb were already eating breakfast. Certain he had simply lost his way and had invented some outlandish tale, they showed little interest. Exchanging winks and smiles, they refused to listen to Claude until they'd finished their fried salmon, pone and black tea.

Claude allowed them their good-natured jests. Then he stunned them with his discoveries of the night before. As he described the earthen gates and underground passages, Chubb and Alexander realized they were sharing a secret as old as the Kutenai themselves.

That, however, was nothing, Claude told them, compared to the other secret he had to tell. He promised his companions great wealth and spoke of a grass-fire stone, an eternal green flame. Chubb and Alexander were incredulous. From under his shirt, Claude pulled out a worn leather pouch that hung from a strap around his neck. He shook the pouch carefully. The extraordinary stone tumbled out. The three men gazed at the fortune in the palm of Claude's hand.

Furthermore, Claude told them, the Indian boy had promised to lead him to the source of the stones. But there were conditions. The young brave no longer wanted to live with the Kutenai. He had no family in the tribe and he felt alien to its ways. Indeed, he hardly spoke the language. The Kutenai, however, forbade him to leave because their tribe was small and every brave counted for two. The boy was virtually their prisoner. With Claude's help, though, he could escape. If Claude would hide him in a wagon until the caravan reached its rendezvous, the brave would take him to the grass-fire stones.

When he'd finished, Claude sipped noisily at his tea. Before Alexander or Chubb could comment on the bargain, Claude added bluntly, "I told him hokay."

His two friends shrugged and shook their heads. Hokay?

"You may get us rich, me lad, unless you get us killed. Somehow, I fear," answered Alexander.

Claude laughed. Instead of Alexander's sarcasm, he heard approval of his plans.

"And now, *mes amis*, I'm very tired. Today I will sleep and tonight our Indian friend will make us all rich men."

He crawled into the wagon. Before they had started rolling, Claude was snoring loud enough to scare the horses.

That same morning Marcel visited Alexander. Marcel had kept his distance during the entire trip, and Alexander had decided to forget that they had shared the same dinner table for almost three months. To Alexander, Marcel was only the wagon master, and just a so-so wagon master at that.

Marcel asked Alexander to climb down from the wagon and walk with him. Unfortunately, Marcel also heard Claude snoring. He flared up instantly. "Why is this man sleeping during the day?"

"He was up all night tending to two horses with colic Monsieur Dentere," replied Chubb, reminding Marcel that Claude was the caravan's only veterinarian.

Marcel peered into the wagon and sniffed for the smell of whiskey. "Tell Claude not to snore so loudly. And how are the horses?"

"Fine, Monsieur Dentere," Chubb answered without hesitation.

"Come, Alexander," Marcel said brusquely. "We must talk."

Alexander was completely perplexed. For almost a month Marcel had not spoken two words to him, except to upbraid him for almost getting killed, and now he wanted to talk to him in private. For a while they walked in silence.

"I want you to know, Alexander, I have not written in my log of your encounter with the Sioux hunting party," Marcel began.

"Exactly what do you mean, Marcel?" shot back Alexander.

"I mean that Papa will not hear about this incident from me and that there will be no record of your failure to obey a company rule, a rule which explicitly forbade you to make explorations that would endanger the rendezvous in any way." Marcel spoke officiously.

"You're making it sound as if I risked the entire venture by taking a ride. Marcel, that isn't . . ."

Marcel interrupted him. "That is precisely what you did. Don't you understand? I, however, am officially forgetting it."

"Thank you, Mr. Wagon Master," Alexander replied caustically.

Either Marcel chose to ignore the affront or else it simply escaped him, for he merely stated, "It's about time you said that.

"I trust you haven't forgotten your lessons, the lessons I taught you before we started the trip." Marcel changed the subject so quickly that Alexander was caught completely off his guard.

"I think I still remember."

"Think?"

"I remember, Marcel. It takes no genius to remember what I have to do."

Again Marcel ignored the sarcasm. "Papa has asked me to look out for you. I trust you're happy? Without grievances, problems?"

"Thank you again, Marcel, for your concern." Though the point of this charade eluded him, Marcel's empty words needled Alexander.

"We rendezvous, Alexander, in three, perhaps four days. Tell that to your friends." With that news, Marcel mounted his horse and galloped back to the head of the caravan.

He's mad, thought Alexander, absolutely mad.

Alexander didn't tell Chubb about the rendezvous. He was becoming as petty as everyone else, withholding information to gain an advantage over the other men. He chastised himself that night as he unrolled his sleeping gear. Tomorrow, first thing, he would tell Chubb and Claude the news. Chubb and Claude were his good friends. Tomorrow, too, Alexander remembered, the three of them would be wealthy men. Chuckling to himself, Alexander fell asleep.

He didn't sleep long. Someone was shaking him violently and calling his name. He awoke with a start.

Instantly alert, he descried Marcel, a groggy Chubb and one of the wagon leaders. "What's the matter?" he asked.

Marcel shielded the light from his small lantern with his body. His voice was hushed, brisk. "Come. Walk with us beyond the wagons. I don't want to wake the camp."

Alexander pulled on his boots. He shot a quizzical glance at Chubb who responded with a shrug.

"Quickly," Marcel pressed him.

The four men walked in silence. When they'd passed through the circle of wagons, Marcel turned to Chubb and Alexander. "Your friend Claude is in great danger. The fool. Idiot!" he snapped.

The wagon leader put a hand on Marcel's shoulder. "Calm," he said. "Calm."

"A few minutes ago a young Kutenai arrived in camp. He told us that Claude dived into a spring for some sacred stones hidden in a secret cache. What a fool to believe such a story. He hasn't surfaced."

Alexander became agitated. "If he's underwater, why are we wasting precious time?"

"He must be gone by now, Alexander," said Chubb sadly.

"Keep still, both of you. You'll wake everyone," the wagon leader commanded them. Then, to Marcel, he said, "Continue, monsieur."

"He isn't dead. That is, we don't think he's dead. He may not even be underwater! Listen closely now. The boy says that under the spring lies a chamber, a passage that's wide enough for a grown man to clear and that leads to a cave. We assume Claude is in the chamber. Any attempt to rescue him will require a powerful swimmer and I know of no other swimmer as powerful as you, Alexander.''

"Ah, so you do remember, laddie?" Alexander spoke louder than he'd intended.

"What was that, *mon ami*?" asked Marcel.

"Nothing. Take me to the boy."

Fear had unnerved the young brave. If Claude was lost, so were his chances of escaping the Kutenai. His own life was now in danger, too, for should the stir created by Claude's rescuers awaken the Kutenai, they would discover he'd revealed their tribal secret to the white man.

Marcel lowered his lantern to the ground. Chubb lighted two more, but still they could barely see the near bank of the spring. The night was moonless. Marcel dispatched Chubb to the wagons for torches.

Alexander managed to determine from the stammering young brave that the spring formed an almost perfect circle of water perhaps twenty feet in diameter.

"It looks calm, but truly it is treacherous," said the boy. "That's why it's called Devil's Mouth."

"How deep is it?"

"How can Claude, or any man, stay under this water and live?" Alexander spoke quietly, deliberately. He wanted to soothe the young boy's nerves, for his success depended on the accuracy of this brave's information.

"There are secret caves. In several of them grow the grass-fire stones."

"Draw these caves for me." Alexander gave the boy his dagger and with his hand swept clear some ground at the edge of the water.

First the boy drew a long, vertical shaft. On its left side he indicated an opening that led to a chamber behind the wall of the shaft. From the farther wall of the chamber the boy drew a tunnel that sloped sharply downward, then veered upward and narrowed. Water entered the tunnel, the boy said, but it only covered its floor. The tunnel opened into an enormous cave. There the green stones glowed, so brightly, the boy added, that you didn't need a torch.

"Have you been in the caves?" Alexander asked the boy.

"Yes."

"Can you stand up down there?"

"Not in the tunnel. But in the first room, yes."

"Is there air?"

"Yes."

"Have you yourself seen the stones in the cave?"

"No. I couldn't get through the opening."

"Good Lamb of God, man! If you couldn't get through, how could Claude? He's three times your size!"

"There are rocks and stones down there. The pebbles shift. Sometimes the opening is large, other times you cannot pass. The day I went under—"

Alexander cut him short. "How many of me is the spring deep?"

"Ten of you," the boy judged.

"That's pretty deep," Alexander said to Marcel.

"And Claude is lost. No one can dive that far under the water." Marcel seemed already resigned to his loss.

"No, not necessarily. According to the boy, the opening Claude sought is here, about three-fifths of the way down. That's still a long way down, but it's not impossible."

"*If* the Kutenai boy is right," added the wagon leader.

"It's your decision, Marcel. Should I go down to see if I can pull old Claude out of that hole he's squeezed himself into or not?" Although Alexander sounded cavalier, he had himself decided to try at least one dive to rescue his good friend.

"Two tries. I'm asking you to make two tries. If the boy is wrong and the opening is too far down, we stop. But I ask two tries."

A twig snapped in the pines. The Kutenai brave prepared to run and the three men turned to face the intruder or spy. They saw Chubb returning with the torches.

"Is it possible, do you think, to strap some wicks and flint to my body, so that if I do get to the dry chamber, I might have some light?"

"I can fix it for you," the solemn wagon leader said with a certainty that barred all doubt. He wrapped the tapers and flint in several layers of oilcloth and then tied the package tightly around Alexander's chest. The tapers would be easily accessible to Alexander and the tidy bundle wouldn't interfere with his dive.

Alexander also tied a line around his waist. Its slack was strung around a sapling, and Chubb took hold of the other end. If Chubb felt two distinct tugs, he, Marcel and the wagon leader were to pull Alexander up as rapidly as possible. The Indian boy, meanwhile, was to dive into the spring, clear the line of rocks and crevices and pull from below.

The dawn had begun to break. The surface of the spring, which in the dark had looked so calm, everywhere bubbled. Alexander thrust his face into the icy water and drank the sulfurous water. He belched loudly. "What kind of water is this?" he asked the boy.

"Sacred water. It's best not to drink of Devil's Mouth."

Alexander waited no longer. Clutching a boulder to aid him in his descent, he plunged feet first into the water. Neither was the boulder heavy enough nor the dive forceful enough for Alexander to reach the Devil's Mouth thirty meters down. And the sapling that guided his line fell. Alexander swam back to shore.

While Chubb wound the line around a sturdier tree, Alexander prepared for his second dive. With a larger boulder and a running leap, he plunged into the bubbling spring. He sank rapidly. Sooner than he had expected, he saw Devil's Mouth. He let go the boulder and squeezed through the opening into a narrow passageway. His breath failing, he forced himself upward. Suddenly his face was above water. Alexander climbed into a musty chamber. Water swirled about his feet and ankles. The air reeked of an odor like rotten eggs. Though certain a man could stay alive here, Alexander wasn't so sure about how long.

"Claude!" he shouted. He heard no response. He shouted a second time. An eerie sound answered, or echoed, him.

"Claude!" he yelled one more time. The walls echoed the name of Alexander's friend. Then the chamber fell silent again.

Alexander was debating his next move when his own name penetrated the gloom. "Alexander!" he heard. "It's me!"

Alexander undid the bundle tied to his chest. When he lighted one of the tapers, an acrid puff of yellow smoke sent him into a fit of coughing. It took him several minutes to catch his breath. His eyes adjusted to the eerie, amber light, and then he saw them—the bones. He was standing not on rocks, but skeletons. He vomited.

He tried to ignore the bones of the Kutenai who'd been swallowed by Devil's Mouth. He tried to ignore the noxious fumes and the dizzying motion of the water reflected on the chamber walls. And he tried to concentrate on his task.

Alexander inched his way into the tunnel. Water trickled down the walls. The candle went out. He lit another, and across the ceiling of the tunnel he saw long streaks of dried blood. On the rocks below lay the bones of fingers broken by Indians who'd tried desperately to claw through solid rock.

Slowly, Alexander advanced. The water deepened. At some places it gushed through the walls and poured silt and pebbles into his path. The debris formed makeshift columns and false walls standing between him and the entrance to the cavern of grass-fire stones. Without the light of his taper, Alexander might easily have mistaken these shaky pillars for a sound hold or support and like many Kutenai before him, perhaps like Claude, he would have been buried in a pile of pebbles, rocks and silt.

A mound of rocks had collapsed into the cavern's entranceway. Once Alexander had managed to worm his body through the narrow opening, he saw another pile of rocky debris not too far from him. Beneath it lay Claude, trapped face down. A faint whimper answered Alexander when he called to him.

Alexander pulled himself forward. His taper flickered and he heard it before he felt it. A flood of water, silt and stone swept him into the cavern. It left him buried under rocks and sediment next to Claude. He couldn't move. He panicked.

Darkness now compounded their plight. The torrent of water had washed away the package of tapers. The safety line still bound Alexander's waist, but he couldn't move his pinioned arms. When he struggled to free his right arm so that he could signal to Chubb with the line, he felt only more tightly wedged. He groped blindly for any opening and his fingers clawed hopelessly at solid rock. Breathing was becoming more difficult. Alexander tried to conserve air and control his panic by breathing as regularly as he could.

Alexander finally managed to calm himself and to concentrate on survival. "Claude, Claude," he whispered.

"*Mon ami*, we're lost," he muttered.

Alexander ignored Claude's despair. "Can you move? Can you move anything?"

"Only my arms forward. Only my arms forward," he repeated wearily.

Alexander rested his head for a moment on the chamber floor. Sulfurous water bubbled up into his mouth and nose. Startled, he picked his hand up, shaking it and felt a sudden surge of strength. He heaved his body up. With a convulsive force his muscles strained against the rocks until, miraculously, he felt himself sliding backward.

As Alexander shoved himself back into the tunnel, the life line went taut for a second. Then, on the sharp edge of a rock, it snapped. Nevertheless, he'd escaped the pile of rocks and in the tunnel he could breathe freely again.

Alexander recovered his breath. The torrent of water that had buried him in silt and stone had also widened the entrance to the cavern. He moved quickly now. Forcing his strength, he pulled Claude feet first out of his trap and dragged him across the gravelly floor. They gulped the air in the tunnel and wasted none of their little strength on words. They inched their way through the darkness back to the chamber, where at last they could stand erect. Once they had stretched their long-cramped muscles, Alexander signaled to Claude that they were ready to start their ascent. As they crossed the chamber to the Devil's Mouth, Alexander for the first time noticed the bulk around Claude's stomach. The treasure Claude had stowed there apparently outweighed all risk. It also hindered his passage into the spring. Three times Claude tried to squeeze through the opening and each time failed. Each time, too, he swallowed more of the spring's acrid water. Finally, with Alexander supporting his friend's back, Claude succeeded in entering the spring feet first. Alexander followed.

Claude broke through the surface of the water, followed quickly by Alexander. Chubb, Marcel, the wagon leader and the young brave cheered them on. Claude, however, doubled over in pain, and Alexander had to drag him ashore. Claude's ordeal had only begun.

When they stripped off Claude's clothes, the men discovered no treasure under them. Claude's stomach had swelled to almost five times its normal size. Chubb raced into the woods and back to the camp for the doctor traveling with the caravan. The brave forgot his fears and ran to his village for the Kutenai medicine man. Half sick and thoroughly exhausted, Alexander fell back onto the grass. He did not stir until the shrill pitch of angry voices awakened him.

The Kutenai medicine man and the wagon doctor were arguing vehemently about water, gods and Claude. Because the spring was sacred, the Kutenai insisted, its bubbles would kill the white man who had defiled it unless the gods were appeased. The wagon doctor, on the other hand, believed that the gas from the water had become trapped in Claude's stomach, which expanded when he surfaced.

The witch doctor danced to placate his wrathful gods. The wagon doctor, meanwhile, took out his surgical blade and with one swift incision cut into Claude's swollen stomach. The foul gas and stomach fluids erupted so violently that they rent irremediably the lining and wall of Claude's stomach. And Claude was lost.

They buried Claude that morning. In his hand, Alexander clasped the grass-fire stone, the luminous green flame that had brought Claude to this unfortunate end. He would, he decided, present it to Juliette. He longed for her warm sympathy and he mourned the death of his good friend.

Chapter 7

When Alexander first heard the noise, he thought they were nearing a raging river or waterfall. He listened more closely. He'd heard rapids and cataracts before, but this wasn't nature's roar. It was the din of human voices and Alexander realized that they were approaching the rendezvous. Yet he could see no sign of it, not even a distant cloud of dust, when he stood on the wagon seat.

"Can there be that many people, Chubb?" he asked.

"I tell you, *mon ami*, it gets bigger every season. First two wagons go out, now eighty. First we go one week, now three months. First we rendezvous with a dozen trappers, now only *le bon Dieu* knows. It gets bigger." Chubb sighed. They'd been traveling a month. Another hour made no difference to him.

Alexander, however, watched eagerly for any sign of the rendezvous. When he saw something he rose from his seat and shouted to Chubb. "Look directly ahead!"

"Welcoming party. You forget they're more excited to see us than we are to find them. Good finding Marcel made. He made good finding."

The greeting party turned out to be two Indian braves racing their painted ponies to the caravan. Alexander judged it a dead heat, but the braves contended hotly over whose was the victory. Circling each other, they prepared to do battle.

"Fight!" someone yelled from the first wagon. The wagoners laughed and cheered. The braves, however, were scuffling in earnest. The sun flashed off their short knives.

"Now it's official," said Chubb. "We have our first knife fight. That, my journalist, is how you know we are officially at rendezvous. By the knife fight."

Their wagon passed the two combatants. It rattled with the caravan past the steep face of a cliff and Alexander needed no further clues.

The caravan was moving into an orderless throng of trappers, Indians, men on horseback, ponies, ruffians, busy squaws. Without any design trappers had pitched their tents and Indians their tepees anywhere in the shadows of the purple hills. Raucous voices, shrieks, curses, drunken laughter and drunken song deafened Alexander as Chubb strove to drive their wagon into one of the four circles that would be their camp.

The rendezvous, like the departure, shattered Alexander's dreams. He'd expected order and civility. He'd imagined tents set up in orderly rows and pelts neatly stacked for appraisal. Although he had fully expected the trappers to be coarse and boisterous, he hadn't thought that they would lack all civility. Nor had he thought the agents would be as rudely mannered as they were slovenly dressed.

As Alexander and Chubb walked through the camp, a young brave accosted them with his sister. Although Alexander had heard of Indian maids being bartered for a rifle and two tins of biscuits, the brave's offer shocked and embarrassed him. Chubb, however, asked her to disrobe. He deliberated a moment, then to the dismay of her brother he refused her.

"It's a miserable trip back, *mon ami*. You, too, will need companionship, you'll see."

"And when we get back to Montreal, do you bring her home to meet Louisa? That I would like to see."

"You will learn, *mon ami*! You will learn!"

"Tell me what was wrong with her. Why did you turn down so pretty a girl?"

"Too skinny. I like big mama with lots of meat." Chubb laughed heartily at his own joke.

They passed a group of trappers playing cards and backing their heavy bets with pelts. Their card game quickly declined into a shouting match and soon they were backing their curses and recriminations with bare fists, hefty punches and knives. No one paid them particular attention, least of all a trapper who was taking his pleasure with an Indian girl under a nearby tree.

The brawling trappers, the barter, all the color and excitement of the rendezvous fascinated Alexander. He was eager to see everything at once. The clangor of a brass bell, however, cut short his tour.

The bell signaled the men to return to their wagons. In the center of the campsite, Marcel stood on a makeshift platform. After reminding the men that profit was the sole purpose of their arduous journey, he ordered them to prepare immediately for the next day's business. Before nightfall he expected them to unload the wagons, erect stalls and set up stocks so that trade could begin at the break of dawn.

The wagoners grumbled. The trail had wearied them and they would have preferred to relax, to talk with new comrades and drink with old friends. Nevertheless, they set to their tasks.

Alexander helped Chubb unload the tea from their wagon. As they stacked tin after green tin, Alexander wondered how Chubb planned to account for the tea they'd shared on the trail. As tea merchant for the caravan, Chubb had had to sign a voucher for his stores. Experience had taught him how to vouch for the pilfering too.

Alexander's own preparations took little time. He had only to set up a table for the pelts he'd be appraising the next morning. As he surveyed the campsite that tomorrow would be a bustling market, Alexander noticed seven other men completing the same chore. They, too, were appraisers, he discovered, and again he felt humiliated, used, misled. He'd studied, he'd practiced and he'd believed his skills necessary to the success of the rendezvous. Any importance that had attached to his position was diminished by the sight of these other unimpressive men. He was merely one of them. He was furious with himself, with Papa Louis and his empty promises, but most of all he was furious with Marcel who had succeeded so thoroughly in demeaning him. Fuming, he kicked wildly at his table. It toppled.

Chubb appeared over a stack of tea. "Careful, *mon ami*. You break it, it comes out of your wages." Chubb failed to joke Alexander out of his ill temper.

Alexander stormed off. One day he would lead a rendezvous, Papa Louis had promised him. And his boorish son, the ineffectual leader of the caravan, had seen fit to train him only to grade pelts, had led him to believe this insignificant task was a crucial assignment. Their duplicity overwhelmed him. None of them had even bothered to tell him that Papa Louis wouldn't be traveling with the caravan, not even Juliette. He distrusted all of them, and twice now he had risked his life for these self-serving French. The whole venture mocked his dream of opportunity.

Alexander had wandered far from the camp. He halted in a pathless woods. It was dusk. The silver birch caught the last light of the sun. He relished the solitude, the tranquility, the rich smells and faint sounds of the forest.

A faint ripple of girlish laughter startled him. Then he thought he heard the sound of water splashing. Alexander trod through the underbrush. He paused, listened and then followed again the sound of water and laughter.

She was bathing in a shallow brook. Tossing back her lustrous hair, she laughed as the icy water shimmered over her firm, young breasts, down her supple body and over her shivering thighs. She faced him boldly when Alexander stumbled upon her in the dusky light of the glades.

That afternoon she'd tried to tempt Chubb by raising her deerskin dress over her head. She didn't have to try now with Alexander. Desire overwhelmed him. Her shameless gaze, her immodest smile, every quiver of her sensuous flesh aroused the passion long pent-up in him.

Her arms outstretched, she beckoned him. Then her hands were stroking his sinewy arms and shoulders and back. He trembled more at her touch than at the water's iciness. Her fingers followed the line of the angry scar across his chest, a scar as awesome as that of any brave honored by her people. She knelt before him, this white man godlike to her. Firmly her hands massaged his buttocks, his hips, his sturdy thighs. Her ardor fired his lust.

With a religious solemnity, she led him to her outspread blanket. She lay down on her back. Her smooth skin, still wet with the brook water, glistened in the twilight.

He came to her with a fury he could not control. He explored every curve of her yielding flesh. In his fingers he tangled her dark, sleek hair. He conquered her tender breasts. And when his mouth took hers, she surrendered all resistance. She clasped him to her. Her body cried for him and, feverish, rose to meet him. In their fire they consumed each other.

Crickets and the evening songs of mockingbirds had lulled him briefly to sleep. When he awoke, she was kneeling beside him in her deerskin dress. He reached up to touch her face. She bowed her head in modesty. They might have been strangers to each other, waiting to be introduced, and the passion they'd shared seemed not a memory but a dream.

Juliette's image suddenly flew into his head. His thoughts leapt back to departure day, to the smile that concealed her duplicity, and again her family's secrecy and Marcel's continual mistreatment of him distressed Alexander. He grimaced.

The Indian maid interpreted Alexander's frown as displeasure with her. Pointing to the blanket, she shook her head. Alexander tried to reassure her. The more he smiled and nodded yes, however, the further she sank into despondency. To prove that she hadn't displeased him, Alexander reached into the pocket of his trousers and extracted Claude's old leather pouch. He signaled the girl to come to him.

The grass-fire stone tumbled onto the palm of his

hand. Its rare glow held her gaze. Then she looked at Alexander with surprise and disbelief. When he tried to press the stone into her hand, she pulled away. Several times he tried and each time she refused his gift. Finally, grasping her tightly by the wrist, he forced her hand open and then closed her unwilling fingers around the grass-fire stone.

"For you," he said. He pointed to the gem and then to her. "For you."

Alexander pulled on his clothes. She didn't move. She stared at the luminous stone, turned it over in her hand, admired it. She seemed transfixed.

Alexander left her like that, silent and motionless in the darkening woods. He returned to the wagons. He felt renewed, ready now to seize opportunity and fulfill his promise without the help of the Denteres or anyone else.

Alexander awoke the next morning to the sound of Chubb's raucous laughter. No hour was too early for Chubb to indulge in some practical joke on one of the wagoners.

Rubbing the sleep from his eyes, Alexander growled, "What's so funny, laddie, to wake the devil with so loud a laugh?"

"So you went out and bought yourself a companion, eh? And you called me vile!" Again he burst into laughter. "Ah, *mon ami*, we are all victims of the flesh, all brothers under the skin." He continued to laugh.

"I don't understand you at all, Chubb."

"Voilà! I point to the evidence." Curled up on the ground in front of the smoldering campfire slept Alexander's Indian maid. "So don't you point any fingers at me, *mon ami*. And don't tell me I had so much brandy that I don't remember and she's mine because she's not mine. And if she isn't mine . . ." Chubb swept his hand toward Alexander.

Alexander was more angry than he was embarrassed. He feared, too, that Marcel would hear of his adventure with the Indian girl and would in turn tell Juliette.

He awakened her rudely with the toe of his boot. Seizing her by the wrist, he led her to the edge of their campsite. "Go," he told her. He pointed at the pine forest, and when she failed to move, he pushed her roughly toward it. Without turning her head, she walked off slowly.

She was back within the hour. Alexander had barely finished his breakfast when he spotted her. He threw down his tin plate, strode over to her and virtually dragged her beyond the circle of wagons. Again he commanded her to leave and again she did.

Again, too, she reappeared. When Alexander looked up from his morning chores, he met her brown, unwavering eyes. When he walked to the lead wagon, she followed several paces behind. If he went into Chubb's wagon to check on supplies, she waited outside. He could ignore her, but he couldn't rid himself of her. He could only hope that, spurned, she would wander off, and would do so before Chubb noticed the magnificent green stone sewn to her deerskin dress.

Alexander had more to worry about than this stubborn Indian maiden. Today would test his skill as an appraiser. He didn't know what to expect. He'd set two chairs at his table. A journal lay open on its top. His quill was ready. But not one trapper came to him or anyone else with bundles of pelts.

The trappers crowded around the stalls for supplies. They were buying everything in sight, although they had yet to receive any money for their furs. They were paying in chits, and the prices they were paying were exorbitant. Whiskey sold for eighty times what it did in Montreal and besides it was diluted with water. Tobacco, tea, sugar, lead and gunpowder all were twenty to thirty times more at the caravan tables. Whiskey, food and Indian girls would absorb every last penny these trappers made on their furs. A rendezvous was a profitable venture indeed, but only for Hudson's Bay Company.

Alexander would have lingered longer among the company's rowdy customers had he not heard Marcel shouting his name. Marcel stood at Alexander's table with a scruffy old man and several large bundles of pelts.

"Monsieur, *s'il vous plaît*, will you accommodate this gentleman?" Marcel spoke to Alexander like a master to his servant. Alexander resisted the impulse to punch Marcel and sucked in his breath instead.

"Of course, Marcel."

"Monsieur Dentere, *s'il vous plaît*," Marcel corrected him with pure contempt. "And you will please rid the caravan of that piece of Indian baggage. Such accommodations are not allowed by the company, you know." He pointed at the Indian girl, whose eyes, expressionless till then, opened wide with terror.

Alexander ignored Marcel's admonition and decided to concentrate on his first customer. They both sat down. The codger began to unknot a burlap bundle of pelts and Alexander was repelled by his stench. When he turned away for a breath of fresher air, he noticed that Marcel was standing behind him. Other trappers had gathered around his table. They too had some estimating to do, to see which of the appraisers would give their furs the best and most lenient evaluation.

Alexander spread out the pelts before him. He examined them. "These are all AA," he pronounced.

The old man smiled at the excellent rating and nodded his agreement. The other trappers voiced their approval. They'd found a good man, it seemed.

Before Alexander could proceed to the second bundle, however, Marcel shouted at him from behind. "You must be mad, *mon ami*," he spat out. "From here, even from this distance, I can see that all the pelts are cut along the rear right edge. And look how badly they're seamed. You must have been drunk that week, eh, Pierre? Half value," he told the old man.

The old trapper wailed and the others shared his disgruntlement. "That's not bad seaming, monsieur. Come, look closely, it's the animal itself."

"Marcel, I . . ."

"Quiet, Alexander. Half value."

The trapper protested further.

"Half value," Marcel cut him off with finality.

Angry and embarrassed, Alexander stared straight ahead. It had been years since someone had told him to be quiet in public. After a long silence, he spoke to Marcel without turning to face him. "Perhaps, Marcel, you would prefer this job?" he asked.

"So you could do mine? No chance, Scottie. You get on with what you're being paid to do and be attentive as to how you spend the company's money. And, Scottie, it is Monsieur Dentere."

Alexander wanted to strike this supercilious milksop who owed his life to him. He'd risen halfway out of his chair when he felt a firm hand forcing him back down.

"It's too long a walk back, *mon ami*. Stay calm, stay calm. I'll help you." It was Chubb.

Chubb rested his hand on Alexander's arm. Alexander took several deep breaths and slowly regained his composure.

Then Alexander continued his appraisal of the old man's furs. He found no more perfect pelts, but still a year's work had earned the trapper seven hundred and thirty dollars. In one year the mayor of Montreal earned a tenth of that, but then the lord mayor didn't have to undergo the hardships that this poor devil surely had suffered. And once he'd paid Hudson's Bay for his next year's supplies, he'd be lucky to walk away with any money at all.

The old man proved to be Alexander's least difficult customer that day. The trappers became more ornery by the hour. They threatened him with churlish words, with virulent curses, with murder, knives and razors. They vilified him and they shouted him down with unsparing obscenities. Nor did Marcel and his assistant Reynard, whose name meant fox but who was more of a weasel, in any way boost Alexander's self-esteem. They constantly argued his decisions, and as the three of them not once agreed on the quality of a pelt, every appraisal became a compromise. Their wrangling stalled Alexander's progress and undermined his confidence. By nightfall he was numb.

Exhausted and apprehensive, Alexander returned to his wagon. He didn't want to face the dark, staring eyes of the Indian girl. He'd ignored her the entire day, but still she stayed. That she would have to leave was unquestionable, although the worst had already happened. Marcel had found them out.

The girl had fallen asleep at the wheel of his

wagon. As quietly as an Indian himself, Alexander climbed into the wagon, unrolled his blankets and promptly fell asleep. For the second night in a row, he'd written no entry in his journal.

That first day set the pattern for the rest. Every morning Alexander awakened with dread. All day he haggled with foul-smelling, scurrilous trappers and argued with Reynard and Marcel, who continued to treat him like a dimwitted child. Each night the impassive girl waited outside his wagon. Her presence only irritated him more.

No matter how often Alexander led the girl out of the camp, no matter how wildly he pointed first to her and then to the distant mountain, no matter how roughly he thrust her onto the forest path, inevitably she returned within the hour and again he was suffering her blank-eyed stare. He tried to ignore her, tried to bury himself in his work. But the monotonous hours, the tedium, the endless contention and frequent outbursts battered his spirit and drew him closer to despair. Time lost all significance for him, and he hadn't written in his journal since the day he'd arrived at the disheartening rendezvous.

He didn't know when it had happened, or how. Alexander had thought that he'd simply ceased to care both about his work as an appraiser and about his grander aspirations in the fur trade. But then he realized he'd become more dispassionate, more businesslike in his dealings with the trappers. Without qualms he haggled with them over their pelts, and whatever his appraisal they respected him neither more nor less. The trappers expected argument and contradiction. They assumed the first call of any appraiser to be contended by Marcel and his assistants, for no one person alone determined the value of a fur. Alexander's anger over a common bargaining procedure had been a waste of his own energy. He noticed that being contradicted never ruffled Marcel. Voted down on the grade of one pelt, Marcel briskly moved to the next. Alexander's growing familiarity with everyday practices at the appraisal tables made him view himself more as an integral part of the company. And if he didn't value his role in the rendezvous, no one else would either.

One morning Alexander demanded that all the trappers call him Monsieur Mackenzie. "Monsieur, *s'il vous plaît*, if you want my full attention, or you can take your pelts somewhere else." As there was no somewhere else, the trappers could choose only to call him Monsieur Mackenzie. He succeeded in commanding their respect and that day passed more easily.

Alexander began to learn the tricks of his trade. He observed the ploys of other appraisers and devised games of his own, the rules of which he alone knew, in order to snare the trappers into the deal most profitable to the company. Alexander played to win, though often he lost. Nevertheless, he always relished the sport.

The days no longer tired Alexander. At night he lingered by the campfire and listened to the stories the trappers had to tell. These rugged mountain men had battled arctic winters, wild beasts and hostile Indians, sometimes all three at once, and they'd survived. But mostly they'd conquered their overwhelming odds. Conquest was their beast and theme.

Alexander had conquered a few odds himself. He too had some tales to tell. One night, long after the camp had gone quiet, Alexander opened his journal. He began again to write.

Chapter 8

Like giants, indomitable in spirit and fierce in courage, fur trappers had stalked through the northern wilds in Alexander's imagination. At the rendezvous, for all their bluster of incredible deeds, he discovered they were, in fact, ordinary men. And they seemed all the more remarkable to him, these army men who'd fled regimentation, order and authority, these farm hands who'd wearied of plowing, seeding, harvesting. A trapper, they told him, needed only a strong back and a strong stomach or else, some of them said, a strong back and a weak mind.

The wily beaver had led these remarkable men into situations that painfully tested human endurance. Neither cunning nor skill had enabled one of the trappers and his partner to survive an especially dire winter. Their stomachs had, for they had had no other choice than to eat beaver skin. Another trapper had spent three years in the wilderness with a Blackfoot arrowhead lodged in the thick of his back. He'd eventually met up with a white man who gave him a bottle of whiskey to kill the pain and dug out the barbed head with a fiery hot blade.

Each story topped the one before it. One fellow had known a trapper whose leg was wounded by a rifle ball. Gangrene set in. To save their partner's life, the trappers had to amputate his limb. Their tools were crude. With a butcher's knife, they cut through the flesh and with a hand saw cleft the bone. From the fire they took a red-hot iron peg. They cauterized the trapper's bleeding stump and then wrapped it in bandages. A few weeks later, their partner was hobbling about on a makeshift crutch.

More bizarre was the story told of Marcel's assistant, Reynard. He'd led trapping expeditions until a great misfortune ended that career. Reynard had negotiated a major trade with the Mohawk Indians far to the south. To show their appreciation, the Mohawk presented him with a young maid from another tribe. She, however, denied Reynard her pleasures, and when he insisted, she bit off his offensive member.

Then, one night, Alexander heard the tale that fixed his destiny.

Company whiskey had loosened this unusually young trapper's tongue. He slurred his words, constantly repeated himself and jumbled the sequence of events. Sometimes, lost in the tangle of his own narration, he simply stopped talking and promptly fell asleep. The meandering tale fascinated Alexander nevertheless, for in it he found his long-awaited opportunity.

The young trapper and his partner were trying to track down trapping grounds which were reported to be particularly bounteous. At post after post they'd met a grizzled old trapper, and envied the size of his trappings. They concluded that the man must be working in California Island, the far, lush western land beyond the impassable Rockies, and that he must therefore have discovered the secret of the Northwest Passage.

Wily though the old buzzard was, the two of them managed eventually to pick up his trail. They often went without food or drink just to keep him in sight. One morning, however, he gave them the slip. He must have broken his camp long before dawn and continued his westward trek.

The sun had barely risen when the young trapper and his partner headed west, but they failed to find any trace of the cunning codger. Nevertheless, they were sure that he'd taken the river route they were following. Then the river forked into two. The trapper and his partner decided to split up. Each of them would run one of the rivers, try to determine the old man's route and then, the next night, meet once more at the river's fork.

The young trapper ran his river longer than the single day allotted. Positive that he'd spotted another canoe, he rode the rapids and eddies until the river calmed and then opened into a bay. He tasted the water. It was salty. As swiftly as he could, he made his way back to tell his partner that he hadn't found the old trapper, but that he had reached an ocean. He'd discovered the Northwest Passage.

He waited at the fork in the river for almost an entire week. His partner did not return. The young trapper never saw him again.

Had he not decided to wait one more day, the trapper would have escaped his capture by the Blackfoot. They knocked him unconscious and must have carried him miles away, for when he awoke, he was hopelessly lost in the northern wilderness.

Since that time, the trapper reported, he'd been

searching for the fork in the river that would lead men to the bountiful world of the great Northwest.

After the young trapper had fallen into a deep, drunken sleep, some of the wagoners scoffed at his tale. Some doubted its credibility, while others admitted its possible truth. Most of them had heard stories like it before. Alexander, however, believed the man. He was certain, too, that the trapper never would have divulged his secret of the forked river had the whiskey not unleashed his tongue.

To discover the Northwest Passage, to travel its waterway beyond the Rockies and chart its route, had captured Alexander's imagination. For a long while, he sat alone by the smoldering campfire. He was eager for tomorrow, eager to question the trapper when he was sober. Alexander shivered with excitement and the cold. The fire had burned itself out. He returned to his wagon. He would succeed where others had failed, he thought as he laid out his blankets. He dreamed most of the night, but he didn't sleep until dawn.

Chubb's noisy preparations for breakfast soon awakened him. Icy creek water cleared his head and sharpened the excitement he'd felt the night before. Eager to find the trapper and to interrogate Chubb about the Northwest Passage, he couldn't eat. He sipped at a large tin mug of company tea.

"Chubb," he asked finally, "what do you know of this Northwest Passage?"

"Ah, *mon ami*, you are now officially part of the rendezvous."

"Explain that." Alexander left off his customary please and hoped Chubb would spare him a long lecture.

"Since I was a little boy, I've heard men talk of a

river through the mountains to the west. Many claim they've discovered this magic river. Yet when they try to find it again, poof, the river is gone, disappeared.''

Alexander took a long sip of tea and said nothing.

''Look at that, will you?'' Chubb pointed his knife at the far end of the camp.

There stood a Sioux chief, splendid in his feathered headdress and richly beaded deerskin. He carried a decorated lance. Slowly, the chief and seven husky, young braves, began circling the camp.

''What you think those fellows want?'' Chubb asked.

The Sioux didn't interest Alexander. ''A trapper told a story last night about a river that took him to salt water. He tasted it. Now, Chubb, I'm no fool. I know when a man is spinning a tale and—''

''Oh, *mon ami*! Men have searched for that waterway since Champlain! Find it and you are immortal. Find it and you are as rich as Croesus.'' He glanced up then and pointed to the Sioux. ''Look. The Indians have your little friend with them.''

Dark-eyed and solemn, the Indian girl walked between the chief and the braves. She did not, however, deter Alexander.

''She's unimportant. That trapper is important. I want you to hear his story. Then you decide if it's just another campfire tale inspired by too much whiskey.''

''But he can't find the river again, can he?''

''It's in Wyoming territory, he said.''

''That is days, weeks to the south. But I ask you one more time. Can he find the river again?''

''He told us Blackfoot attacked him and carried him away. He lost all sense of direction but—''

Chubb laughed. ''I told you, *mon ami*. They all tell the same story.''

"But don't you understand, Chubb? These Blackfoot must know where they found him," persisted Alexander. "They found him by the river, right? Once we find them, the Blackfoot in that raiding party can lead us to it."

"Just like that?" Chubb snapped his fingers.

"Just like that. We have to talk to that trapper when he's sober."

"So now it's we, eh? We'll find the Blackfoot, who would as soon cut off our heads as look at us, and you expect them to tell us politely where the river to California is? Aiee, Alexander, sometimes you are daft, as mad as our old friend, Claude."

"Chubb, I'm going to find the river. And you know what?"

"What, *mon ami*?"

"You're going to help me."

"Perhaps monsieur," Chubb almost consented. "But right now, I think you'll be helping out some Indians, not the Blackfoot but Sioux."

"Sioux?" Alexander turned to see the Indian party heading directly toward him. The young girl raised her arm and pointed her finger at Alexander.

"Sioux don't wander this far north. Cheyenne, maybe," speculated Alexander.

"Sioux, *mon ami*. I've seen them many times before."

"What can she want now?"

"I think," said Chubb, "she still wants you."

"They look like they mean business," muttered Alexander, alarmed now by the braves, their war paint, their determined stride and their cold, brown eyes.

"War paint for a—" Chubb had no chance to finish his sentence.

Whooping loudly, the braves leapt forward. They surrounded Alexander and thrust their lances at his neck. They were yelling incomprehensibly.

The wagoners gathered to watch. None of them knew quite how to react, for the situation, despite the threat to Alexander, was almost comic and certainly bizarre. The company men so far outnumbered the war party that the young braves couldn't even hope to survive a skirmish. Indeed, the Indian haters happily would have fired their ready rifles and wiped out the party in one round had they not been restrained by the wagon leaders. No trading company wanted hostile Indians in a territory rich with fur.

The problem was strictly Alexander's. With seven lances not a hairsbreadth from his neck, he had every reason to fear for his life. More than frightened, however, he was mortified that the entire caravan would have nothing to talk about but his peccadilloes. He felt thoroughly bewildered and helpless. Neither he nor anyone else could make sense of the warriors and sign language failed to make them withdraw their lances.

Finally Chubb shouted to a runner. "Go fetch Charley Broken Toes. And hurry!"

Alexander, the fiercely painted braves, the Indian girl expressionless, the chief, Chubb, the expectant crowd, everyone stood still. Minutes dragged by. Sweat poured down Alexander's brow. Then, at last, Charley Broken Toes appeared. He limped through the crowd, into the circle, and he gasped at what he saw.

"Find out what the trouble is, Charley. Fast," Marcel ordered him.

"I second that," Alexander croaked through his tight, stretched throat.

The braves started shouting again.

"Are they Sioux?" Chubb yelled to the interpreter.

"Cherokee," answered Charley. "My people."

Charley outshouted the warriors with an explosive barrage of words. The braves fell silent. Gradually lowering his voice, Charley spoke to the braves. He was almost whispering when, finally, the warriors drew in their lances and took one step back.

"Thank you, laddie," said Alexander with relief as he rubbed his neck.

"It ain't over," whispered Charley. "It ain't over by a long shot."

Alexander studied the Cherokee maiden who, he was sure, had brought him to this pass. But he didn't know how, for as a rule Indians did not regard a woman so highly that a chief and seven braves would risk their lives for her. She stood proud and silent. Defiance marked the set of her jaw and glinted in her dark brown eyes.

Charley began interpreting the Cherokee message. "The chief says Winter Flower, that's the girl, is his first-born, a princess of the tribe. He also says . . ." Hesitant to insult a white man, Charley paused. "He says, that, uh, you abused her."

"That's a strange word for it, Charley. I . . ."

"I must answer him only 'Yes, it's true' or 'No, it's not true,' and that's all," whispered Charley.

Anger flashed in Alexander's eyes. Again anxious to seek out the young trapper, he had no patience for this interrogation. "No, it is not true. Tell the old geezer that for me."

After another exchange with the chief, Charley reported, "Chief says you offended the princess and so you offend him and you offend the tribe." Seeing Alexander's anger turn to fury, he hastily added, "Only answer, 'Yes, it's true' or 'No, it's not true.' " After a long pause he begged, "*Please*."

Alexander fumed, and his refusal to reply seemed to have brought the parley to a dead halt.

Then Charley continued. "The chief says you gave a jewel stone to the princess and didn't take her to your bed or home." Charley didn't wait for an answer but in an aside told Alexander, "Among my people, exchanging a gift is a symbol of union. This girl is your wife and, like it or not, yours for life. But also tribal law forbids this union, for you will defile Cherokee blood. That is why the chief is angry."

"My wife! She's not my wife!"

"She claims you gave her a rare jewel. When you did that, you married her."

"Then tell her to give me back my jewel and we'll get unmarried." He held out his hand.

"I think that's what they wanted you to say. I'll tell them." Charley turned to speak with the chief. Their discussion became more heated. Their gestures, their nods and frowns, the rising intensity of their voices all suggested a difficult compromise, concessions gained and demands lost. Charley looked agitated, the chief dissatisfied. Then, with finality, the chief folded his arms and shook his head. All discussion stopped.

Charley slowly backed away from the chief until he stood halfway between the two adversaries. He turned to face Alexander. He wet his lips and seemed about to speak, but the right words apparently escaped him. He stood there perplexed, pondering.

"Come on, Charley, spit it out! I won't eat you," Alexander shouted at him.

"Yes, well, uh . . . Well, the chief says you can

dissolve this union easy enough, but if you want the jewel back, you must fight for it."

"Yes, I want the jewel back."

"Then you must fight Bright Star."

A strapping young brave with fierce eyes and powerful arms tossed his fringed, deerskin shirt to the ground.

"I don't want to fight anyone."

"You will, I think, whether you like it or not," said Charley. "It's the only way he can honestly tell anyone that the jewel is his. My people aren't thieves."

"I'll fight him then."

"Have you ever fought Cherokee style?" asked Charley.

"Of course, I've never fought Cherokee style."

"Look at Bright Star. You see what he's doing?"

The brave rolled and twisted a long piece of cotton cloth tightly into a rope with a stone in the middle of it. Then he knotted both ends of the rope and stretched it out on the ground. At each knot he placed a dagger.

"What you do now," Charley explained, "is take the knotted end, put it in your mouth and bite down on it with the knot behind your teeth. When you're ready, you signal the start of the fight by picking up the knife. If you drop the cloth, the other braves will run you in."

"And if Bright Boy drops the cloth?" asked Alexander.

"Bright Star," Charley corrected him. "Then, with their lances, the braves will run him in."

Alexander took off his short vest and shirt. He rubbed some dirt into both his hands. He walked slowly to his end of the rope. Crouching low, he toyed with it. Not for a second did he take his eyes off Bright Star, who'd already put the cloth in his mouth and the knife in his hand. Pretending to test its slack, Alexander pulled on the rope and jerked his opponent forward. His friends applauded. Smiling to himself, Alexander bowed his apologies.

With no further ado, he put the knotted end of the cloth into his mouth, again rubbed his right hand in the dirt and picked up the dagger. The fight began.

Bright Star started circling Alexander. Jerking back his head, he tugged at the rope to keep his opponent off balance. Then, when Alexander expected another tug, Bright Star fooled him. He let the cloth go slack, and sweeping his arm in a wide arc, he took a swipe at the unsuspecting Alexander.

Bright Star struck Alexander forcefully in the throat with the back of his hand.

Struggling to regain his breath and to prepare for his own attack, Alexander pulled the rope taut and began to circle Bright Star. Then, lunging forward, he surprised Bright Star with a powerful kick in the stomach. The Indian fell to one knee.

Swiftly, Alexander moved in to finish off his stunned opponent, but the wiry brave yanked him to the ground with a fierce tug on their tether. Bright Star's sudden pull almost wrenched the knot from between Alexander's teeth and the sharp blade of the Indian's knife cut through his chaps. Alexander's leg was bleeding. The crowd was shouting. The two opponents scrambled to their feet.

Once more the two of them squared off. Warily, they began circling each other. Flinging his knife from one hand to the other, the brave took two quick jabs at Alexander. Both fell short of the mark.

At the same time he pulled in the tether, Alexander rushed headlong at the brave. Losing no momentum, he threw himself in a running slide to the ground and sent

Bright Star flying over him. Before the Indian could recover, Alexander started pummeling him. The shortness of the rope, however, prevented Alexander from landing a severe blow.

Bright Star resisted Alexander's kicks and jabs. Although his own swipes went wild, he managed again to get to his feet. Backing away from Alexander as far as the tether would allow, the brave fought for his second wind.

Again Alexander attacked. He dropped to the ground and pulled the Indian down with him. They scuffled, and in a flurry of backhand blows to Alexander's head and neck, Bright Star gained the advantage.

Bright Star dragged Alexander over the ground. Hauling him erect, the brave forced Alexander to stand on his unsteady legs. The glinting blade slashed at the air between them. Alexander backed away, and with surprising dexterity, the brave started tossing the knife from hand to hand.

Alexander timed his next move carefully. He raised his leg and deftly kicked the handle of Bright Star's blade. The knife went flying into the crowd.

Bright Star stopped dead in his tracks. Feigning defeat, he started to cave in at the knees. His play did not fool Alexander. With a powerful kick to his stomach, Alexander sent the young brave reeling. The knot fell from Bright Star's mouth. Alexander rushed to the writhing Indian, seized a fistful of his hair and snapped back his head. He put the tip of his blade to Bright Star's neck and ran its keen edge over the Indian's flesh. He drew blood. The crowd went quiet.

Alexander strove to catch his breath. "What I am going to say is simple, simple . . ." He stopped, realizing Bright Star couldn't understand his words, and yelled for Charley.

"Tell him," Alexander ordered Charley Broken Toes, "tell him that I claim his life, but that I don't want it now. If I see him or her again, anywhere ever again, I'll skin them both alive and feed what's left to the wolves."

Alexander couldn't measure the full power of his message, but with relief he watched the Cherokee unceremoniously leave. In his hand he held the grass-fire stone.

The wagoners and trappers cheered Alexander and patted him heartily on the back as he worked his way through them to the creek. He leapt into the water. He bathed his wound and washed away the dirt from battle. The water soothed and then invigorated him. It felt good. He would have stayed in the creek longer had Marcel not shouted to him. Alexander moved toward the shore and asked Marcel to repeat his words.

"If you're through with the morning entertainment, perhaps you won't mind giving us the pleasure of some work." Marcel spoke brusquely, bowed to Alexander, turned and left.

The man is mad, thought Alexander. Absolutely mad.

Chapter 9

Chubb concentrated on the trail and the frisky team of horses that would pull their wagon back to Montreal. Alexander surrendered to his wretchedness.

For two weeks Alexander had searched for the young fur trapper who claimed he'd discovered the Northwest Passage. Each day Alexander had grown more anxious until finally he was frantic. No one had seen the trapper since the night he'd told his drunken tale. No one knew when, or if, he had left the camp. He simply had disappeared, it seemed, without a trace. Nevertheless, Alexander had continued his search, had refused to acknowledge its futility. The quest for the Northwest Passage would never let him rest. Then the rendezvous had broken up. Alexander had learned only that the name of the man might be Vincente.

There was the slim possibility this Vincente might be traveling in one of the small bands of trappers that the caravan passed on its homeward trek. With little hope, Alexander sought among them an unforgotten face, but it was to no avail. Otherwise, he rode in heavy silence beside his sympathetic friend, Chubb.

Several days into their journey, the axles of two of

133

the wagons broke. The caravan stopped for repairs. That day, as Chubb put it, Alexander returned to the world.

The wagons had broken down in the very area where they'd buried Claude. Chubb and Alexander decided to visit his gravesite and pay their last respects. Although they'd marked the grave well, to their amazement they were unable to locate it. Indeed, they'd begun to doubt they were anywhere near the site when they stumbled upon the sacred spring that the Kutenai called Devil's Mouth.

"The entire land has changed with the season," Alexander remarked.

"If you told me I'd never been here, I'd believe it. It's incredible, *mon ami*."

A clanging bell called the men back to the caravan. The wagons were ready to roll again.

"Adieu, *mon ami* Claude, wherever you are. Goodbye, good friend," shouted Chubb.

"Do you think he hears you?" asked Alexander as they were walking back.

"I do, yes. Or else, *mon ami*, it isn't worth it at all, is it?"

Alexander didn't comment. He didn't want to encourage Chubb who had a predilection for lengthy homilies.

"The hardest part," continued Chubb, "will be telling his wife."

"I didn't know he was married."

"Oh, yes. Children, too. Nice family. It's the world we live in that's not so nice, or the way of our world."

The caravan was moving again. Chubb asked Alexander to spell him as his arms were aching with the strain of driving the horses over the rocky terrain.

"You know, Chubb, trying to find Claude's grave proved something to me. You said it wasn't possible, but now I see it's very possible."

"What is it you're yapping about without making any sense?" asked Chubb, happy that his partner had broken his gloomy silence at last.

"You said that no mountain man who claimed he discovered the river to the western shore has ever been able to prove that claim because he's never been able to find this mysterious river again. Now, I ask you, why should you expect them to? You and I couldn't even find Claude's grave, a grave that we ourselves dug and marked. Think about what I'm saying!"

"There's nothing I can say to argue with you."

"I don't want you to argue with me. I want you to reason with me, to help me solve this puzzle."

"If what you say is right," reasoned Chubb, "and our search this morning seems to prove it is, then the land up here must change her clothes very fast."

"And very often. That's the clue. That's why no one has ever been able to return to the same spot twice."

"But you would think, *mon ami*, that anyone looking for so important a route would mark his trail."

"But didn't we leave markings on Claude's grave?"

Chubb again recalled the wooden cross he'd forced into the earth. "You're right again, *mon professeur*. You feel better for all this unriddling?"

"I feel wonderful," Alexander answered honestly. "Now we can get down to planning our expedition without worrying if someone lied to us or not."

"You're still saying 'we' *mon ami*," Chubbed wailed ruefully.

135

"That's right, Chubb, we are, I mean, I am, aren't I?"

They both laughed.

During the long, tedious days that followed, Alexander and Chubb talked of little else. Alexander's plans for an expedition through the mountains of the great Northwest offset for him all the boredom of their journey back to Montreal. Chubb's reservations failed to daunt his enthusiasm.

"And who will finance such a venture?" Chubb one day questioned Alexander and his practicality.

"Monsieur Dentere himself! I told you what he thinks of me. Indeed, he himself said that I was most qualified to lead a rendezvous."

"He actually told you that?"

"More than once. In fact, Marcel was there on both occasions."

"That cannot have sat well with Marcel. Now I see why he talks to you the way he does. I wish you'd told me this sooner. It explains a lot."

Alexander, however, had no interest in discussing Marcel. "So, money won't be our problem, Chubb. That's one trouble we can put out of our heads."

In his fervor, Alexander put many a trouble out of his head. Chubb had to rein in his friend's imagination more often than he did their lively team of horses.

"Well, we have at least four months to plan this expedition in any case," Chubb remarked during one of their sessions.

"Four months? My God, Chubb, you saw how much *one* month changed the land! And you think we can wait for four?"

"No one, not even you, my hearty friend, can survive the winters this far north. People freeze to death right outside Montreal. Up here you would go like this.'' Chubb snapped his fingers.

"Maybe we can find a southern route, through the colonies, where there is no snow.''

"Don't be foolhardy. Foolhardy don't pay.''

Tomorrow Alexander would forget Chubb's sound advice. For all of Alexander's bold spirit and determination and manly strength, his impatience would defeat him yet, Chubb was sure. Continually, Chubb had to force his partner to consider his human limitations and to plan this daring expedition more slowly, carefully, rationally. With blunt words and often harsh advice, Chubb wanted only to help his friend's chances of success.

Practicalities did eventually distract Alexander from his grand plan. In two days the caravan would arrive in Montreal. The wagoners would return to their wives, their children, their homes, and he would again see Juliette. He'd been faithful to his promise, and almost daily he'd recorded in his journal the experiences, the impressions and wonders he wanted to share with her. He longed for Juliette, for the happy hours they once more would spend together, but he wouldn't move back into the Dentere mansion.

Alexander remained ambivalent toward Juliette's family. He felt that Papa Louis had betrayed his trust and that Marcel had at every opportunity abused it. Alexander couldn't bear the thought of long dinners at the same table as Marcel or the prospect of his pompous conversation in the drawing room. Nor would he be able to conceal for very long his contempt for this incompetent Dentere while his family adulated his witless accomplishments. No matter that Alexander had no home in Montreal—the Denteres, so far as he was concerned, were not possible hosts.

Chubb, however, was another matter. He and his wife had a spare bedroom above their apartment. At a minimal rent, which would nonetheless help his accounts enormously, Chubb offered it to Alexander. Alexander's gratitude was surpassed only by his appreciation of this man who in the past few months had become his lifetime friend.

The twilight was already dwindling into night two days later when the caravan began to pull into Montreal. No cheers and banners, no brass band, no crowds greeted the weary wagoners. Squirrels scampered out of their paths. A dog or two barked. The city slept. Disappointed though Alexander was by the lack of ceremony, he could still contemplate a bath. At least he hoped he could.

"Chubb!" he yelled above the rattle of wagon wheels on the newly cobblestoned streets. "Your house, does it have a bathtub?"

"Not only a bathtub, *mon chéri*, but someone to bathe you if you wish." Chubb laughed. He was thinking of his wife's cousin, a woman as ugly as any alive, but could she ever scrub backs.

Alexander ran an uneasy finger beneath his highly starched collar. Gripping the journal tightly under his arm, he walked up the driveway to the Dentere mansion.

The trees had been budding when he'd left for the rendezvous months before. Their naked branches now made the grand house seem all the more vast. Its brick walls stood a full three stories high under a gambrel roof. Rows of mullioned windows with white shutters looked out over the expansive ground of the Dentere estate. Alexander found it hard to believe that he'd once lived there. Had he not saved the lives of Marcel and Juliette that day on the St. Lawrence, he was certain he never would have crossed the threshold of the Denteres' stately house.

Alexander walked past the front entrance to the house and headed for the stables around the back. Juliette, he figured, would be out riding at this time of the afternoon. He was right. Daisy's stall was empty. Nor was Joseph, the blacksmith, anywhere about. A sullen boy glanced in his direction and then continued soaping a saddle.

Although Alexander wanted to undo his collar and loosen the jacket that buttoned too tightly around his chest, he decided to bear his discomfort for another half-hour. As it was, he didn't know how long he waited for Juliette at the gate to Daisy's stall. The familiarity of the place, the smells of hay and leather and horses, recalled those long, happy days he'd shared with Juliette. He daydreamed and memory made him yearn for her and their carefree hours together all the more.

The clopping of horse's hooves and shouts from the courtyard roused Alexander. He ran to the doorway and saw Juliette on Daisy cantering toward the stable. She looked radiant. Flushed and smiling, exhilarated by her ride, she was calling for Joseph to lift her down from Daisy.

Alexander rushed into the daylight. "Juliette! Juliette!" he shouted to her. "I'm home!"

At the sound of his voice, Juliette straightened in her saddle and raised her hand to shield her eyes from the sun. "Who's that?" she cried, and then answered her own question with delight and surprise. "Alexander, my Alexander! You've come back!"

She was looking around for Joseph, for a groom or stableboy or anyone to help her dismount, when Alexander was by her side and offering his hand. "Allow me, or else I'll have to leap up there to claim the hug I've been waiting for all these months."

She jumped down lightly and rushed into his open arms. "Oh, Alexander! Alexander, Alexander!" She wrapped her arms tightly around him. Without guile or embarrassment, she confessed, "Oh, how I've missed you, my dear Alexander. And yesterday, when you didn't come home with Marcel, I thought—"

"You're more beautiful than ever, my Juliette."

"Then kiss me. Kiss me, please, Alexander. Marcel did."

"You're bold." Alexander said no more. He pressed his mouth to hers and her lips met his in a kiss that spoke their long desire for each other.

"How many months I have waited for that, my Alexander. Too many months." Juliette's eyes sought his, held them, and happily she would have drowned in his sea-blue gaze. Then she asked, "Why didn't you come yesterday?"

"Yesterday Daisy would have smelled sweeter to you than I."

"Had you grown a beard like Marcel?" She stroked his smooth face.

"No, but I discovered there are no bathtubs on the trail."

"You haven't told me you missed me yet." Juliette feigned a pout.

"But I didn't."

Tears almost instantly filled her eyes. "Alexander!"

"I spoke to you each night and then I dreamt of you with something of you beside me." Alexander picked up the journal that had fallen to the ground. " 'Each night as you take down this book . . .' "

"Then you didn't forget?"

"It was my salvation."

"Come, come inside. Mother is there and I know she'll be almost as happy to see you as I."

As they walked to the house, Juliette told him that her father and Marcel had gone to the market to set prices for their goods. Their profits would be higher this year than any before, she'd overhead her father say. They entered the kitchen from the small garden behind the house.

"Monsieur Alexander! Welcome, welcome home."

"Thank you, Mariou. I'm happy to be back."

"Already I have the chocolate."

"You are a witch, Mariou."

"I saw you through the window waiting for mademoiselle. So tall you are today, so strong."

"You think he's changed, Mariou?" asked Juliette. "Maybe you did grow, Alexander."

Embarrassed by their discussion of him, Alexander peeked into the cozy alcove off the kitchen where he and Juliette had passed many afternoons sipping chocolate and sharing their dreams. It was a cheerful room with whitewashed walls and a red brick floor. Its curtains matched the blue of the tiles that framed the fireplace.

"Fetch Mama, Mariou," Juliette told the maid who set before them two steaming mugs of chocolate and a plate of croissants. "Tell her our old friend has come home."

"You keep saying home, Juliette. I won't be staying

here. I . . .'' Alexander halted, sought for more tactful words. ''I won't impose on your family any longer.''

''Impose? Nonsense!'' Juliette exclaimed as her mother came into the room. ''You're expected. Mama, tell him he must stay.''

''*Bienvenue, mon chèr* Alexander. *Bienvenue*.''

''Mama Marie,'' he said and awkwardly kissed her proffered hand.

''You two, not together five minutes and already as sympathetic as ever. Ah, Juliette, that you and your brother got along as well.''

Mama Marie assured Alexander that in the Dentere house he would always have a home. To Juliette's disappointment, Alexander promised Mama Marie only that he would visit again soon.

Juliette and Alexander sat together in the pleasant alcove long after Mama Marie had left. Indeed they talked well into the middle of the night. Then, when Alexander insisted on returning to his cramped quarters above the Chubbs' apartment, Juliette had Joseph awakened to drive him home in their carriage. ''It's a brand new one,'' she said. Then she added pertly, ''You'll ride in more style than you'll sleep.''

Chapter 10

The weeks that followed kept Alexander busier than he'd ever expected to be. He had little time to explore the bustling city of Montreal. When he wasn't planning his expedition to the mysterious forked river with Chubb, he was attending to the whims and biddings of Juliette. If he became so engrossed in his plans with Chubb and neglected to call on her, Juliette did not hesitate to visit him. Her stylish carriage never failed to elicit shouts and cheers along the less than fashionable streets of the Chubbs' neighborhood.

Alexander enjoyed his time with Juliette. Her enthusiasm over his journal and her close attention to every detail of his experiences in the wilderness flattered him. He basked in her admiration of him, even though he knew that the success of the rendezvous hardly had depended on him, as Juliette liked to assume. Nevertheless, no matter how much stronger, wiser and happier Juliette made him feel, Alexander had more to contemplate than an adventure already past. He had a future to plan too.

That plan required maps. Alexander and Chubb couldn't afford to buy maps of the Northwest Territory, which were sketchy and inaccurate in any case, nor could they fund a team of scouts to map the region for them. They had to rely on their memories, or, more accurately, on Chubb's memory, for he'd been traveling for years into the northern wilderness. Also, Chubb knew other wagoners, some trappers and even a few explorers who were familiar with the territory. These men could corroborate the landmarks that Chubb and Alexander remembered as well as add new details to their rudimentary maps.

Alexander and Chubb spent tedious hours and sometimes days trying to track down these rootless men who might be out of reach in the wilderness or holed up in a dingy room with a week's supply of cheap whiskey. Their time was often wasted. So was their money. A former cartographer for the Crown, who'd been drummed out of service for drunkenness, demanded whiskey as payment for information that proved to be useless. Occasionally, though, luck and their diligence took them to men sober enough to recall the exact location of a lake, a hill or an Indian village, or to describe a particular tree that marked a trail or the bend of a river. Chubb and Alexander gradually filled their maps with details essential for their expedition.

Juliette knew that Alexander was dividing his time between her and something else. What bothered Juliette was that he refused to discuss with her the something else. Before the rendezvous Alexander had shared all his plans with her, all his successes and disappointments, his secret fears and secret hopes.

Juliette noticed other changes in Alexander too. He'd grown more certain of himself. He'd become firmer in his opinions and he revised them far less readily than before. Although she praised his accomplishments and truly admired his new self-assurance, his occasional pomposity disturbed her. She missed Alexander's gentleness and couldn't understand the determination and impatience that now seemed to drive Alexander from her.

Nor could Juliette understand why Alexander had made no attempt to see her father since his return from the rendezvous. "I've run out of excuses for your bad manners," she bluntly told Alexander. "Why don't you want to see Papa?"

"I do want to see him, but I want to be ready to see him before I do."

"To say hello and tell him how you are? You need to prepare for that?"

"Of course not, silly girl. I want to propose a venture to Papa Louis and I want to have all my facts so I can talk to him about it intelligently. You know how he is."

"I know how he is and I know he's wondering when you'll come by to say hello."

Alexander wanted to reply that her father could have found him in his own kitchen on any number of days. He wanted to say that Papa Louis probably felt no more pressed to see him than he had to confide in him that he, the managing director of Hudson's Bay Company, wouldn't be leading the rendezvous. Indeed, Alexander tried to change the subject. "I haven't seen Marcel either, for that matter," he said.

"Oh, but you saw *him* every day for months." Alexander did not respond. "You did, didn't you?"

"Of course, yes," he lied. "And besides your father has been traveling."

"He went to the American colonies to see about

some shipments that went astray and arrived in Boston harbor by mistake.''

''What did he say of Boston? Of the colonies?''

''Nothing much.'' Juliette's offhand reply disappointed him.

''Alexander, in two weeks it'll be Christmas. Will you come to the house for the holiday? It'll be so pretty with all the decorations.''

''Decorations?''

''Yes, decorations. Especially the tree. We always set it up in the parlor and trim it with all sorts of beautiful ornaments.''

''A tree?'' He was astounded. ''You bring a tree into your house?''

''Have you never heard of this?''

''I'd remember if I had.''

''Marcel and I had a tutor who came from the Old World. He taught us the custom.''

''This indeed, I'll have to see.''

''Oh, how good! Papa will be there, everyone will be there. I'll tell Mama, she'll be so happy. Everyone will. Especially Papa.''

Another custom crossed his mind. ''Juliette? Do you give gifts?''

''Gifts? No.''

''In my home Christmas is a time for giving gifts to the people you love.''

Juliette was touched. ''Many things about you may have changed, my Alexander, but one thing I'm happy has not.''

Alexander smiled. ''What is that, Juliette?''

''That you still care for people.''

''Only certain people, my Juliette. Only certain

people." He took her arm and led her to her carriage. "Until Christmas?"

"That's two weeks from now. Won't I see you before then?"

"If I'm going to see your father in two weeks, I have a lot of getting ready to do."

"You sound as if he's a stranger to you."

Alexander didn't comment. He squeezed her hand, kissed it and repeated, "Till Christmas."

When Alexander told Chubb that they had only two weeks to finish their maps, Chubb was more agitated than pleased.

"But we're far from ready, *mon ami*. Most of our maps are still incomplete," Chubb objected.

"We already have more maps to find one river than Champlain had to open up this entire world. I have no qualms about presenting our maps to Papa Dentere as long as I know that they're accurate."

"Have you decided what territory you're going to tell him we want to explore?"

"Wyoming Territory."

"Wyoming Territory? Who can tell us anything of that place?"

"Who then can tell us that our maps are wrong? Can anyone in the Dentere household refute their accuracy?"

"No."

"That is precisely why we tell him Wyoming."

"Then I suggest we get to work immediately. Christmas, *mon ami*, is but two weeks from now."

Their work quickly became frustrating drudgery, for neither Alexander nor Chubb was a skilled cartographer. Their carefully drawn rivers turned into smears of blue ink and their forests and hills into green blotches. Unless it was thoroughly dried, the red ink designating Indian villages rubbed off at the slightest touch. Constant erasures rubbed through the parchment that Chubb and Alexander had purchased at great expense.

"The part we paid least attention to has proved to be our undoing," remarked Alexander when they'd inked the last of their maps.

Still, the maps were legible enough to show that the two men had some idea as to where they were going, how long it would take them and what they could expect along the way. And Alexander felt ready and confident enough to convince Papa Louis that Hudson's Bay Company would not be risking money on this expedition but rather would be investing it in a very profitable future.

The French believed in Christmas and the Denteres had spared no expense on the holiday. Alexander approached the house with a childlike awe. Wreaths of holly leaves and evergreen with red ribbons, pine cones and cranberries decorated the windows of the Dentere mansion. A candle glowed in the center of the magnificent wreath on the front door.

Mariou greeted Alexander in the front hall. Eyeing the rolls of charts and maps Alexander had brought for his presentation to Papa Louis, Marcel commented to him, "Plans for a new wagon, I suppose—one, I trust, with a softer bench for your wagoners."

Alexander did not laugh with Marcel. Extending his hand, he said, "Happy Christmas, Marcel. Am I too early?"

"On the contrary, everyone is already around the tree."

"Ah, the tree. Juliette told me about that. You actually have a tree in your house?"

"And a village. Come, see for yourself."

A tall spruce stood in the center of the parlor. From its branches hung strings of popcorn and cranberries as well as nuts, pine cones, cookies and fruit. Around its base a village of cardboard houses stood on a hilly terrain constructed out of rocks and moss and papier-mâché. Twigs became trees. White sheets and confetti created the illusion of snow, while mirrors passed for ponds and streams. Tiny porcelain figurines peopled the miniature scene.

But more beautiful than any adornment for the season was Juliette herself. In a pale green dress of watered silk bound at the waist by a bright red sash, she welcomed him. "Happy Christmas, Alexander."

"Happy Christmas, Juliette."

"Do you like our tree and village? Marcel and I make one every year, but this year it was mostly Mama and me. Marcel has become too important now, you know. Papa says it's the best ever."

Her remark about Marcel surprised Alexander, until he realized it was merely a sister's affectionate gibe. Then it bothered him.

Mama Marie greeted Alexander with a kiss on the cheek and Papa Louis with a warm bear hug. "You came back to see everyone but me, huh? I should be insulted," Papa teased him.

"You went to the colonies, I heard."

"That's true, but not for the entire time that you've been back from the rendezvous."

"I've been busy on my own."

"At what?" Work never failed to arouse Papa's curiosity.

"With your permission, I'd like to discuss it with you after dinner. If that's all right with everyone else."

"It's plans for a new wagon with softer seats, I swear it is, Papa. Alexander thinks big." Marcel enjoyed his joke and laughed long after everyone else.

"Marcel!" Mama whispered disapprovingly.

"After dinner it is," Papa raised his glass and noticed Alexander's empty hand. "Mariou, have you been swigging at my wine? Our guest has no glass. Shame on you!"

Alexander's hand wasn't empty for long. Raising a glass of red wine he saluted his host. He drank the wine too fast. The temperature in the room seemed to rise and he felt woozy. He reached for a candied fig. He'd downed a fistful of them when Juliette came over to him.

"Come with me, Alexander, and let me show you the preparations for our Christmas dinner." She took him by the hand and led him out of the parlor.

"Don't get lost, you two. We have other guests, you know," Mama called after them.

"Other guests?" Alexander asked with a note of surprise.

"Yes. There's Papa's partner, Monsieur Desmoines, and his wife. And Monsieur Reynard, whom you know from the rendezvous."

"Reynard from the trail, of course." Alexander smiled as he toyed with the idea of telling Juliette the story of Reynard's misfortune with the Indian maiden. He resisted the impulse, however, and followed Juliette into the kitchen.

Fancifully prepared vegetables, quiches, cakes, pies and puddings filled the long, planked tables. Soups bubbled on the stove. A goose stuffed with sweet potatoes and apples was roasting in one of the huge ovens. Thick lamb chops were baking in another. The aromas overwhelmed Alexander. Juliette, however, had something other than food on her mind.

Tightly holding his hand, Juliette led Alexander into the alcove. From a bottle opened by the kitchen staff to celebrate the holiday, Juliette poured champagne into Alexander's glass. In one gulp he emptied it and Juliette slid into his lap. Drawing her closer, Alexander wrapped her in his arms and kissed her hungrily on the mouth. His unexpected passion startled them both. Juliette flushed, and happily his captive, she rested her forehead on his.

"I have something for you," Alexander told her huskily. "Something one man died for and another man twice risked his life for. I can think of no one on this earth who could do more justice to this beautiful jewel than you."

Alexander placed the grass-fire stone in Juliette's delicate hand. In the flickering light of the fireplace its green flame glowed even more fiercely than it had under the wilderness moon.

"Alexander, it's magnificent, more magnificent than any gem I've ever seen. Each jewel you give me is more beautiful than the one before."

At first Alexander didn't understand Juliette's compliment. Then he remembered the three diamonds and his grandmother's gold cross, which he'd entrusted to Juliette. But he hadn't given them to her. Now, however, was hardly the time to correct the misunderstanding.

"Happy holiday, my love."

"Your love?" whispered Juliette, surprised as much by Alexander's tender words as she had been by his hungry desire. Passionately she kissed him and he her.

They stole each other's breath, and lost in each other's kisses and arms, they didn't see or hear Papa Louis come into the kitchen. Nor did they see him leave in a silent rage.

Dinner was served and each course tempted Alexander's palate more than the last. He tried to eat sparingly, and if he was losing the battle, he was enjoying his defeat enormously. It was a glorious feast.

Only the seating arrangement bothered Alexander. Usually he was seated next to Juliette, but today he sat opposite her and the oafish Reynard sat in his place. So, rather than sharing private jokes with Alexander, Juliette politely bore the attentions of Marcel's assistant. Nevertheless, Alexander felt she need not bear them quite so politely as she was. When Reynard wasn't fawning over Juliette, he was chatting busily with Marcel. The elder Denteres engaged Monsieur Desmoines and his wife in lively conversation. Generally, Alexander concentrated more on the dinner than the company, although he occasionally caught Juliette's eye and won her smile.

More disconcerting to Alexander was Papa Louis' eye. Several times during dinner, Papa Louis glanced, indeed almost glared, at Alexander, and each time a flush reddened the old man's face. Alexander wondered why. If he'd insulted Papa Louis, he didn't know how.

After dinner it happened again. Reynard was accompanying Marcel and Juliette on the clavichord in some French Christmas carols and Alexander asked Papa Louis if he might take this opportunity to speak with him. Papa Louis' face flushed as he virtually glowered at Alexander. He said yes, however, and the two men withdrew to the study.

Papa Louis sat down behind his massive desk and

took a long, black cigar from the humidor. He didn't offer one to his guest. The slight surprised Alexander.

"All right," Papa said gruffly, after he'd lit the cigar, "what's on your mind?"

Papa's brusque manner baffled Alexander. He concluded that he must unknowingly have insulted Monsieur Dentere to be treated in such a way. He suddenly realized he'd neglected to bring his maps and charts into the study.

"Excuse me, Papa, but I've forgotten some very important material to show—"

"No, no, no," Papa Louis interrupted him. "First you tell me what you expect from me and then you can get your important material."

"What I'd like you to do, sir, is finance an expedition, which I will lead, to find the Northwest Passage." Alexander spoke with clarity and determination. He paused for a response, but Papa Louis said nothing.

"I have maps and charts which I'm prepared to . . ." Alexander's voice trailed off and still Papa Louis said nothing.

"They're in the hall, these are . . ." Alexander faltered. "I mean, the maps and charts are what I forgot to bring in."

"And these are your intentions?" Papa Louis almost scoffed at him. "I thought they would be of another nature."

"What do you mean, sir?" Alexander's question was barely audible.

"How can you sit there and tell me that you, not a year in the wilderness, can succeed where other men for years have failed?" Papa Louis' face turned red. "You couldn't even tell me how to get to Ottawa, let alone how to cross the Big Mountains. And you expect money from me, money for some . . . some folly?''

''It's hardly a folly, sir.''

''Are you planning to take Juliette with you also?'' Papa Louis' flush deepened.

''No, of course not . . .''

''Why not? What have you promised my little girl to make her behave so disgracefully this evening? How long have you been misleading her this way? Under our very own roof you have deceived me and my wife. We opened our home to you and you thank us by seducing our daughter!'' Outraged Papa Louis was shouting at Alexander.

''What are you saying, sir!'' Alexander tried to calm him. ''Juliette and I have done nothing a brother and sister wouldn't do.''

''That's what you would like us to think, wouldn't you, you blackguard? I trusted you like another son. I sent you on a rendezvous, provided opportunities. And this is my reward? Am I so bad a judge of character? You repay me by spoiling my daughter!'' Papa Louis' wrath terrified Alexander and his vivid flush alarmed him.

''Monsieur! Please, monsieur. I have not, not in any way, taken advantage of your daughter.''

''We've treated you like a son, better than a son, and you dishonor our daughter with treachery and debauchery. She's an innocent, meant for men finer than you or I will ever be.''

Alexander could do nothing to mollify Papa and little, at the moment, to answer the accusations concerning his relations with Juliette. Although it might take years, Alexander felt sure that the truth would eventually bear his honor out. Right now, however, he needed Papa's help to implement the expedition.

Papa Louis gulped down a large brandy, then another. Uncertain of his next step, Alexander buttoned and unbuttoned his jacket.

"Sir, I have not seduced your daughter!" Alexander blurted emphatically. "In no way have I deceived you or dishonored her in this house. Juliette is too dear to me for that."

"Where then? Where have you dishonored her? In the forest? In the market?"

"Take hold of yourself, monsieur."

Alexander poured him another brandy. Papa drank it down in three fast gulps. Then Papa Louis sank into the chair behind his desk. He buried his face in his hands. He was silent.

Alexander moved toward the door. He'd already reached it when Papa stopped him.

"What is this expedition of yours about?" He sounded subdued.

"To find the Northwest Passage." Alexander spoke slowly, confidently.

"I won't finance such a venture."

"I have maps, charts. I even have a man who's been through it."

"I don't care if you had the hand of God in yours to lead you to the West. I will not finance such an expedition."

"May I ask why not?"

"For many reasons." The color had returned to Papa's face and he was breathing normally again. "You have no experience, you know nothing of any territory except the rendezvous." When Alexander started to protest, Papa raised a hand to silence him. "You couldn't get from here to here if you weren't riding on the seat of a wagon." From here to here, Papa indicated, was from one edge of his desk to the other.

The gibe insulted Alexander. He wanted to tell him that Marcel couldn't get from any here to anywhere without the help of guides and Indians who knew the territories. He didn't however. He tried to ignore the insult and hold his tongue because all his hopes rested on this man's power and influence.

"It might interest you to know, my sneaking Scots friend, that Hudson's Bay has already made large commitments for an expedition to find the Northwest Passage."

"And they will all fail because—"

"Fail! Have you learned rudeness as well as slyness?" Papa paused to refill his brandy glass. "Maps and charts, charts and maps. They are the playthings of silly children. You must have firsthand information. Firsthand. Do you think I don't have charts and maps? I have a roomful of charts and maps and every one of them is wrong. You need people who have been there, men who have lived in its forests and traveled its streams. There are such people."

Alexander didn't tell Papa about the young fur trapper he'd met on the rendezvous. He feared that another interruption would end their interview.

"And who are you to sit in *my* home and declare any expedition of mine a failure? My men may not have found the river west, but they have discovered the richest fur trapping lands in the entire world. And, you, you pompous ass, dare to call them failures?"

"I meant, with all due respect, milord, that they didn't find you a passageway to the West."

"And you will? You? Hah!" Papa Louis scoffed

and his cold eyes bore into Alexander's. "Allow me to inform you that we ourselves are now readying just such an expedition at great cost. It will leave this spring and it will be led by experienced and *honorable* men."

Again Alexander suffered Papa's insults.

"We already have firsthand information, the information of a man who has actually tasted the waters of the ocean in the West. With his knowledge, our men will find the forked river. They will sail it west. They will reach the great Pacific. It shall all be as I predict."

Alexander's stomach sank. "May I ask the names of the men who will lead the expedition?" He was afraid he already knew.

"I don't think you'll be invited to join the party, if that's why you're asking. In fact, I'm sure you won't."

"I want to lead an expedition, not be in one."

"Wake up, Alexander, wake up! You have too much to learn."

"There are others who are interested."

"Who? McGill, your contryman? He cannot have grown so foolish in his dotage that he would seriously consider an expedition led by you."

"He's no fool," Alexander muttered noncommittally. He didn't want to risk Papa Louis using his connections to thwart any chances he and Chubb might have with McGill.

"A man must do what he has to do. But I wager that Marcel and Reynard will be swimming in the ocean long before you put on snowshoes."

"Marcel and Reynard will lead the expedition?"

"This spring," Papa Louis gloated.

"They have an eyewitness to . . ." Suddenly it was clear to Alexander why he and Chubb hadn't been able to find the trapper. Marcel and Reynard had hidden him, tied up or drunk, so that he couldn't tell his story to any possible competitor. The wily French had euchred Alexander out of his dream.

In the Dentere household, the only thing left for Alexander to do was to say good-bye. He did, and then added, "You disappoint me, Papa, when you accuse me of mistreating the person I am fondest of in all of Canada."

Papa couldn't believe the effrontery. He exploded into a stream of curses in both English and French that stunned the unsuspecting Alexander.

"Pig! I saw you . . . You bastard, I am . . . I am . . . I saw you in the kitchen with my Juliette, my baby. I'm not so blind, old or stupid that I cannot interpret the meaning of such embraces."

Now Alexander turned red, but not in anger.

"You are forbidden in this house! You are forbidden to see my daughter, and if I see you anywhere near this house I'll shoot you! Do you understand?" He grabbed Alexander's collar. "Am I clear?" He twisted it tighter. "Am I clear?" he rasped.

Alexander fought for his breath. "Yes, milord, but—"

He never finished the sentence because Juliette came bursting into the room with a smile to light up all of Montreal.

"What are you two old trappers up to? Come in, everyone wants to see both of you." She rushed to Alexander's side and entwined her arm in his.

"Juliette!" screamed her father, as if she had thrust her arm into a basket of vipers. "Juliette, what are you doing? Come over to me."

Perplexed, Juliette let go of Alexander's arm. She

looked at him and then at her father, his body rigid, his face beet red, and covered with perspiration.

"What? What's the matter?" she asked as she moved toward her father.

"You, my Juliette. You and me," answered Alexander.

"What—" she began to question them, but Papa Louis cut her short.

"I'll answer my daughter. You've said and done enough. Leave her alone, leave us both alone. Get out of our lives."

"Papa, what are you saying? I don't want Alexander out of my life. I love him, Papa! I love only him."

"Juliette, you don't know what you're saying. You're being silly, this is all new to you. He's poisoned you against us."

"That's not true, Papa. He loves you, and Mama and Marcel. Oh, Papa, please don't send him away. I wouldn't survive."

"You'll survive his deceit and lies. This man has betrayed the very family that made him a son."

"Alexander, please. Say something," pleaded Juliette. "I want to be with you."

"Stay. Stay here, my Juliette. For now. When I come back for you, I'll be able to give you all you deserve."

"I've forbidden you to see her. Do, and I'll have you shot like the dog that you are. Do you understand?"

"In our journal we'll always be together. There, no one can keep us apart, my Juliette." He made his way to the door.

As he opened it, she cried, "Alexander, I love you! I love only you!"

Chapter 11

They'd been sitting on the hard bench for almost an hour. Their backs were stiff and their haunches ached. Chubb shuffled his feet. From behind the oak banister the clerk snapped at him to be quiet.

Right from the old sod, thought Alexander, when he heard the clerk's brogue. And he thanked God for any divine intervention that had spared him a clerkship in the office of Joseph McGill. The office door opened. A spindly, dyspeptic looking man peered at them, then asked the clerk, "Are these the two, Jonesy?"

"Aye, Mr. Coombs."

"Send them along shortly then."

Chubb and Alexander started to rise. Jones motioned for them to sit back down. "He's on his way to the privy. When he comes back, *then* he'll call you in."

"I'm surprised he didn't ask us to meet him in there, *mon ami*," whispered Chubb.

"Quiet, Chubb, he'll hear us." Alexander had a mission and he didn't want anyone offended in any way.

Coombs returned. He eyed them both suspiciously, for his duties included screening crackpots and troublemakers for McGill. His instincts told him these two filled both bills. When Alexander spoke, however, Coombs' suspicions began to ebb and his face lit up.

"Aha. You're the Scot who traveled with the French!"

"I am sir," Alexander admitted, exaggerating his burr.

"And your partner?" asked Coombs, pointing to Chubb. "You're a Scot, too?" The disbelief in Coombs' voice indicated he already knew the answer.

"I'm Canadian," said Chubb. "I was born in Montreal."

"You weren't born in France, Chubb?" Chubb's reply had taken Alexander by surprise.

"So, gentlemen, enough of this talk. What scheme do you two propose to make some money for McGill? That's all that interests us, you know. Making money." He leaned back and let out a dry, crackling laugh.

Alexander had learned his lesson well from Papa Louis. He told Coombs just what an experienced fur trader would expect to hear committing huge sums of money to an expedition. He told him that they had firsthand information from a man who had actually tasted the salt water of the Pacific and that they themselves knew the territory well enough to cross it by landmarks only a day apart.

"And this trapper who drank from the Pacific, if McGill wanted to meet him, could he?" This was the critical question that Chubb and Alexander had anticipated.

They answered it as glibly as they'd rehearsed it. They looked at each other, shrugged and in unison lied. "Of course," they said.

Two days later, Alexander received a message from Coombs. Within the fortnight McGill would see him.

McGill and Coombs might have been brothers, except that Coombs had thick, coal black hair. McGill was bald as an egg. It struck Alexander odd that he kept running a hand over his naked scalp.

"So, you've met Coombs, eh?" asked McGill.

How could I have not, Alexander was tempted to answer. Instead, he replied politely, "Yes, I did, sir."

"He's not one of us, you know." Alexander looked puzzled. "Scots! He's not Scots."

"I didn't know that, sir," said Alexander and thought the man not only odd but also balmy.

"He's Welsh."

"I'll be." Alexander wanted for any other comment.

"Good man though, for a Welshman. Did you like working for the French? Crafty bunch, tricky. Can't be trusted. Did you learn any of their tricks? Good for you if you did. Indians hate them too, you know."

The man prated on. He waited for no answers to his stream of questions. Alexander nodded yes or shook his head no. Whichever, it didn't seem to make much difference.

McGill stopped to sip some tea. He hadn't bothered to offer Alexander any.

"Coombs says you have an interesting scheme. Interesting, he says. Not good, mind you. Very cautious, the Welsh. Very cautious. Too cautious, I say. Well, laddie, are you going to tell me your scheme or no?"

"Well, milord," began Alexander.

"Milord, is it? You don't call me lord, laddie. You call me McGill like everyone else. Milord is for those fat, pillow-bottomed English."

"Well, McGill," Alexander made another try.

"Better," McGill interrupted him, again.

It was exasperating, but finally the man allowed Alexander to speak for five minutes. Alexander presented his proposal as he had to Coombs. He also showed him the maps and charts that he and Chubb had so painstakingly drawn. McGill, however, showed no interest in them.

"Charts and maps, laddie. I've learned not to trust charts and maps. I have no use for them."

No one did. Alexander waited in another uncomfortable silence for McGill to continue.

"Why didn't you take this plan to Dentere? You worked for him. You saved the lives of his children. Dentere could have sent any Frenchman in Montreal on the rendezvous and yet he chose you."

Astounded by how much McGill knew, Alexander answered, "Dentere told me that he was already planning an expedition and two at the same time would be too costly."

"He's wrong, you know. One has nothing to do with the other. They've sent out dozens at the same time. Were you aware that he was lying to you? Why was he lying to you? No matter. His reasons are his own. What's important is that Marcel heard your trapper too. He did. Did Dentere tell you that?"

The man was uncanny. "How do you figure this, McGill? How do you . . ."

"Watch your accent, laddie. You sounded like a blasted Frenchy just then. How do I know? I can add two and two, laddie. You and Marcel were on the same rendezvous." No man in his dotage, McGill then reconstructed shrewdly not what might have happened, but what actually did happen.

"So, milad, let Dentere chase some drunken trapper's fancy," McGill concluded. "Northwest money stays here." He pointed to his pocket.

Alexander was crushed.

"Don't be so sullen, laddie. It's a lot of money you're asking and I have infinite better ways to spend mine. But, if you're interested in finding a passage through the mountains, I have a plan that might interest you."

Mountains did not interest Alexander. The magic river did. He started to rise.

"Sit, sit, sit," McGill ordered him. "You're a strapping lad from Dundee, eh? I had an uncle with a shop in Dundee. Impatient people. Are you impatient, lad? Don't be. If you're itchy because you're thinking Marcel will have the edge on you, you're thinking wrong. It'll be months before he's packing for his trip. You can put money on that."

The old ram was reading Alexander's mind.

"Besides, Marcel's French. They give up, the French do. You wouldn't though. On that I'll stake gold."

After pausing to stroke his bald head, McGill continued. "I was born in the mountains, the Cairngorm Mountains, so I know one thing a lot of people don't. There's more than one way to get over a mountain. You understand what I'm telling you?"

Alexander nodded a definite yes.

"Cat got your tongue, laddie?"

"Yes. I mean, yes, I understand what you're telling me."

"But do you understand what I'm aiming at? So what if the boy wonder Marcel, that sly, eely Frenchy, does find the passage? You think there's only one? If there's one, there's two, and if there's two, there's hundreds." The old man began stuffing a pipe almost twice the size of his fist.

"What will it serve him to find the way? Him or his father. The route is here." McGill pointed to the near edge of his desk. "And Hudson's Bay is here." He plopped himself across the desk to reach its farther edge.

"Too far, too far to service. But only the mountains seal off my company from lands rich in fur. And if someone in my employ found a passage to them, it would benefit Northwest tenfold more than Hudson's Bay. Am I clear, laddie?"

"Yes, McGill, I think so."

"The mountains can fool you, laddie. They're tricky. You can think you're going eastward home and you're on your way farther west than where you've been. I know the mountains. Do you?"

"I think so."

"Think so! I won't risk my company on a think. When you work with me, laddie, you're sure, sure of every river, scarp and crag, every crack in every crag. You won't be risking my company, but your life. Would you risk your life, laddie, on what you know about the mountains? Think on it. I'm not as hard a man as those piles of rock and clay. Here's what I propose."

Acrid clouds of smoke rose from McGill's huge pipe. He stared at Alexander. When he started speaking again, he pitched his voice low and almost whispered. He spoke slowly, more deliberately.

"I have every reason to believe the best chance of finding a passage lies not in Wyoming Territory or in any of Hudson's Bay Company's territory, but in our territory, Northwest's territory." Then, without any warning whatsoever, he rose to his full height and thundered, 'Do you realize that Dentere put together his last rendezvous on Northwest territory? That son of a bitch, that French scum chose to ignore our boundaries!" He fell silent, then sat back down heavily.

"I didn't know that, McGill." Alexander's tentative words did not fill the silence.

"The passage. You may be the one to find it. A Scotsman could. First, you must learn the area. Walk it, walk it in winter and spring and summer. Study it, learn it. And when you know it like the back of your hand, walk it again. Then, me laddie, you'll be ready to strike out and by God, you'll win. Now, I can help you, Allie, me lad. I can help you and Dentere can't. But if I do, I expect something in return."

"I'm willing, McGill, I'm willing. God knows I am," Alexander replied eagerly in a thick Scottish burr.

"The company has a trading post. Deserted now it is, though it was built at great expense of gold and of men. Of men, you hear, laddie? But it still stands. Reopen this outpost for the company. Reopen it and let all the trappers know you're there."

McGill stopped to relight his pipe.

"You'll settle in faster than you think." He puffed out billows of smoke. "Get settled there. Learn the territory, I tell you, and when you're ready to risk your life, wander where you choose. I'll keep you on my books as long as your expeditions begin and end at Lake Athabasca."

So Alexander wasn't turned down after all. McGill not only had faith in him but was also willing to spend some of that money in his pocket. Alexander was overjoyed, but for one very important matter that had to be resolved.

"McGill, you've not invited Chubb to this meeting, nor have you mentioned him in all of your plans for me. Is there a reason or was it an oversight?"

"Of course, there's a reason, an excellent one. He's French. And learn it now, laddie, he will always be loyal to the Frog."

"His loyalty is to me. I can vouch for that."

"You will discover that Northwest employs no Frenchmen. I would wager that tonight your loyal friend will be meeting with Dentere himself to tell him what we discussed here this afternoon."

"I would find that hard to believe."

"He means that much to you, that Frenchy?"

"*My friend* means that much to me," Alexander corrected him.

"A man does what he has to do." McGill might have been quoting Dentere, thought Alexander. "But let me tell you this. One day your life may be in his hands. As he is French, let me assure you that he will betray you. It's a national characteristic."

With that he pushed himself up from the desk and stretched out a bony hand. "Let's end the morning on a happier note. The next time we meet, we'll be discussing the river route to the West."

They shook hands. As Alexander, elated, moved to the door, McGill encouraged him. "You're in charge, milad. Do us proud. Mr. Coombs has all the details. Any troubles, any problems, and there will be plenty, you tell him. Now, leave me alone to dream."

That night Alexander and Chubb clanked many a tankard of ale to celebrate their good fortune. By the early morning hours, they were spilling more than they were drinking and they might have awakened half of

Montreal with their exuberant rendering of French drinking songs. Their spree obliterated the next day for them.

Hard work and careful planning filled the weeks that followed. The two friends had to reach the outpost at Lake Athabasca by February, the territory's harshest month. Coombs suggested they travel by dog sled, but neither of them had ever driven a team of dogs before. So they decided to ride on horseback as far north as possible and then walk the rest of the way. Three mules would carry their supplies.

"One thing we definitely will not need, *mon ami*," Chubb laughed, "is our maps."

Once they'd estimated their needs, they had to battle with the Northwest Company's bureaucracy. Coombs insisted on clearing their list of supplies before it went to the commissary. He questioned almost every foodstuff and every bit of hardware on it. Not only did he eliminate a dozen or so of their requests, but also one of the mules and the spare horse they'd ordered.

"Just like that you can tell me what I'll need on my trip? Just like that?" Alexander asked the clerk furiously.

The dour Coombs stood his ground. "Take the slip to that dock and they'll give you what I've marked here."

"Are you going to answer me?" Alexander might as well have shouted at the doorpost. He ripped the sheet off the counter and stormed out of the office.

Alexander and Chubb consoled each other. One thing, however, that Alexander never mentioned to his friend was McGill's reluctance to hire him because he was French. It would have embarrassed Alexander to discuss it. Nor could he confess to Chubb his pain.

Alexander yearned to see Juliette. He wanted to

share his plans with her, now that so many of his dreams were being put into action. He wanted, too, to touch her, to kiss her again. A month had passed since that disastrous Christmas dinner and Alexander's fatal interview with Juliette's father. Their passionate kiss, Papa Dentere's ultimatum, Juliette's tears and her bold declaration of love all haunted his memory. And at night he dreamed of the day when he would return to the Dentere mansion and claim Juliette for his bride. They were long, lonely nights.

Unable to tolerate the anguish any longer, Alexander took Chubb into his confidence. Chubb offered more than sympathy. He also devised a tactic, astounding in its simplicity, by which Alexander could meet with Juliette secretly. When Joseph, the Denteres' blacksmith came into town for groceries, Chubb would slip him a letter to Juliette along with a small packet of bills to seal Joseph's lips.

Chubb's plan worked perfectly. Alexander was watching from his window when the Dentere carriage drove up to Chubb's house. Juliette quickly alighted. Her face glowed as radiantly as the early afternoon. She dashed into the doorway and Joseph clattered off to the shopping district. Alexander ran to the hallway. He heard her footsteps on the narrow, creaking stairs. Then he was holding her in his arms, kissing her. They were together again.

"Come in, my Juliette. I've waited for this moment so long. How I've missed you!"

"And I you, my Alexander. How did this happen to us? Why?" She looked for a place to put her cape and bonnet. Alexander took them from her, carefully folded the cape and lay it with the bonnet on his only chair.

"This is where you live, Alexander?" Sadly she contemplated his comfortless room.

"Only for a few more days. Tell me . . ." Alexander led her to the bed as there was nowhere else to sit. Juliette sank down at its foot. He sat beside her. "Tell me how you've been." Then leaping up, he apologized. "I'm not a very good host. I have some wine, some cider, or Louisa can make us some chocolate. You like that still . . ."

"No, no, nothing for me, Alexander. I only want to see you. I've missed you so much. Will you be away a long time?"

"I'll be back before the new snow. Isn't that what the Indians say?"

"Now you know more about them than I, Alexander." The odd look she gave him made Alexander worry that Marcel had told her about his conduct with Winter Flower on the rendezvous.

"I want to hear all about you," Alexander changed the subject, "what you've been doing, and your family. Have they been mean to you?"

Her tears came quickly. "Oh, Alexander," she sobbed, "home has been awful. I've been so miserable. Papa shouts constantly at me, and when she's not crying, Mama is dragging me to church. Worst of all is Marcel who makes up simply awful stories about you."

"What stories?"

Juliette didn't tell him at once. Instead, she spoke of that awful Christmas night. The family had managed to be civil to their other guests, but as soon as they'd left, the shouting and the tears began.

Livid, Papa Louis kept shouting that Alexander was forbidden ever to enter his house. Juliette was sobbing, and for a different reason, so was Mama Marie.

Then, when Papa found Alexander's gift, the grass-fire stone, he became even more enraged. An Indian hex stone, he called it, and Marcel told a horrible story about how Alexander had stolen it from an Indian girl. Papa seized the gem from her. Despite Juliette's pleas, her father hurled it from the balcony into the night.

Juliette was sure she'd lost the stone forever. Snow covered the garden below the balcony. With little hope she begged Luca, the gardener, to search for the stone. Five days later, to her amazement and delight, he brought it to her. Juliette rewarded him handsomely. Since that moment she'd worn it next to her, hidden beneath her bodice.

Juliette undid the fine gold chain around her neck. She handed the magnificent stone to Alexander. It held the warmth of her body.

"It hasn't been happy for you, my Juliette. I'm sorry I've caused you so much misery."

"It's unbearable." Juliette could not hold back her sobs. "Take me with you. Please take me with you, no matter where it is."

"Now, that's impossible," he told her gently.

"And Marcel," she continued, "he struts about as if he were the man of the house because he's going to open up new lands rich in fur and gold. He's going to be famous. Let him be. But why must he make me so sad?"

Marcel's name perked up Alexander. "When is he leaving on his expedition?"

"Whenever he can get his trapper sober for a day." She managed a small laugh.

"What do you mean?"

"Marcel has found this beastly trapper . . ." Juliette paused to dab her eyes and then proceeded to tell

172

Alexander all that he suspected and that McGill apparently knew. As she spoke, Alexander wondered if McGill had a spy in the Dentere camp. One thing was certain: Marcel and Reynard were having more difficulty controlling this man who claimed to have sipped the waters of the Pacific than they'd anticipated.

"If it weren't for the very charming Monsieur Reynard, I think that I'd have gone out of my mind by now. He's so nice, Alexander. Do you remember him?"

Her affection for Reynard alarmed him. Before Alexander could respond, however, Juliette rose from the bed and crossed to the chair for her purse.

"I haven't come to you empty-handed, Alexander." She pulled out a journal like the one she'd given him for the rendezvous. "Now I know you'll take me with you," she said. Alexander absent-mindedly flipped through its pages.

"Not yet," remarked Juliette. "I haven't thought of the the right words yet. But I will before you go."

Alexander, though, wasn't looking for an inscription. He was thinking about her and Reynard.

He thought about Juliette and himself, about the gulf that separated them. This beautiful young woman lived in a world of afternoon teas and musicales. There were rooms in the Dentere mansion larger than Chubb's entire house and works of art on the Denteres' walls worth more than any block in his district. Juliette may love him, but she would soon tire of carrying water three floors up these narrow stairs to make a cup of tea. Here she'd have no Mariou to attend to her needs and her whims. Juliette took for granted comforts that most people never dreamed. Before he could wed her, he would have to narrow the gulf between them, would have to make the riches that Marcel sought in the West his own.

He cradled her small, white hand in his. He covered it with dozens of tender kisses. She thrilled at every one of them. Then, abruptly, Alexander rose and walked to the door.

He called down to Chubb's wife Louisa for two cups of chocolate. Lost in each other's eyes and smiles, they waited for Louisa in a comfortable silence.

Louisa brought them two steaming drinks in clumsy, chipped mugs. The chocolate was bitter. Sugar was a rare, expensive commodity in Montreal. Embarrassed, Alexander recalled Mariou's sweet beverage served in fine, English bone china.

As they drank, Alexander told Juliette all the details of his recent good fortune with McGill. The news of his expedition delighted her, but she was shocked to learn that he and Chubb would be venturing north in the middle of winter.

"It's unheard of!" she exclaimed. "What kind of man is this McGill?"

Alexander assured Juliette that trappers, Indians and camping men had been living in the Northwest Territory for decades. As strong and hardy as any man, he'd soon learn their tricks of survival. "But now you see, my Juliette," he added softly, "why I cannot take you with me. It would be madness."

She moved closer. She rested her head against his. Caressing him, she whispered, "Oh, my Alexander, what you do for me!"

He kissed her gently. Her soft lips parted and the tip of her tongue brushed his. She kissed his face, his hair, then surrendered to the fervor of a long, impassioned kiss. She trembled. Her warmth, her scent of roses and lilacs and the press of her body overwhelmed Alexander.

They tumbled back onto the feather bed. Louisa's mugs hit the bare floor with a crash.

Slipping her hand under Alexander's loose shirt, Juliette rubbed his expansive chest. The touch of her fingers ignited his desire. He crushed her against him and began kissing her with the passion that had long sought release. A strange tremor passed through her body into his.

Juliette moved swiftly to undo her hooks and buttons. Her gown fell in a heap beside the bed. She shivered, but not from the cold. She took his outstretched hand and gently he pulled her to him. Their ardor bound them. Their passion quickened, and wrapped about each other, they expressed their love.

Chapter 12

Even Louisa stayed home, the day was that brutal. A blizzard was raging over Montreal. The wind whipped the snow into them as they trudged through the empty city streets. Alexander and Chubb had tried to wait out the storm, but their two horses couldn't remain immobile another day.

Once outside the city they traveled with the blizzard at their backs and covered a greater distance than they'd anticipated. They had long passed the ridge of the Blue Mountains when they pitched their low tents in the hard-packed snow that first night. By stringing tarpaulins to several trees, they also rigged a shelter for their animals. Everyone at Northwest had cautioned them to take as much care of their mules and horses as they did of themselves.

Secure in the canvas tent and the warmer for good, hot tea, Alexander asked Chubb, "Did you bring any of our maps?"

Chubb laughed and fixed himself another cup of tea.

"I'm serious. We should have thought to bring them."

"Why?" asked an incredulous Chubb. "Of what use would they be to us? We're going farther north and farther west than any region we charted."

"I'm not thinking of us. I'm thinking of Marcel, of where he'll make his first thrust across the big mountains."

"Put him out of you head, *mon ami*. He'll drive you crazier not being here than he would looking over your shoulder."

"Juliette said he was having trouble."

"And didn't I tell you he would? McGill makes more sense in five minutes than any trapper who talks all night of floating through the mountains to the Pacific."

"You still think that trapper's story's only a pipe dream?"

"I do."

"Then Marcel is in for a bad time, isn't he?" Alexander brooded. "Juliette told me they won't begin their expedition until the thaw."

"And we are this far ahead of them. Sleep, *mon ami*," said Chubb, regretting that his partner's rivalry with Marcel hadn't ended, "we have a lot of figuring and freezing to do before we get to this Fort Fork."

"We'll cross the mountains before Marcel, Chubb. Indeed, we will." Then Alexander took his friend's advice. He fell asleep.

The cold but clear weather the next day allayed many of their apprehensions about the journey. No calamities befell them and they encountered no more difficulties than they had when they'd crossed the plains in a wagon. Food was surprisingly plentiful. Indians traded deer meat and prairie rabbits for trinkets and beads. Fish abounded beneath the icy surface of the streams. Alexander and Chubb crossed the wintry prairie more quickly than either of them had expected two men on horseback with mule-drawn sleds could.

When they turned north, however, severe weather impeded their progress. Snow blocked the narrow passes through the cliffs. Chubb and Alexander often spent days dragging their horses, mules and sleds along an uphill trail, only to discover it was ultimately impassable. They lost more days dragging their animals and supplies back down. Nor could they risk cutting across frozen lakes and ponds, because beyond the shores the ice thinned treacherously. Long detours wearied the two explorers.

They had trudged through deep snow to the top of a bluff and, for what seemed to be the hundredth time, had discovered their trail impassable, when darkness stranded them. That night a storm blew down from the north. Fresh snow and bitter winds confined Chubb and Alexander to their tent the entire next day.

The storm cost them more than a day. While they huddled inside the tent, one of the mules still tied to its sled chewed through its tether and wandered blindly into the thickly falling snow. At the edge of a bluff, the mule fell with its sled and supplies deep into a crevice. When they lost the mule, Alexander and Chubb also lost their tea, dried fish, jerky and, most necessary of all, the bags of feed for the animals. They would now have to forage for food under the heavy snow.

The snow swirling around them, the wind driving it into their faces, Alexander and Chubb struggled with their animals. They pulled, they pleaded, they kicked, swatted and pushed at the horses to get them back down the difficult trail. The mule, however, resisted all their prodding. When Chubb struck it with the wooden pole that held up their tent, the stake snapped like a twig and still the mule refused to move. When he whacked it bare-handed, Chubb succeeded only in breaking a bone in his hand. They finally had to abandon the stubborn animal to the heavy, drifting snow which threatened to bury them all. They attached the mule's sled to one of the horses and slowly, step by laborious step, they slogged their way through the storm.

When neither the men nor the horses could trudge any farther, they set up camp against a large snowbank. The bank shielded them from the storm better than did their tent, which no longer had its center support. All night the canvas snapped like a whip in the roaring wind.

Chubb and Alexander had nothing to eat that night. Nor did the horses. The animals could not survive much longer. Rather than abandon them, Alexander thought it would be more humane to end their lives with a shot from a rifle. Chubb, however, argued that they couldn't afford to waste any of their limited ammunition. Reluctantly, Alexander agreed to abandon the horses. Then both men slept fitfully.

Their bedrolls, knives, rifles and ammunition strapped to their backs, Chubb and Alexander left the horses behind them the next morning. They plodded through a white nightmare of snow. Their every step broke through a thin crust of ice. The snow was freezing as it hit the surface. Chubb's broken hand ached the more for the raw cold and Alexander, who had wrenched his shoulder and back, trudged on in dull but unrelenting pain. If they stopped for more than five minutes their perspiration would freeze. Frostbite would be their undoing. On they plodded. Movement at least kept them warm. They had nothing to eat but the snow.

Three days later, Chubb spotted the fresh carcass

of an animal. Wolves had done their predatory work and evidently then had scattered, perhaps at the sound of their footsteps or the scent of human beings. Blood trailed in every direction. Alexander cut out the animal's stomach and kidneys. Chubb boiled them in heated snow. The broth was nourishing, but they nearly froze in the time it took them to light a fire.

They walked. And walked. They lost all sense of time and direction. The weather was their enemy, their battleground a wilderness, white and cold and vast.

Late one morning, on the white horizon, they thought they saw Indians running in long coats of fur. Alexander and Chubb plunged toward them in the knee-deep snow. They shouted. The Indians disappeared. Alexander fired a round of the rifle into the air. For minutes the shot echoed off the frozen landscape. But the Indians did not return.

They began to spot traps. Unfortunately they were empty, yet to be baited and sprung. A rotting fish did still lie in one of them. Foul though it smelled, the fish tasted better than the fanciest meal money could buy in all of Montreal.

Hunger shrank their stomachs and food constantly occupied their minds. When Alexander wasn't thinking of food, he was thinking of Marcel, who, by this time, would be packing supply wagons for his expedition. Marcel wouldn't be traveling with a couple of feedbag mules and crippled horses. Nor would he lack for food and supplies. But he would be weeks behind Alexander and Chubb. Time was their edge, and as long as they could walk, Alexander vowed they would not lose it.

They walked on. The arctic winds howled and the snow, relentless, tortured them. They walked lost. They walked blind in a world empty and white.

They thought, at first, that they were hearing things. They heard them in the distance, yelping and whimpering. Then they saw them. A team of ten huskies pulling a sled of fur-clad Indians burst into view.

In hooded coats and high, fur-lined boots, the Indians bowed and then approached Alexander and Chubb decorously. They led the two men to their long sled and wrapped them warmly in caribou pelts. When the Indians caught sight of the rifle, they became jubilant and even more hospitable to the two weary, cold and very hungry travelers.

Chubb and Alexander rubbed their stomachs and pointed to their mouths. The Indians seemed to understand. They nodded and the sled began to move.

In the middle of an endless field of snow, abruptly, they stopped. They could see nothing for miles. One of the Indians tended to the dogs. The others leapt off the sled and began thumping the snow. Then they put their ears to the ground.

"Good God, Chubb," whispered Alexander, "more Kutenai?"

These Indians, however, weren't thumping at homes underground. They were looking for drifts of solid snow. When they found one, they sawed out square blocks of snow with long, sharp knives. Two of the Indians, meanwhile, were digging a trench. In a matter of minutes they'd dug out a perfect circle, knee-deep and about as wide as two outstretched arms.

The Indians then slid blocks of snow into the trench and piled a smaller circle of blocks on top of them. Soon they'd fashioned a dome. After shearing off the square edges and pressing snow into the cracks, they covered the entire shelter with a layer of snow. From the inside one of the Indians carved out a doorway.

Over the floor of the shelter they spread out fur pelts in layers. An oil flame in a clay jug, foul smelling though it was, warmed the room further. Alexander and Chubb took off their jackets. Comfortable for the first time in weeks, they forgot their hunger and promptly fell into a sound sleep.

The weather cleared the next day. The bright sun and the Indians' crude oil heater warmed the igloo so well that Chubb and Alexander were able to remove their boots and slick chaps. They shouldn't have. Their feet ballooned to almost three times their normal size. They tried to soak them in melted snow warmed slightly over the oil flame, but even tepid water seemed to scald their feet. After swabbing them with oil and wrapping them in skins, Chubb and Alexander could only wait for the swelling to go down. At least neither of the men suffered frostbite.

They did, however, suffer gnawing hunger pangs, which sips of warm water could hardly abate. They hadn't eaten solid food for days. When Alexander finally did manage to convey their plight to one of the rescuers, the Indian could offer no more than sympathy and a shrug. Hunger was a way of life for him. He consulted with his friends and then, with some reluctance, left the igloo. He returned with some fetid chunks of animal flesh that the Indians fed their dogs. Nevertheless, to the two men, barely conscious in their hunger, the rotten seal meat was more than palatable. They ate it greedily. They were revived.

And they would survive. Shelter, these Indians had taught Alexander, was the key to survival in this cold, desolate land of winds and snow. With seal or rabbit or fish a man could combat his hunger. But without shelter, when the piercing winds lashed into a leather jacket and chaps and the snow fell so thick it obliterated all horizons, a man could hold no hope for a tomorrow.

Hunched over his journal, Alexander recorded the experience of the past few bitter weeks and the lessons he'd learned from it. Fascinated, the Indians watched every stroke of the pen. And Chubb knew that if Alexander had the strength and faith to write in his journal, the two of them would indeed continue their expedition.

Their swollen feet confined Alexander and Chubb to the igloo another two days. On the second day Alexander cleared some of the fur skins from the floor and in it he scratched a crude map. He hoped the Indians would understand. He wanted to find out both where they were and how they could get to their destination.

He and Chubb had planned to travel north, then north by northwest, from Montreal to Fort Fork, an encampment occupied by employees of the Northwest Trading Company. The fort stood at a bend in the meandering Peace River which connected the Bad River to Lake Athabasca. Once Alexander and Chubb had reported to the men at the fort, they were to proceed north to the lake and re-establish the trading outpost at Fort Chipewyan. Both the fort and Lake Athabasca were due south of a large body of water called the Great Slave Lake.

Again and again Alexander scratched these landmarks in the igloo floor. Each time he rearranged their geographical relationships, the Indians studied the lakes, the fort and rivers with interest. They failed, however, to grasp Alexander's point. To no avail Alexander drew a larger map to include Montreal, the St. Lawrence

River and the Atlantic Ocean. Then an idea struck him that was simplicity itself.

Alexander ripped a page from his journal and sketched a beaver. The Indians nodded. One fell to his hands and knees to imitate the animal, while another pretended he was eating it. They also understood Alexander's rough drawing of a beaver pelt, and when he drew supplies, a whiskey bottle and beads next to it, they knew exactly what he meant. Smiling broadly, he turned to the exhausted Chubb and said, "When we get home, we'll frame and hang this picture in our parlor." Chubb smiled back weakly.

The Indians, meanwhile, scraped Alexander's maps from the floor and drew their own. Alexander realized that he and Chubb had gone too far north. The Indians agreed to guide Alexander and Chubb to Fort Fork. Although the sign language seemed to indicate a short journey directly south, the two explorers were soon to discover they had traveled almost a hundred miles too far north.

Their feet were still too swollen to fit in their boots when they left the next morning. After wrapping them in sealskin, Alexander and Chubb covered them with fur blankets in the dog sled. They rode in comfort through a world of white cliffs festooned with long ribbons of ice. In the thin wintry air they could hear the steady beat of the dogs' paws against the snow. Their master's commands crackled over the frosted lands.

Then a new snow began to fall. Gradually it built to a fury of biting winds and stinging flakes. The lead dog quickened its pace. It veered suddenly and almost dumped the sled's human cargo. Alexander and Chubb held on tight as the dogs careered toward higher ground in the blinding white snow.

The Indians had to leap onto the sled's runners because they couldn't keep pace with the dogs. They soon realized that the dogs were chasing an animal. One of the Indians threw himself across the sled and managed to release the taut tether. Freed, the dogs barreled into the storm. Yelping and barking they disappeared.

The Indians jumped down off the sled. One of them signaled he wanted a rifle. With the slightest hesitation and a nod from Chubb, Alexander handed it over to him. The dogs drove two small caribou into their field of vision, then circled the frightened animals.

The Indian with the rifle quickly dropped to a kneeling position. He squeezed off a shot and despite the short distance missed. He reloaded and Alexander feared that the animals, alarmed by the men, the dogs and the shot, would dash off into the wilds. The caribou, however, calmly stood in the circle of yapping dogs. The second shot found a mark. The larger of the caribou ran off as the smaller dropped.

They butchered the animal then and there. They fed its innards and head to the dogs and the five of them dined on a leg and some of the ribs. The Indians showed Alexander and Chubb how to crack the bones, suck out the marrow and drink the broth. They feasted greedily. When Chubb absent-mindedly went to lick some bits of meat off the blade of his knife, however, the knife froze instantly to his lip. He pulled it off and lost a large chunk of skin which bled for a long time.

After several more days of travel, eating caribou by day and sleeping warmly in ice houses at night, they noticed that the ice at the mouths of the rivers was starting to break up. The snow fields were dotted with pools of water and the dogs kicked a cold spray back over the men and the sled. When the sun went down and temperatures dropped, the spray froze into a thick coating of ice.

Despite the hazards their progress was excellent. The sled shot southward through ice field after ice field. When faced with open water, their guides pushed together huge blocks of ice to make a bridge between the two icy shores. After taking the whining dogs across, they pushed the sled, laden with the still-bootless explorers, over their ingeniously constructed bridge.

At the end of a long day of traveling, one of the Indians shook Alexander's shoulders and signaled him to mount his back. The Indian carried Alexander to the top of a high ridge where the guide pointed out a thin file of smoke and kept repeating, *"Taavani, taavani."* Alexander never forgot that evening, for it taught him how deceptive distances were in this remote northern territory. It took them fully two more days of travel at maximum speed to sled their way from that ridge to the threshold of Fort Fork.

Alexander had imagined Fort Fork to be just that, a fort, a grand encampment with ramparts and great wooden gates. What he and Chubb found, however, after their long, cold weeks of exhausting travel, was no more than a simple garrison, the kind of blockhouse the early settlers built to protect women and children during Indian attacks. The square building, no bigger than a fair-sized house, had a second story that overhung the first and a roof in the shape of a pyramid. Its few windows were small and heavily shuttered. A cupola extended over the roofline and only an unmended picket fence surrounded the dilapidated garrison.

Three men, armed but looking very drunk, greeted the dog sled. When they discerned the sled's cargo, two of the men, apparently on orders from the third, laid down their long guns and helped Alexander and Chubb into the fort. No one spoke.

Inside the fort Alexander and Chubb suffered new tortures. The dry air in the hot, stuffy room stung their faces and hands and pained their swollen feet unbearably.

A squat, bearded man with one bad eye and diseased skin ordered the other two to heap snow into a washtub and to pull it up to a massive, roaring fireplace. Then keeping his head cocked so that his good eye was on Alexander, he asked, "Where have you been trapping?" He spoke without emotion or surprise, as if two half-frozen and half-starved men who arrived at the fort by dog sled were an everyday occurrence.

Feebly Alexander answered him. "We aren't trappers, we've been traveling from Montreal to join you here."

"Say again," said the squat man in charge while another served Alexander and Chubb bowls of soup.

Alexander began the tale of their adventure north from Montreal. Unable to resist the aroma of the soup, however, he stopped midsentence and started slurping it.

"I don't know whether to laugh or to cry," muttered One Eye. "Who in their right mind would cross this territory in the middle of winter?"

"We were told, monsieur," replied Chubb, who'd already finished his soup, "that it was done all the time by people in your company. Mr. McGill himself told us."

"McGill! McGill, is it?" The three men started laughing and pounding the table or their thighs. "McGill, indeed. For your benefit, laddie, when you work for Northwest, the first rule everybody learns fast is never take the word of McGill," chuckled One Eye. Then he said suspiciously to Chubb, "You're French. McGill wouldn't hire no Frenchy."

"He's with me, lad." Alexander broadened his accent to let them know that a Scotsman had hired Chubb and traveled halfway across the continent with him.

"Canadian, I was born on Montreal Island," answered Chubb.

"And I am Rose La Rose!" Laughing, One Eye mimicked a dance hall girl before telling Chubb bluntly, "You're a Frog and I don't trust ye."

Suddenly One Eye exploded. "Get those bloody bastards out of here," he shouted, pointing at the three Indians who'd saved Alexander and Chubb from certain death.

Responding to One Eye's command, his two men ran the rescuers out the door. The next thing Alexander and Chubb heard was a round of shots, then the yelping of dogs as the sled rushed off.

"Those Indians saved our lives! You could have at least let us feed them or thank them properly," Alexander protested.

"Eskimos," muttered One Eye.

"What's that?" asked Chubb.

"Eskimos. Those aren't Indians, they're Eskimos. They were just fattening you up to sit down and eat you. That's the thing they do up here when the grub gives out. They eat the likes of you and me in tiny pieces. The parts they can't cut up they feed to the dogs."

"They feed you anything you didn't catch?" asked one of the others.

"Some seal meat," answered Alexander uncertainly.

"Seal meat?" One Eye laughed slyly.

"Probably some trapper they chopped up last summer."

Alexander and Chubb lost their appetite and put down their soup bowls. The three men laughed uproariously as they passed around a jug of whiskey and momentarily ignored the two guests.

"Well, we got plenty of time to tell you all about your new home, because it smells like there's more snow coming. But before you two open your yaps, get out of them clothes and into that tub. Talk about seal meat. I don't think they'd come close to you." Again the three men laughed.

One Eye pointed to the tin tub his two men had hauled up to the fire. Alexander and Chubb saw that the snow had not only turned to water but also that small wisps of steam were rising from it. After rubbing themselves with whale blubber to make their skin more pliable and to keep it from cracking in the steamy water, Alexander and Chubb stepped into the bath. They might have stepped into a vat of boiling oil. The remedy was far more painful than any cold they'd endured.

That night the wind was rising when they climbed the ladder to the dormer. When it faded, it was so quiet that Chubb swore he could hear the fresh snow falling. One Eye had been right; they would have plenty of time to talk.

During the next several days Chubb and Alexander settled into the fort. Heat, food and whiskey gradually thawed them out. That it was already April astounded them. They'd been traveling two and a half months since the day they'd left Montreal. And they'd thought the five weeks it took the Dentere wagon train to reach its destination was a long time! The men at the fort laughed at Alexander's trust in McGill letting them set out on such an impossible journey in the dead of winter. Nevertheless, Alexander's faith in his Scottish benefactor never wavered.

Alexander and Chubb bore the company of the three men at the fort while they waited for the thaw that would enable them to continue on to Lake Athabasca and Fort Chipewyan. Most nights they retired early to the upper story and left the gang of three, as they called them, downstairs with their whiskey.

"I wonder what kind of men we'll find at our fort," asked Chubb one night.

"Not much better I think," answered Alexander.

"I hope it's better, *mon ami*, I certainly hope so. But one thing I want to do before I die is learn how to pronounce the name of that Fort—Chip-a-wan, Chip-oo-yan? On my tombstone you carve . . ." Chubb looked over at Alexander who was staring at the ceiling and not listening to him at all. Softly he said, "He's not even thinking of what to put into his wagons yet, let alone moving out."

"Can you truly read my mind so easily, Chubb?"

He ignored the question. "I think that's all you think of. Don't worry. We have enough problems to think about besides what some ill-mannered rich kid is doing."

"No, this time you're wrong, Chubb. This time I was thinking what a big jump we have on old Marcel. What a jump we have on him."

"I hope so, *mon ami*. Now, let me sleep, huh?"

Chapter 13

Indians of every nation were milling about the fort. Some wore colorful deerskins stretched like a second skin across their bodies while others were wrapped in bright woolen blankets from head to toe. None of them wore the great furs of Alexander's rescuers. To thank and reward them for saving his life, Alexander searched in vain for the Eskimos among the Shoshone, the Cherokee and Kutenai who'd gathered at the fort. When the winter broke, they came there to look for work, and their arrival marked the start of the June thaw.

Chubb and Alexander could now prepare for their journey upriver to Lake Athabasca and Fort Chipewyan. One Eye Ralston insisted that they sign a voucher stating they'd brought no Northwest Company goods to Fort Fork. He didn't want to have to account to McGill for anything they might say had been left with him. "Better figure out something to tell the old bastard or else he'll have you paying for everything you lost. I owed him once and worked a whole season for nothing."

Ralston also told Alexander that as most of the Indians had come to work, he should choose a dozen or so to take with him to Chipewyan. Alexander sought out the strongest braves and maidens he could find. Not only were all of them willing to accompany him upriver and help him restore the camp, but also they could speak either English or French. Among them, too, was a mysterious young squaw with corn silk woven into her hair, which she almost concealed under a brightly colored blanket. Fearful that their place might be taken by other braves as willing to work as they, Alexander's band of Indians shadowed him and Chubb everywhere they went over the next few days.

Although the Indians were an annoyance to Alexander and Chubb at Fort Fork, they proved to be invaluable guides and skillful hunters once the trek northward began. Ralston allowed them no provisions for the trip to Lake Athabasca, but Alexander's braves kept the small company well supplied with fresh deer meat and fish. Their familiarity with the terrain further simplified the journey, which seemed to be complicated only by an occasional walk in mud.

One thing, however, bothered Chubb. "*Mon ami,* something has been on my mind since I heard that one-eyed bastard laugh about it."

"What's that, Chubb?"

"How will we trade for pelts? How does McGill expect us to do that?" he asked plaintively.

"We aren't going to trade for anything, not for pelts, skins or beavers themselves. We are, I tell you, one more time, a post, a post where trappers come to leave their pelts. We're a storage house and only a storage house for now."

"For now?"

"Chubb, we can't get tied down trading and making deals every day if what we're being paid to do is find the rivers across these mountains!" Alexander waved at the mountain ranges looming around them. "That's our job. Not trading skins."

"And that's the part I cannot bring myself to believe. *Mon Dieu, mon ami*, we're getting wages for that? *Sacre bleu*, it's incredible. We're living on the easy street, no? That's fun."

"Fun, hey? You call this winter fun, my man? You call crossing the wilds with only melting snow to eat fun? Then remind me to stay away from you when we're going to have some fun."

At first Chubb thought Alexander was joking with him. Then he realized he was steaming angry.

Nor did Alexander let Chubb forget his definition of fun. Any mishap, accident or cause for complaint along their way brought the same response from Alexander: fun, he'd mutter or growl at Chubb. Then one afternoon, with the sound of racing water in their ears, he poked his partner in the ribs and proclaimed, "Well, milord, get ready for a houseful of fun." Alexander pointed in the direction of a fort, their new home for who knew how long.

Countless storms, seasons of neglect and a tangled overgrowth of dead vines had ravaged Fort Chipewyan. A huge tree had fallen across the roof of the ell attached to the main building, which was little more than a rectangular log cabin. A second, smaller ell had been built behind the first so that successively smaller cabins constituted the entire fort. The tree had damaged the second cabin beyond repair and Alexander estimated that they would have to rebuild the entire structure from the ground up. They would begin the next day.

Their first night at the fort, Alexander and his small company dined on fresh trout caught by their expert fishermen, the Kutenai. As they sat around the campfire that evening in late spring, the tribesmen talked of preparations for the winter. They suggested building a smokehouse to store fish, a plan to which Alexander readily agreed. Indeed, all kinds of ideas for the little settlement occupied Alexander's mind and he wanted nothing more than time alone to mull over them.

Chubb, however, had more pressing news for him. *"Mon ami, mon ami!* I have something most interesting to tell you."

"What is it, Chubb?" asked Alexander wearily.

"Do you recall long ago on the rendezvous with Claude," Chubb crossed himself rapidly, "poor Claude, and we spotted a strange creature?"

"I don't know what you're talking about."

"That Indian girl, or at least we thought she was an Indian girl. She was swimming and she had flaxen hair. Yellow hair, not black like every other Indian in the world."

"No. No, I don't, I . . ." Then Alexander remembered. "Yes. Someone came out of the woods and whisked her away. We couldn't find them."

"Disappeared right before our eyes. But that was before poor Claude discovered they lived under the ground."

"What about this creature?" Creature, though, was a harsh word, Alexander thought, for that beautifully strange, almost eerie maiden with golden tanned skin and long, yellow-streaked hair.

"She's here! In our party! She is right now, at this moment, in the stream washing. Come."

"No. The last time I saw an Indian girl washing . . ." Alexander made a sign of slitting his own throat.

"Her hair is the color of corn silk and she is the same all over."

Although Alexander felt a twinge of jealousy and the pang of desire, he dismissed the feelings immediately. Indian girls were trouble. If he didn't know that by now, he never would. Still, her golden hair lingered in his memory and her golden skin stirred his imagination.

"I thought you'd like to know, that's all, *mon ami*," said Chubb, disappointed by Alexander's seeming indifference.

She was working the next day with Tatanee, the brave who owned her and three others. They were building the smokehouse that Tatanee had suggested the night before.

Alexander walked over to rebuke them. "We'll build a smokehouse after we rebuild the second cabin. Yes?" As he talked, he tried to ignore the flaxen-haired maiden, whose beauty could be his undoing.

"Yes, my lord, sir, Alexander," Tatanee said haltingly.

"Alexander will do."

"Yes, my lord, sir, Alexander," he repeated, as he bowed and set down his handmade tools. His four maidens followed him, also bowing in acquiescence. Alexander walked away, the image of the golden Indian girl firmly planted in his mind.

It took Alexander, Chubb and the band of Indians half the summer to rebuild the outpost. Trappers came infrequently at first, but word spread and more came more often. Some left their pelts, most did not. Alexander's trained eye valued their mangy, badly cut furs at very little. If the trappers were leaving such pelts with him to test his honesty, they would soon discover that honesty prevailed at Fort Chipewyan.

One of the trappers also brought Alexander news of Fort Fork. One Eye Ralston and his two partners were dead. All that could be determined was that they'd been drinking extraordinarily hard for a week and fallen to fighting among themselves. Who shot first hardly mattered as the three of them now lay dead outside the fort.

Alexander dispatched word to Montreal, but it would take months for a reply. Rather than lose Ralston's goods to scavengers or unfriendly Indians and desperate himself for supplies, Alexander sent out a party of men to carry back whatever stores remained at the fort. That expedition took what was left of the short, sweet summer in the North.

"Chubb, we've wasted an entire season getting ready and we haven't seen anything yet," lamented Alexander.

"But, Alexander, we're getting a good feel for the territory, no? We're learning it better than anyone before us. Those drunks at Fort Fork never set a foot past a whiskey bottle. What did they learn?"

Alexander didn't realize the truth of Chubb's words until he began making his journal entries once again. Page after page of description and hand-drawn maps proved to him his familiarity with the territory, its natural landmarks, its trails, its freshets, brooks and streams, its rivers that ultimately, he knew, must lead to the ocean.

Alexander felt more confident than ever that he would discover the magic route to the West. Marcel ceased to bother him, but not Juliette. He expressed his longing for her passionately in his journal every night, but he knew that until his name was on the river that took trade and commerce to the West, she would be no nearer to him than the Northwest Territory was to Montreal.

Alexander's success, however, depended upon a craft reliable and flexible enough to sail the waterways. He'd had been so sure that the fort would be equipped with a boat that he hadn't even thought to ask. But Chipewyan had no boat and he would have to improvise. Without the materials, tools or know-how to build a keel, Alexander decided to construct a raft outfitted with a mast and sail.

Alexander's labors quickly drew a crowd. His band of Indians watched him wrestle with wood that splintered, joints that separated and ties that burst. "You can't build anything without proper tools!" he yelled out when he wasn't sputtering his frustration to himself. Chubb tried to help, but he, too, lacked all skills in the building of boats. The Indians stood by astonished, fascinated and perplexed by white man's magic. They chattered, they pointed and they pondered with great awe everything that Chubb and Alexander did.

The raft was, at best, a series of compromises. Deep in his heart Alexander knew that no craft would sail straight or true or long when built by compromise. Even if it failed, however, Alexander didn't view his raft as an exercise in futility. It was a first and necessary step toward his goal.

Chubb begged off when the time came for launching. Had he been able to tell if it was a sailboat, a dory or a raft, Chubb would gladly have gone, but mongrels of any kind scared him.

Alexander gave up trying to convince his partner to join him and one of the Indians helped him move the raft to the water's edge. No one, though, would venture any farther. Alexander was alone. He couldn't back down, but he had a funny feeling he was about to get soaking wet.

He gave his craft a firm kick and watched it bob with the current of Lake Athabasca. At least it floated. He then climbed aboard his contraption with a long pole to guide it. Almost immediately he lost the pole. When one of the Indians prepared to dive in to rescue it, Alexander waved him off. He would navigate by sail.

Once Alexander got the little sail raised, his troubles started. A gust of wind ripped through the cloth, tore it from its pinnings and rendered it useless within minutes. The gust also sent the craft careening toward a sousehole, a whirlpool created by a large rock hidden underwater. While Alexander's raft barreled toward the swirling water, everyone on shore watched in helpless horror.

The maelstrom caught the craft. A torrent of eddies swept it up, then swirled it in every direction. Whirling faster and faster, the raft spun into the rock. For a brief moment it rose above the churning water and then capsized. Safe, but embarrassed, Alexander bobbed up and down in the water. He made one last, futile attempt to save the raft before the rough current smashed it into splinters and oblivion.

Alexander swam to shore and threw himself onto the riverbank. He coughed up water and laughed while Chubb and the Indians clapped hands for him. After taking his bow, Alexander raised his arms, shrugged and walked back to the main house to change his clothes.

That night by the fire, Alexander's amusement with himself and his ill-fated raft gave way to panic. To meet the challenge of these fierce, hazardous rivers, he needed a suitable craft. Without it his expedition was doomed to failure. Suddenly his goal seemed no closer than it had been six months before.

One morning shortly thereafter Tatanee came bowing into Alexander's room and asked in his most formal English, "If my lord, sir, Alexander, would come with him to the stream with two names?" Curious and apprehensive about Tatanee's unusual request, Alexander followed him to the rivulet in the woods behind the main house. As they approached, Alexander saw the other Indians kneeling on the bank, looking and pointing at something he couldn't make out. Fearing the worst, he quickened his step.

What captured the Indians' attention, however, was no quirky accident, but a child's toy, a miniature boat floating freely in the swift current of the rivulet. Tatanee stepped into the water and pulled out the toy canoe which he showed to his chief. "Is much nice for river," he said.

Alexander found the miniature canoe, hollowed out of an ash branch, surprisingly heavy. He studied the simplicity of its line and symmetry of its hull. It greatly impressed him.

"We can make big one with permission of my lord, sir, Alexander," offered Tatanee. "It is best this way to tread Waters of Peace and Waters of War." Alexander assumed he was referring to Peace River and the Bad River, the two rivers that flowed into the lake.

Alexander had seen canoes on rivers before, and

he had seen the flimsy, small vessels sink as soon as they collided with an obstruction. Obstructions lay in the path of any vessel at every turn of the rivers in the Northwest Territory, but if he understood Tatanee, this canoe would not only be strong enough to navigate the waterways but also big enough to carry both supplies and men. Tatanee and Providence were smiling at him and Alexander seized the opportunity. "Build one, Tatanee. You build one and we, Chubb and I, will help." They would also learn a valuable lesson.

Tatanee went to work right away. He selected a long, straight tree that Alexander didn't think would be wide enough to be dug out. Tatanee told him he wasn't going to dig out the trunk but use the wood. "It would be better you watch. I cannot talk about canoe in words," he added.

The men felled the tree, then began to hollow it out as thin as possible without breaking or splintering the wood. The women, meanwhile, were heating water over a fire. When the men had finished carving out the tree, Tatanee called for the hot water.

Alexander watched the flaxen-haired Indian girl carry pot after pot full of boiling water, which she pounded into the hollowed tree. Her beauty and grace captured his gaze and her watchful eyes returned it. When they met on the path to the tree, she dutifully waited for him to pass. Their eyes met too, and he held her there as long as civility allowed. Then, abruptly, she turned away and continued with her work.

When the water was overflowing the hollowed-out trunk, Tatanee signaled for the women to stop. The men proceeded to pull at its sides, to press them even thinner. The water began to cool. The women threw hot rocks from the fire into the hollow until it started to bubble again. Once more the practiced hands of the men pressed against the pliable edges of the trunk, pushed them back farther and farther. The wood began to assume the shape of a bow.

The process continued for days. When the Indians had gutted the tree trunk completely and spread its sides into the shape of an elongated bow, they had to allow the wood time to dry out thoroughly before sawing it into the curved ribs that would give the canoe its final shape. The ribs, joined together by transverse bars, became the skeleton of the canoe, which was then covered with deerskin. After they'd sewn the pieces of hide together carefully, the women pressed chewed gum into each seam to waterproof the canoe even further. The completed canoe would be a lot broader with a bottom a lot flatter than any Alexander had seen before. "Better," Tatanee explained, "for the white waters and wild rivers of the North."

Chubb, meanwhile, had been kept busy by the rush of trappers who'd started using the outpost. The furs were mounting in the storehouse daily while their stockpile of goods continued to diminish. When Chubb learned that two of the trappers were going south to Montreal before the snows, he immediately informed Alexander so that he could write letters to McGill and Coombs. Not only did the outpost need wagonloads of supplies for the upcoming winter, but it had a houseful of pelts waiting to be picked up and accounted for as well. Otherwise, the message continued, all goes well.

Alexander also wrote a long letter to Juliette, which he sealed securely with wax. He instructed the trappers to deliver the letter to Chubb's wife Louisa at the exclusive Beaver Club in Montreal where she worked as a maid.

The business of the outpost and his personal affairs attended to, Alexander hastened to the riverbank for the launching of the canoe. Chubb followed on his heels.

Longer than Fort Fork was wide and easily as heavy as the combined weight of three men, the canoe was larger than either Chubb or Alexander had imagined. Alexander reckoned it could carry six to eight people and at least two tons of supplies, while Chubb doubted it would carry anything at all. He doubted indeed that it even would float.

It took five men to carry the canoe, or manage the portage, as Chubb put it. Alexander held his breath as they eased it into the water, but he had no cause for worry at all. The canoe floated as if it belonged to the river.

With Tatanee and three other braves paddling and Alexander and Chubb as passengers, the canoe skimmed along the white water of Slave River. They maneuvered it easily through whirlpools and surges, and even rode a three-foot waterfall without tipping. Then Tatanee warned everyone that he was going to tip the canoe to test its true seaworthiness.

After attaching a coil of rope to its bow, Tatanee stepped back to the middle of the canoe in order to get a view of the river. Every eye in the boat was on him. As they approached a huge waterfall, he grasped the side of the canoe and tilted it. At the foot of the waterfall he swung the canoe into the rapids. The white water swamped it. The canoe capsized and came down over their heads like a lid on a kettle.

In the darkness and confusion under the boat, six

bodies thrashed about in the icy water. Alexander and Chubb bumped heads, then, bobbing up and down, managed to free themselves from the boat. They worked themselves back to the capsized canoe and joined the braves who were clinging to its sides. They all waited for Tatanee's next move.

Recovering the rope secured to the bow, Tatanee threw it over the upturned bottom and led it to two bosses on one side of the canoe. After fastening it to the bosses, he used the rope to climb onto the overturned boat. Standing on top of it, he pulled with all his weight on the rope in an attempt to turn the canoe right side up.

Understanding exactly what he was trying to do, Alexander and Chubb scurried aboard to add their weight to the rope. Slowly the boat began to turn. Grabbing for the far side as the canoe flipped over, Tatanee clambered aboard. Once settled, he began pulling everyone else back into the canoe.

Alexander thanked God for Tatanee. Not only did his canoe float, it even floated when capsized. Furthermore, it was maneuverable by one man, could carry six and had room enough for several months' worth of equipment and supplies. The canoe answered Alexander's prayers for the craft he needed to cross the mountains to the West.

That night after dinner Alexander kept Tatanee by the fire to discuss plans for the journey. Proud to have helped his white chiefs and eager to continue his usefulness, the brave agreed to build three more canoes over the winter months. He also offered two of his women to his leaders, the girl with the golden hair and a shy maiden neither of them had noticed in camp before.

Although the flaxen-haired maiden aroused Alexander's curiosity and desire, he resisted the temptation of Tatanee's offer. He wouldn't press his luck. The trouble he'd had with the Indian princess Winter Flower had far outweighed the pleasure. When he rejected the golden Indian maid, Alexander thought he read relief in her blue eyes.

Alexander now had a winter to dream not of an Indian maid but of a waterway. He had the know-how, the help, the equipment, the funding. He would have three more canoes in the spring. Then all he would need to do was discover the magic river.

That there was such a river, he was sure. Every trapper who'd worked on the far side of Great Slave Lake directly north of Lake Athabasca had reported it to be the widest, longest river they'd ever trapped. It was fed by the Slave River, the very river on which they'd tested the canoe. The nameless, big river fascinated Alexander and he was impatient to explore it. The cold, dark winter would pass slowly for him.

The arrival of the supply wagons later that fall heartened Alexander tremendously. It told him that McGill hadn't forgotten them and that he'd reached Juliette. A message from Coombs indicated they were still expected to look for new lands and, if possible, to find a passageway to the West. It also said that no reports were circulating in Montreal about the discovery of such a passage, and that exhilarated Alexander. It meant Marcel hadn't made it after all.

Alexander rushed out to yell the news to Chubb and they celebrated it with a little jig on the dock. "I wonder what happened to the boy wonder?" laughed Alexander.

"I tell you, *mon ami*, that trapper was making it all up in his head. He found that river in his jug of whiskey. Never believe a trapper, that's my advice to you." Chubb roared. "And to you," he added, as he tapped the shy Indian girl under her chin.

Chapter 14

That winter came. It was strangely idyllic for Alexander. It allowed him time for introspection and self-discovery, for Chubb's tales and Tatanee's Indian legends, and for his journal which was daily becoming fuller. Nothing satisfied him more than to prop up his feet next to a roaring fireplace and write down all his observations after a good day of hard labor.

For as long as the weather held, he and Chubb practiced with the canoe. When Tatanee wasn't supervising the construction of the other three canoes, he instructed Alexander and Chubb in various techniques of paddling, poling and bracing. He taught them how to spot a vortex, how to avoid surges and how to ride with an eddie. They learned too, how to portage the canoe when waterfalls or rocks made the river impassable. Every day they could, Chubb and Alexander worked with the canoe. They mastered it and when the river froze over, they missed their daily exercise.

With the first heavy snows came an unexpected problem. Tatanee's behavior became erratic and his moods unpredictable. His unbounded friendliness might suddenly give way to surly indifference or even outright defiance. Alexander and Chubb began to notice bruises on his women's faces and bodies. At first they thought Tatanee had started drinking. When that proved not to be true, they couldn't come up with any other reasonable explanation for Tatanee's strange conduct. They could only hope that the situation would rectify itself because Tatanee was invaluable to them and their expedition.

When the weather cleared for several days, Alexander and Chubb decided to trek to the Great Slave Lake and try to find the origins of the nameless, great river that so many of the trappers had talked about. They could cross the lake easily now because it was frozen solid, and both Tatanee and his shaman assured them a storm was most unlikely. After extracting a promise from Tatanee that he would control himself in their absence, Alexander and Chubb set out on their journey.

It took little more than a week. Although uneventful, the expedition did convince Alexander that the nameless river would lead them to the West. The river water had not yet frozen, nor would it until the dead of winter according to all the trappers, probably because of the salt content. By the time they returned to camp, Alexander was certain that the river without a name would narrow the chasm that separated him from Juliette.

A more immediate problem awaited them back at the outpost. Tatanee had gone on a rampage. Not only had he smashed everything in sight, but he'd also beaten anyone who'd tried to stop him. Two of his braves finally had overpowered and restrained him while he slept.

When he came face to face with Alexander, Tatanee became contrite and begged forgiveness. Alexander accepted the apologies of his most valuable aide, then cut loose his hands and feet. "Remember, Tatanee, I need you," said Alexander, as he prepared to leave. "We all do. But we value the fort more than any one man. If you would destroy that, we will have to destroy you first. Do you understand?"

Tatanee bowed and lowered his head. "Yes, my lord, sir, Alexander," he answered.

As Alexander walked through the compound, he passed the flaxen-haired girl. Her blue eyes followed him until he disappeared into his cabin.

Three nights later, she came to his bed. She stood before him naked. In the light of the full moon, Alexander could see that her body was red with welts. Then, for the first time, he heard her speak.

"Among my people, if a brave strikes a woman, she may leave him. If he strikes her again, he is put to death. No one strikes anyone in my tribe." Light, almost musical, her voice trembled with the wonder of a small child. "I have chosen to leave Tatanee and I ask to come to your bed."

Alexander's heart skipped once and for a second his stomach tightened. He faltered, but decided to deal with Tatanee in the morning. When he threw back his blankets, she didn't hesitate to accept the invitation. He couldn't lie close to her as her body still ached from Tatanee's blows. Indeed, she had been so badly pummeled that she could barely stretch out. Holding his desire in check, Alexander turned his back to her, so that Lea, the Kutenai name for small, golden bird, could get some sleep.

The next morning he insisted that Lea stay in bed. He also had one of the other maidens attend to her by soothing her wounds in a hot bath saturated with the leaves of medicinal herbs and plants. Until she recovered completely from Tatanee's beating, Alexander would not allow her to work or even to leave the sanctuary of his cabin.

Alexander didn't know quite how to deal with Tatanee himself, although he assumed it punishment enough for Tatanee to have lost the companionship and favors of Lea. Each time they passed in camp, Tatanee held his head low in shame and said nothing. He neither questioned Lea's desertion nor mentioned it. He accepted it and seemed more afraid than vindictive.

Chubb reminded Alexander why. "Do you remember, *mom ami,* during the first days of our rendezvous, the wagoners who were always drunk?"

"That means everyone, Chubb."

"No, no. The ones who lost the wagonful of lamps and lamp oil trying to ford the river backward." While Alexander tried to remember, Chubb continued. "Claude asked the Kutenai chief what he would do to men like ours. Not whip them, said the chief, not whip them because no one in our tribe strikes anyone."

"I recall it, but only vaguely, my friend," said Alexander.

"Then Claude asked him what he would do and the chief said he would kill them! Perhaps Tatanee thinks his days are numbered."

"Let him think what he wants. For what he did to that girl, he should be flogged for a day. Let him worry, it'll do us all good."

Alexander's nights with Lea became more painful for him as gradually she recovered from her wounds. Nights slipped by into weeks, and Lea made it clear that she intended their bed to be for sleeping only. Although Alexander honored her wishes and didn't force himself upon her, he hoped that someday she would want him as much as he wanted her. Deep within him he knew that the impulse that brought her to his bed would blossom into full passion. Until then, he had to curb the desire that she awakened in him every night by the fire and in bed.

Alexander began reading to her from his journals. His entries about crossing the wilderness to Fort Fork astonished her with their vivid descriptions and detailed observations. She told him what he longed to hear. She felt that she'd journeyed with him, that she too had discovered this land, its rivers and mountains. His words made her see anew the very territory in which she lived. A path finder, she called him, and no higher praise could she have given him.

One night Lea told him about herself, about the mystery and shame of her fair skin, her flaxen hair and pale blue eyes.

Her mother had been a runaway, or white Indian as her kind was called by the early settlers. Like other runaways she wanted only to escape the drudgery of pioneer life. The Kutenai had discovered and adopted her. Contrary to the legends of the white man, the Indians did not ravage helpless white women. They hadn't mistreated Lea's mother in any way. Instead they had revered her, honored her with gifts, deerskin clothes, decorated moccasins, beads and kindnesses. In return she had only to trust her new-found family and adjust to a comfortable life as a white sister. Three times Lea's mother had been "rescued" from her Indian family and three times she'd made her way back to the Kutenai village.

Lea, however, did not share her mother's honor in the tribe. Her pale hair and pale eyes set her apart from the tribal family, although her father was a full-blooded Kutenai brave. The Indians interpreted her blonde hair and blue eyes as a symbol of lifelessness. In her birth the spirit of the tribe began to die. Her presence served to warn them that their gods looked with disfavor upon the proud Kutenai. The gods would take more spirits from them.

Lea grew up shunned. Continually denied the love that her black-haired, brown-eyed tribal brothers and sisters received, she was overwhelmed by surprise, happiness and gratitude when Tatanee chose her to accompany him to the far northern territory. Tatanee, however, had become increasingly unhappy in this distant, new land, and she was certain that she was the cause of his misery, she the cursed pale one. Nevertheless, he had no cause to strike her. No one had ever struck her before.

Her story brought hundreds of questions to Alexander's mind, but he couldn't coax any further information out of this strange, wounded golden girl. Had she not been so bright, so alert, so filled with curiosity and wonder, he might have doubted her sanity. He believed her—and he desired her. But he would wait until she chose to tell him more as he would wait for her to share more than dreams in his bed.

The winter passed more mildly than the previous three Alexander had spent in his new land. Even so, he welcomed the spring, the thaw that marked the end of the cold, bleak, sunless season and made the rivers flow free again. Again, too, he focused on his goal, to sail west.

He and Chubb resumed their canoeing eagerly. In a short time they were again as adept at the art as they'd been before the onset of winter. They raced and ferried. Expertly they learned to pole the canoe through shallow rapids where oars proved ineffectual. They perfected their methods, but they were still two canoes short of their goal.

Only one of the other three canoes was near completion. Construction was proceeding more slowly than Tatanee had promised and planned. His lack of spirit had infected the entire crew. Even the appearance of the first trappers of the season, with their tales of the privations they'd suffered during the hard, northern winter, couldn't spark the listless Indians who'd spent the cold months in a warm, well-stocked camp.

Lea was the cause. She'd driven Tatanee close to madness and now she slept in the bed of the lord, sir, Alexander. The pale, flaxen-haired creature would soon drain the spirit from their white chief. She would doom him and then the Indians themselves to a lifeless future. The Kutenai viewed Lea as a bane upon all their lives, and they cursed Tatanee to his face for having brought her with them to their new home in the North.

To mitigate the growing discontent among the Kutenai, Alexander decided to take Lea with him and Chubb on a short expedition to test the one new canoe. Certain that they could handle the craft without Tatanee's help, they would leave him behind to attend to construction and his crew. When he learned that Lea would accompany them to Great Slave Lake, Tatanee's face clouded and his mood became most foul.

The new canoe turned out to be faster, lighter and more stable than the first. It whisked along the northern arm of the Slave River. The ice had broken and every eddie propelled the craft swiftly toward Great Slave

Lake. For four days they traveled without difficulty or the slightest hint of weariness.

Impeded first by souseholes and falls, then by ice too thick to break up, they portaged on the fifth day. The three of them handled the portage easily, and though it slowed their progress, they still managed to reach the western shores of the lake before nightfall. The next day tricky boating got them through narrow channels in the frozen surface of the lake. That night they camped on the banks of the river without a name, the river they hoped would lead them to the Pacific.

While Chubb and Alexander set up camp, Lea began to prepare another feast of acorns and fish baked in parchment and bark. Lea was digging for winter acorns when she discovered a piece of metal tubing with an eyepiece attached to it. At first she thought it was like the magic glass Alexander used to start fires, but closer examination told her it wasn't.

"Chubb, we've had company," observed Alexander, as he studied the glass.

"Where did you find this, Lea?" asked Chubb.

She led them to the spot where they dug out of the snow the gear that neither of them wanted to see. "Surveying equipment," muttered Alexander, and Chubb uncovered a wooden box. When they turned it over, both men let out involuntary gasps. "Hudson's Bay Company" read the inscription on the box.

"What are they doing up here, *mon ami*?"

After pacing around the cache, Alexander answered, "My guess is, whoever was up here left in a hurry."

"Indians? Cree, perhaps?"

"Too far north for Cree, Chubb. More like a bear or wolves. Look." Alexander picked up a handle broken off a knife. "Think he wounded it?"

"Don't look too far for acorns, Lea, you might come across some bones." Lea shuddered at Chubb's joke and moved instinctively toward Alexander.

"Do you think, Chubb? Could it be?"

"Marcel? Impossible, *mon ami*, he's farther south."

"Strange, isn't it, old friend. The one river we're sure will lead us to the West and we find out Hudson's Bay is surveying it."

"Put it out of your mind. It was bound to happen."

"It smells, Chubb. It smells to high heaven, I tell you." Angrily Alexander flung the tube deep into the woods.

"What are you doing? Maybe we could have used that," admonished Chubb.

"Do you know how to use it?" Chubb nodded no. "Well, neither do I, so what'd we lose? This," said Alexander, as he began peeling off the Hudson's Bay label, "is more valuable to me." He stuck it into his pouch with his journal.

Their discovery plagued Alexander for the next two days as they paddled their way through the ice to the mouth of the great nameless river. Alexander would have been elated, had not Hudson's Bay Company beaten him to its shores.

While they slept in their camp the second night, a wet spring snow fell. Alexander awoke to find Lea huddled beside him sharing his warmth. He also found two strange men, half-frozen and emaciated, asleep or unconscious, sharing the last warmth of their campfire. His shout awakened not only the two men but Chubb and Lea as well.

All five of them tensed. All five reached for whatever weapons they had handy to defend themselves. The confrontation lasted only a few seconds as both the

217

strangers could only barely hold a rifle, let alone aim and fire one. When Lea, Chubb and Alexander saw their wretched condition, they rushed to their assistance.

Lea prepared some tea and food, while Chubb rekindled the fire and Alexander tried to make them comfortable. "Poison!" one of them kept saying, as he pointed first to his canteen and then to his swollen lips and mouth. "Poison."

When the two men began wolfing down Lea's breakfast, Alexander, overpowered by his curiosity, investigated the polluted canteen. He uncorked it, smelled it and screwed up his face in disgust. Then, suddenly, his disgust yielded to an expression of wonder, astonishment and disbelief all at once. Without hesitation, he raised the canteen to his lips and drank from it. He spat out its water immediately and jubilantly he yelled, "Salt! Salt! Chubb, come taste this water and tell me it's not salt!"

Chubb tasted, spat and confirmed Alexander's joyful news. It was salt water. Chubb and Alexander stared at the two sick, hungry strangers as if they'd arrived from another world. And they had. They'd filled their canteens with the water that led to the Pacific Ocean and the golden West. They were also too weary to speak, and when they finished gorging themselves on acorns and fish, they fell asleep in the warmth of the crackling bonfire. All Chubb and Alexander could do was wait.

"Mark this spot in your mind forever, Chubb. Etch it there, for we don't want to lose this place," beamed Alexander, then swept his arm toward the river. "They had to come down from here. Of nothing else am I more certain. It's big enough and it's wide enough.

That's the beauty, laddie, it's wide enough for any ship that sails the ocean.''

"We're blessed, *mon ami*. So far we've been right about everything.''

"The only thing that worries me is that Marcel and Dentere himself may have spotted this river. They would be purple with rage if they knew we too had discovered it. And why do you think they have been surveying it?''

"Don't think of them, I tell you," Chubb admonished him. "Think of us! It's you who's making our dream come true. This will be your river.''

When the trappers awoke, they told Chubb and Alexander what the river explorers had hoped to hear. They'd trapped the nameless river all the last year and followed one arm of it hundreds of miles to its end. So wide was it at times that they couldn't see the opposite shore and so it was less than ideal for beaver, but its many tributaries offered exquisite stock. When they finally reached the end of the river, they saw only water—no land, no deltas, no watersheds, only water.

Anxious to escape the wilderness before the onslaught of winter, the two trappers had filled their canteens and water barrel, only to discover that the water was foul. They managed to get to a cabin halfway back down the river and had survived the winter by chewing on beaven skins. Then the weather broke. The two trappers were looking for a company outpost when they spotted Chubb's campfire.

After hearing the tale, Chubb took Alexander aside and broke into the exaltation that both of them felt. "It's a small miracle, *mon ami*. A Marvel! That our fire should bring these two men to us, to give us the proof we need.''

"It's exactly what both McGill and Dentere told

me. You must have a witness. Well, I'll tell you, Chubb, old friend, *we're* the witnesses. *We* tasted the water!''

"Wouldn't it have been better for them if they'd stayed by the ocean to keep warm instead of coming back into the cold?'' asked Chubb.

"Of course, but I don't think they know what they found. I'm sure they don't, and I won't tell them.''

"Nor will I.''

"I thought at first that they were the surveyors who'd been lost all winter but—''

"Forget them, Alexander. Forget them! Think of us. We're here, and where they are only God knows.''

"I'm trying, Chubb, I'm trying.''

That afternoon they broke camp and with the two trappers started homeward for Fort Chipewyan. They'd found their gateway to fame and fortune. Now they had only to explore it.

Chapter 15

The return trip to Fort Chipewyan took two full weeks. Alexander's impatience grew each day. Eager to complete their preparations at the fort and begin the expedition up the waterway, he probably would have paddled their swift canoe through the nights had Chubb and Lea allowed it. Most nights he fell asleep with the canteen of salt water in his arms, as if he feared it and all his dreams would evaporate.

His restlessness only increased back at the fort. It put everyone on edge and hampered rather than hastened the Indians' progress with the canoes.

To expedite matters, Alexander abandoned plans for a fourth canoe and had Tatanee concentrate on completing the third. He wanted it constructed, however, like the canoe he and Chubb and Lea had taken up past Great Slave Lake. Tatanee showed him why it was lighter, more mobile and easier to maneuver than the first canoe they'd built. Its shell was covered with birch bark instead of deerskin. What Tatanee did not tell him, though, was that a bark construction would take several weeks longer. Delay after delay plagued Alexander.

Alexander sent couriers to both Fort Fork and Mon-

treal with messages stating that he'd found the waterway to the West and that his expedition up the nameless
river shortly would be underway. The letter to McGill
also included his discovery of the surveying equipment
that belonged to Hudson's Bay. The Montreal courier
was carrying, too, another long letter to Juliette. In it
Alexander told her how he longed and waited for some
word from her and how her long silence made him
despair of ever hearing from her again. It was a sad
letter and he hoped it would provoke Juliette into writ-
ing to him no matter what the dangers.

The days grew longer and warmer. The weather
was ideal for an expedition and immobility took its toll
on Alexander. He stopped eating. He snapped at
everyone.

Lea was concerned and wondered how she could
soothe Alexander and ease his constant irritation. One
night, after an especially trying day for Tatanee's plodding crew as well as Alexander, she turned to him in
bed and began kneading the muscles of his shoulders,
back and neck. Her small, strong hands worked hard to
ease his tension. They also further aroused his desire for
her, and hers for him.

Lea felt her own flesh tremble as her hands plied at
the taut sinews in Alexander's back. Her fingers worked
diligently. Their every touch awakened strange, new
longings within her and stirred the passion Alexander
had long suppressed. His heart beat quick with it. His
body throbbed against her warm palms. He turned over
on his back, and when she began to rub his firm chest,
she unknowingly tortured him. He battled against himself to stem his passion and suddenly he understood
Tatanee's fury and grief. But he realized, too, that Lea,
imprisoned in her own innocence, had to be led.

His eyes assured and comforted her as he guided her small hand slowly downward to his loins. In her eyes he saw wonder and then excitement glow. Her round, young breasts heaved faster and her breath came short when without warning he pulled her down on him. For one brief moment she resisted the firm strength of his passion before responding to it with all the hungry power of her tender years. His passion burst and he transported her out of herself. With him she crossed a border into a realm of magic and ecstasy. The camp, the territory, even the nameless river ceased to exist that night for them, and they slept peacefully in each other's arms.

For several days after that, Lea stayed away from Alexander. Whenever he came outside to check on the progress with the canoes, she walked to another part of the outpost. At night she slept on the floor. Alexander accepted her behavior and even understood much of her confusion. He didn't press or question her and within the week she rejoined him in his bed.

At last it was time to go. Their preparations complete, the last canoe tested, their supplies loaded, Alexander, Chubb, Lea and Tatanee took their positions in the lead canoe. Two braves and their women would follow in each of the other two.

The clear, sunny days, they figured, should hold for at least two more months. It was early August, but the weather wouldn't become a prohibitive factor until mid-October. By then they should have crossed through the mountains, explored the region and should be on their way back to camp. Even if they failed to beat the snow and ice of another winter, they assured themselves that they wouldn't make the same mistake the two trappers had made. They would wait out the cold winter close to the warm shores of the ocean beyond the river without a name.

The three canoes traveled smoothly down the Slave River, so smoothly that Alexander could write long, descriptive entries in his journal. As the river flowed completely free of ice, portage was unnecessary and they reached Great Slave Lake in excellent time. Without effort or problems they canoed across the placid lake to the broad nameless river. Chubb wanted to call it the Mackenzie. Although several hours of daylight still lay ahead when they arrived at its banks, Alexander decided they would set up camp and have an early night.

"Are you nervous, *mon ami*?" asked Chubb.

"Wouldn't you be, Chubb?"

"Yes, of course. I'm just as troubled as you. We're waiting on the doorstep of immortality, no? That should make anyone nervous."

"What I'm afraid of is that when we get there, we'll find huge settlements of people from the West looking for a passageway to the East."

"It is a giant country, *mon ami*," observed Chubb, perplexed by Alexander's fear and constant worrying. "Don't trouble yourself. If that happens we'll still find something to trade with them. Think of how surprised they'll be to discover us!" He laughed at his own joke. Alexander did not.

The next morning broke bright and clear. Sunlit and brilliantly blue, the river stretched before them, challenged them. It could lead Alexander to fame, fortune and Juliette, or it could prove his every speculation wrong. The longer he studied the wide, rapid river, the more he realized he was procrastinating. He gave the order to shove off and the three canoes started serenely down the nameless river.

The river's strong, sweeping current, however, soon slowed their paddling. Brute strength helped little. They could rely only on skill and strategy. Often they pulled over to the rocks at the river's edge to examine the next stretch of water before running it. When the water ran shallow, they had to pole the canoes. More times than they'd anticipated, they had to portage. Huge rocks not only obstructed their course but also created whirlpools that could drive a big boat to the river's bottom in no time.

Just as Alexander's canoe was passing around one of the sharp bends in the river, he saw the third boat strike a rock. It rebounded and its split side filled with water. Both braves lost their oars. The women were screaming as the canoe swung round and the rapids swept it downstream broadside. It struck another rock. On impact the canoe broke in two and its passengers and cargo were thrown into the river.

The braves and their women latched on to a part of the drifting hull. Narrowly missing rocks on all sides, they smashed into a series of rapids and boulders. The rough water dashed the birch bark into an enormous boulder. The hull splintered. The four desperate Kutenai fought the current, then disappeared from sight. They were lost, beyond even the remotest possibility of rescue.

To no avail Alexander and the rest of the party searched for the river's victims. Once they recuperated from the accident they'd witnessed and taken stock of the supplies they'd lost, they paddled on. The river without a name had shown them its hazards and left them shaken and wary.

*   *   *

As they continued their journey, the current gradually slackened and the water deepened. Long lines of broken cliffs bound the river. Beyond them lay evergreen forests and groves of giant cottonwoods. Alexander reckoned they'd been traveling the river for over three weeks, one week longer than they'd planned for the entire run. The river seemed endless. At some points water spanned the wide horizon while at others it narrowed almost to oar's length.

They fished the river for trout and pike or hunted the woods for venison and grouse, which they ate with wild berries and nuts each night in their camp. Each night, too, Alexander and Lea slept apart from the rest of the expeditionary crew. They explored each other, and the prospects of their journey, the river, the ocean heightened the intimate discoveries of their lovemaking.

After a month and a half on the nameless, endless river, the discovery of the Pacific still remained only a prospect. Temperatures were dropping lower each night and an unseasonable frost often covered their campground in the morning. They also started to notice that trees were getting scarce and fish rare. Beaver tracks had disappeared. Most significantly, though, the shoreline was becoming flatter while the river current was pulling stronger each day. Tatanee concluded they were nearing the estuary and the pull of the ocean's tides, but Alexander and Chubb were perplexed.

"*Mon ami*, shouldn't we have seen higher cliffs and bluffs in the crossing?" Chubb asked, as he walked with Alexander along a desolate shore one chilly evening.

"If we crossed high, if for some strange reason the

river cut through the mountains . . ." Alexander sought an explanation.

"Even here water doesn't flow uphill."

"If we'd crossed mountains," Alexander continued, "the cliffs would have been higher and we couldn't have walked so far inland on our portages. Something's wrong." Then he stated what he didn't want to admit. "I've suspected for some time now that we didn't cross any mountains."

"Exactly," Chubb confirmed the suspicion, "and haven't I been telling you for days what you should have noticed long before now? How many times have I told you that we're skirting the mountains, not crossing them? I think you've been too smitten by your half-breed to notice anything that's going on."

"What does that mean, Chubb?" Alexander challenged.

"Exactly what I said. Each night you play around in the bushes, while Tatanee and I are trying to figure out where we are. I sometimes doubt you're awake enough even to realize we're not in mountains."

"This is a hell of a time for you to tell me your theories, Chubb." Alexander was angry. "Let me give you one of mine to chew on with your new-found Indian pal, laddie."

"Tell me, monsieur," Chubb replied coldly. "I'm waiting."

"Well, have you thought that the mountains might not be mountains this far north, that they might be foothills and the simplest way across is up?"

"You're telling me we've already crossed the mountains?"

"It's a possibility is what I say, Chubb," Alexander snapped.

Chubb, however, was angrier with him. "There's a simple French expression for that theory, monsieur— *merde*. I say to you, *merde*!"

"You have no right to talk to me that way, Chubb."

"I don't? You think you are beyond reproach? Sleep alone one night and plan with us."

"Stop it, Chubb. You sound like a jealous child."

"Well, before I go back to the *men*, let me ask you why, if we've crossed the mountains, is it so cold? Why aren't we basking in the sun of California Island?"

"Because we might be at the Northern Ocean, and in that case we'll see either Unalaschka or Russia."

"Mon Dieu!"

"And if you don't want to see either one with me, turn back. I'll not hold it against you." Alexander didn't wait for Chubb's answer. He turned on his heel and stormed back to the campfire.

He couldn't believe he'd made that dreadful a mistake. Too much of the evidence proved him right. He wouldn't allow Chubb's theories and doubts to blast his hopes. He had to follow the river to its end, to the ocean, and if it led to Russia or Unalaschka rather than the balmy West, only then would he admit to any error.

When they continued the next day, Chubb not only refused to speak to Alexander but also decided to travel in the second boat. With each stroke of the oars, the landscape became more barren and monotonous. Within a few days, too, the occasionally chilly weather had turned into an inescapably bitter cold. It caught them totally unprepared, for they'd thought they were heading for the warm, idyllic shores of the Pacific—not the Arctic.

Nevertheless, Alexander wouldn't turn back. Chubb

finally broke his silence and asked his partner why he wouldn't admit to error.

"You tasted the trapper's water, didn't you," Alexander politely replied with a question of his own.

"Yes, *mon ami*," answered Chubb softly, not wanting to murder his companion's dream. "I did, and it was salt."

"I tell you, Chubb, my friend, there is an answer. The river hasn't forked and we've seen no broad channels on either bank. Those two trappers must have followed this course to the ocean. Do you want to turn back now, now that we may be within five strokes of home, and never know what lies at the end of the nameless river? As far as we've traveled, we must reach an ocean."

His argument convinced Chubb, still remorseful over their falling out, but not the Indian crew. Alexander could no longer treat them as equals or friends. He had to order the Indians to continue on his fanatical expedition.

The land became invariably flat. A cold, sleety wind swept across the dreary plains and down the bleak river. Alexander and his band of Indians huddled against the bitter wind. They were never warm now and still Alexander insisted they continue.

Sleet gave way to powdery snow and the desolate plains to ice-covered fields as forbidding as any they'd encountered on their way to Fort Fork. They no longer camped but sat all night in the canoes and took turns sleeping. Occasionally some of the party foraged for food on the icebound shore. Inevitably they came back empty-handed. Two days after they ran out of solid food, they saw the ocean.

The ocean! The ocean that had cost him lies, pleas,

love and devotion, the ocean that had claimed his dreams for years still eluded Alexander. The ocean that stretched before him was the wrong one. Life had played another grim joke on him. Alexander stared at the salty waters as if he'd been struck by the left hand of God. Failure harrowed him and he was inconsolable. No one, not even Lea or Chubb, could reach him when he retreated into himself and tried to unravel the fatal knot of disappointment that overwhelmed and immobilized him.

Three days later, when Alexander realized his inaction was endangering the lives of seven other people, he decided to return home, not just to the outpost but to Montreal. There he would attempt to right the course of his misdirected life and with Juliette restore his broken dreams and shattered hopes. There, too, he would see Marcel. Alexander's spirits sank further at the prospect of having to measure his failure against Marcel's success.

His three days of isolation had taken their toll on Alexander. Cold, wet, hungry and ill, he lay down in the canoe as they started out on their homeward journey. He was feverish and his every fierce spasm of coughing wobbled the birch-bark craft.

With limited supplies and meager knowledge, Lea tried desperately to prepare herbal remedies for their ailing chief. None of the braves or their women would help pale Lea because to help her would be to help the gods of evil. She'd stolen the spirit of their once great leader who in turn had led them to the wrong ocean. Just as she'd driven Tatanee close to madness, she was enfeebling their white lord Mackenzie.

Lea's attentions and a cold night brought Alexander no relief. The next day the river added to his misery. At first Alexander thought they were caught in some rapids. Then Chubb jolted him with a cry from the next boat. "Alexander, wake up and take an oar! *Mon Dieu*, they cannot keep you on course!"

Alexander pulled himself bolt upright. A sharp wind lashed into his face. Powdery snow covered the hair and shoulders of his crew. It was piling up on the bow and stern of the canoe. The fierce current threatened to capsize or swamp the craft which broke into rising waves of the rough water. They rode the river out of all control.

Tatanee yelled from the bow back to Alexander, "The snow is so thick, I cannot see anything, my lord, sir, Alexander."

With the snow flying at them horizontally, they could barely see fifty feet ahead. Whitecaps broke out of the wall of snow and hit the canoes before they could be detected. Oars could not control the crafts. Chubb and Tatanee tried to slow down the forward movement by jabbing the long poles into the river bottom. The poles snapped.

They battled the treacherous river all night. The next day brought no improvement. Hard, driving snow blinded them. The wind blasted at them and the river raged. The violent water battered the canoes and frazzled their nerves. They were cold, wet and exhausted when, as night fell, the relentless river pitched the bow of Alexander's canoe broadside and exposed them to powerful swells. Fearful they would capsize any second, they all held their breath until the craft miraculously righted itself. Again the swells caught and pitched it. Again freezing water showered them and flooded the inside of the craft.

When day broke on their bedlam, Lea intently studied the horizon. For several hours of their turbulent journey, not once did she avert her gaze from it. Then she told Alexander she sensed that they were approaching a safe place to bring their canoes to shore.

Surf was exploding off the cliffs that towered above them and blotted out the sky. Any moment a broadside swell might smash both canoes against the crags. The roar of the water and howling wind reduced all communication to glances, gestures and pantomime. But they all heard Lea yell, "Shore!" She screamed it a second time at the top of her lungs as she pointed to a break in the cliffs.

Chubb signaled that he saw the patch of flat land and tried to guide his craft toward it.

"No one can help anybody else," Alexander shouted above the din of the water at the Indians whose faces had frozen into masks of fear and dread.

"Don't let the water drag you back when we get close. Just hold on to the rocks!" he screamed to Lea. "Be ready to go when I tell you."

White water swamped Chubb's boat but he managed to land it on a nest of boulders. He and his crew pulled the canoe out of the rampaging water onto the shore.

"We sink! We sink!" screamed Tatanee in Alexander's craft as a wave breaking swamped over them.

"Now!" yelled Alexander, but no one moved. Another wave missed them. "Now!" he repeated and slid into the water. The others followed.

A wave swept the empty canoe downriver. It was lost to the rapids and they were caught in a powerful undertow. Wave after wave washed over them, pinned them against the boulders or trapped them in whirlpools. Coughing, spitting, gasping, they fought for air only to be rolled and pummeled again and again.

They missed the safe shore by two arm-lengths at most when the wild water slammed them against the sheer face of the cliff. The swollen river lifted them, banged and scraped them against the rock. They tried to hold on to a crack in the cliff wall, but the water overpowered them, pulled them back and under.

Then Tatanee made it. He gained a firm hold on the wide crack and managed to scramble up a step or two before the next swirl hit. It missed him by a hand. He wedged himself into the crevice and offered his arm to Alexander. Lea grasped Alexander's free hand and the Kutenai brave completed their human chain. With Tatanee as their anchor, they worked their way out of the pounding water and across the sheer face of the cliff. Slowly they edged over to the shore where Chubb and the other crew awaited them.

The party camped on the dry border of a crescent-shaped beach that night. A mountainous pile of rocks rose up behind them and a thick, impenetrable evergreen underbrush stretched far back from the cliffs and rocks. To continue their journey on land was out of the question.

Alexander contemplated the impassable land, then the river that had led him only to futility. "You said this was the river of no name?" Alexander said to Chubb. "I call it Disappointment River. Now, help me, good friend, to make a mark. This way, if Marcel does come by, we'll give him a good hello."

From his pouch he took out some dry paint and wax which he mashed together in a small cup. Chubb lifted him up on his shoulders, and reaching as high as he could, Alexander wrote on the cliff: "Alexander Mackenzie, from Montreal, by river and land. 28 October 1789."

Chapter 16

Snow fell throughout that bitter day of October 28, 1789 and the river continued to rise. The women helped their braves feed a fire in the shelter of the rocks on the beach, while Chubb, Alexander and Tatanee deliberated their next move.

"Chubb, do you remember where the trappers were coming from the day we met them?" Alexander spoke rapidly, excitedly.

"Upriver, from the ocean," replied Chubb, hesitant to open a newly healed wound.

"No, they didn't!" he shot back.

"*Mon ami*, we found them almost at their end. They still had the ocean water in their canteens . . ."

"No," Alexander interrupted him, "they came from their cabin! Their cabin, Chubb, and by all reckoning it can't be far from here."

Chubb couldn't agree simply because he wanted his partner to be right. A miscalculation now could cost more lives, maybe even their own. Then it struck him, and he practically shouted, "Of course, *mon ami*, I remember! But how do you know it's near here?"

"They described the cabin's location. I'm sure I

spotted it on the way up.'' Alexander stopped and blew on his hands to warm them. "They said it sat near a small stream that shot off westerly from a bend in the river.''

"There's such a bend with a stream,'' Tatanee confirmed. "But to get there we must pass terrible water, my lord, sir, Alexander.''

"And if I remember correctly, *mon ami*, the trappers said that never again would they leave it without supplies for a winter.''

"There will be food then?'' supposed Tatanee.

"Don't be so sure. Trappers have a way of talking and not doing.'' Only Alexander seemed to remember that neither of the trappers had left camp after they were rescued.

"Let's find it and find out.'' Chubb laughed and caught his second wind. More solemnly he confided to Alexander that he, Lea, and Tatanee were worried about their leader's weakening condition.

Alexander, however, turned the tables on Chubb. "You're worried about me? You've eaten none of the little food we've had to share. You can hardly walk and struggle along on the sides of your feet. Do you think you're fooling me? I'm worried about you.''

That night the desolate group huddled close to one another and the fire on the beach. One of the braves stood watch over the fire. Sometime during the night, he dozed off and brutally cold water washed over the flat beach, the fire and the sleeping party. They got an early start.

The current slackened as they paddled down the river in the one remaining canoe and the storm passed over them. They traveled swiftly and covered more distance that day than they had on any other. The weather had lost much of its sting when they pulled ashore at the edge of another sheer cliff to set up camp. The exhausted party got its first full night of true sleep in many days.

"One more day, two days at most, to reach the bend in the stream," Tatanee estimated the following morning.

"We're that close? Good," replied Alexander.

They hadn't paddled far from their camp when a strong wind rose and waves again began hitting their craft with force. The piercing wind brought tears to their eyes. The river soaked them to the skin.

"Let's go back," shouted Alexander. "Back to the beach."

It was all they could do. Back on shore, they lit a fire and tried to warm themselves. Chubb's feet pained him even more and he was finding it difficult even to walk on their sides. When he took off his chaps to dry them by the fire, Alexander saw that Chubb's water-soaked pants had rubbed the skin from both his knees. Raw, red sores covered his kneecaps.

While Tatanee dug for clams on the beach, Lea gathered wood. The other two Indian couples huddled together near the rocks, then suddenly they stood up and walked over to Tatanee in single file. After speaking only a few words, they slowly backed away. When they reached the rocks, they bowed. They turned then and began climbing and clawing their way upward.

"Where are they going?" shouted Alexander, suprised and shocked.

"Let them go," Tatanee replied calmly. "They are fools who wish to go their own way. Let them."

No one spoke of it again, but the desertion haunted Alexander for a long time.

As darkness settled in, the wind died and the river started to run less wildly. The change in the weather provided an opportunity they couldn't afford to miss, not with the cabin so close by, even if it meant traveling at night.

They worked at the oars throughout the moonlit night. Their hands became puffy and blistered and grey. Chubb and Tatanee groaned with pain and exertion. As Lea weakened, Alexander tried to compensate for her. The dawn brought more wind and heavy snow. The water became so choppy that the canoe actually halted in midstream. Immobile, they had to ferry themselves ashore.

They spent a miserable two days and nights waiting for relief from the storm. Merely building a fire now seemed to drain all of them of their energy. In vain Tatanee hunted for clams. Hunger was turning slowly into starvation. The constantly pounding water pounded on their nerves. They became stumbling, plodding snowmen.

When the storm subsided on the second afternoon, they took to the river once again. They rode with the current, and long, sweeping strokes of the oars carried them great distances with relative ease. Tatanee began looking for the bend that would lead them to the trappers' cabin. Even more optimistic, Chubb suggested that they look for smoke, for he was convinced that other trappers must have settled there to wait out the winter. They saw no smoke, nor did they find the bend. Not long after dark they had to pull ashore. Lea had become so weak she could no longer manage the oar and Chubb suffered excruciating physical pain in his legs and feet. They all suffered hunger and exhaustion.

Virtually helpless, Chubb and Lea huddled next to

the rocks, but they found little warmth. Alexander attended to the fire while Tatanee scoured the beach for clams. The fire brought them some comfort. Chubb's condition, however, worsened, and he could barely find the strength to sip Tatanee's clam broth. Then clouds began rolling into the dark northern sky. Soon a fresh snow was falling. With it came a bitter wind and their fire was constantly being blown out. The four of them shared a long, cold, awful night.

In the grey light the following morning, Alexander and Tatanee walked the snowy shore. They searched for a landmark, for something to give them hope. They climbed some rocks and surveyed the river. The snow swirling about them, they strained their eyes to follow the course of the waterway Alexander had named Disappointment. Then both of them spotted it, a line of trees that broke the watery horizon. It had to be the river's bend.

"The bend, my lord, sir, Alexander," whispered Tatanee.

"Yes, it looks that way," Alexander answered vaguely, afraid to hope.

As they headed back to their camp, Alexander told Tatanee, "I think we should leave Chubb and Lea behind. We'll come back for them after we get provisions from the cabin. Food will restore their strength. Then all four of us will take shelter there."

"We haven't found the cabin, my lord, sir, Alexander."

"We will," he said. "We will," he repeated, and meant they must.

Back at the camp, Alexander exaggerated their prospects to Chubb and Lea. "We've located the cabin," he told them. "It should take us half the morning to reach it. Give us time to load up and we'll be back to fetch you before nightfall.''

''I can help,'' mumbled Chubb.

''You will, by protecting Lea and taking care of yourself,'' Alexander answered, but Chubb had fallen back to sleep.

As Tatanee pushed the canoe into the angry river, Alexander glanced back at Lea and Chubb huddled together under their blankets in front of a wavering fire and sheltered only by a wall of rocks. Then he and Tatanee oared into the unrelenting wind and snow.

They did reach the line of trees by the end of the morning, but they did not discover the river's bend. The trees, it turned out, grew in a semicircle around a little cove. ''We go back?'' asked Tatanee.

''No. It's got to be near here. Let's try a little longer.'' Alexander couldn't relinquish this final hope and they rowed on.

Their arms weary and their lungs aching with each breath of freezing air, they rowed against the thundering, white-capped waves slapping at their canoe. Numb, they rowed blindly on until they lost all track of time. Close to total exhaustion, they aimed for a promontory as darkness began to fall.

They hit the rocky shore with a bump that sounded as if they'd torn off the bottom of their craft. Without the canoe they'd be truly lost. Luck, however, hadn't completely deserted them. The bark was still intact. They pulled it onto drier land and Alexander turned to examine the landscape. When he did he found himself facing the cabin. Overcome, Alexander dropped to his knees. They had found shelter at last.

* * *

Tatanee started a fire in the small wood stove that stood against the back wall of the cabin while Alexander searched for provisions he was sure he wouldn't find. He was wrong. In a large wooden crate he found rice, flour, beans, coffee and some dried fish. Trappers other than the two they'd rescued must be using it. Alexander thanked his unknown benefactors.

The room soon felt unbearably hot. Their faces and hands aching with the heat, they had to move as far from the wood-burning stove as possible. Exhausted beyond sense or reason, they fell asleep.

About noon the next day, they awoke in pain. Alexander's fingers were turning black and his feet were troubling him more than they had when he'd been rescued on the icy northern plains by the Eskimos. He noticed that Tatanee too was now walking on the outer edges of his feet like Chubb. Unless they tended to their feet by soaking them in melted snow, they risked losing them.

But Alexander also felt compelled to go back for Lea and Chubb who waited without shelter on the cold, snowy beach miles behind them. He soon realized, however, that it would be impossible to make the return trip in their condition. He wouldn't even be able to walk the short distance from the cabin to the river. "We must soak our feet, Tatanee, or else we'll be useless," advised Alexander, pain evident in his hoarse voice.

The melted snow felt like boiling water. All afternoon they tried to brave the pain of plunging their feet and hands into it, but neither of them could bear it for more than a few seconds at a time. Alexander finally resorted to a gallon of whiskey and half a jug of rum for both an anesthetic and a medicine. After pouring some liberally into himself, he poured some into the foot bath. Although Tatanee refused to drink the white man's poison, he kept his feet in the bath as long as Alexander and not once did he wince from the pain.

After the third day of treatment, Tatanee honed his knife razor-sharp and began cutting away the dead flesh from their feet to reduce the swelling. Sometimes he had to slice almost as deep as the bone in order to reach the festering layers under the skin. He exposed the anklebone of his right foot and the bones of three toes on his left foot. It was a strong measure, but it worked. The swelling went down.

So did food, finally, and they were able to eat without nausea. After six days in the cabin, they were on their way to physical recovery, but guilt and worry over Chubb and Lea agonized Alexander. He couldn't sleep the sixth night. The wind was howling and a fresh snow fell.

"I don't think they could have survived last night," Alexander confessed his fear the next morning. "It was so cold and the snow is still falling heavily." Tatanee said nothing.

Two days later the snow turned to rain. The temperature had risen and Alexander could wait no longer. Although he packed food for four in a gunny sack along with as many blankets as he could carry, he also took a shovel and pickaxe. He expected the worst and couldn't bear the thought of leaving his friend Chubb and dear Lea unburied and prey for wolves or vultures.

Tatanee didn't want to go. He accepted the will of the gods who'd chosen to claim pale, flaxen-haired Lea and the once hearty Chubb on the cold, deserted shore of Disappointment River. He moved out only after Alexander directly ordered Tatanee to accompany him.

They found their old campsite easily, but the rowing strained their sore muscles and the raw, unhealed flesh of their feet and hands. Alexander walked up to the small beach slowly, while a fidgety Tatanee sulked behind him in the canoe. No fire was burning. As he approached, Alexander could see that they'd rigged up a shelter with blankets and sticks, but it had collapsed and fallen on the two motionless bodies.

Only the sound of the rushing river disturbed the silence. Alexander stood quietly beside the two bodies under snow-covered blankets and said, *"Mon ami,* I've come to make you part of your God." He could say no more. His throat was dry and tears brimmed in his eyes.

When Alexander pulled back the blankets and uncovered his friend, Chubb began to shiver. "Chubb!" Alexander gasped in total disbelief and held Chubb's head in his hands. "You're alive?"

"Lea, too," Chubb managed to whisper. Alexander uncovered her, and Lea nodded weakly, then tried to smile.

"Tatanee!" Alexander rose to his feet. "Tatanee!" he shouted with jubilation. "They're alive! Come quick! Help me! They're alive!"

Tatanee bounded from the boat and limped toward them while Alexander dropped to his knees once more. "My friends!" he cried. "My friends, you're alive!"

Chubb couldn't stand up. The severe weather had torn into his clothing and huge sores covered his exposed flesh. Tatanee and Alexander had to drag him to the canoe. They couldn't carry Lea gently enough. She screamed in pain at every touch and her wrist, which must have been left uncovered, was already turning black. But they were alive.

Although Alexander and Tatanee desperately needed

a rest from that morning's row, they decided to try to reach the cabin before nightfall. The weather and light were still holding, but they would have to struggle with the river and their pain. They did, for the rest of the day, even when they were positive they couldn't row another stroke. At sunset, soaking wet and tired, but safe, they beached the canoe within sight of the cabin.

Despite his exhaustion and the bared bones of his toes and ankle, Tatanee first bore Lea and then Chubb on his back from the beach up to the cabin. Alexander, meanwhile, started a fire in the stove and prepared some broth. Both men ignored their own needs and attended to their friends, their wounds and sores and dying flesh. They worked slowly, cautiously, gently. The four of them thanked their gods for each other and for their shelter, fire, and food. They were safe, and now had only to wait for a break in the weather.

Alexander felt no joy at his first sight of the outpost across the lake. He was returning from an expedition to open up the new world of the West that had turned out to be no more than a costly, fruitless trek through a wilderness. He'd survived another ordeal, but his shame and embarrassment lay heavy upon him.

He would have to confess to McGill a waste of money, time and resources. He would have to face Juliette and endure Marcel's jeers. Perhaps, too, he would have to admit that Papa Louis was right, that he had neither the knowledge nor experience to lead such an expedition. He would have to admit failure. Alexander wasn't eager to return to Montreal. The prospect overwhelmed and paralyzed him.

The outpost at least would provide him a short reprieve. Here he could withdraw from a world of galling disappointments and try to mend his broken hopes and dreams. Until the winter passed, he would have to answer to no one, only contend with himself and the fresh wounds his ego had suffered. Alexander had no sooner entered the outpost than he retreated into his room in the main house. He kept apart from his fellow survivors, his companions and friends. He brooded. Silence was heavy.

Nor did Lea speak, though she stayed with Alexander in his room. She veiled herself in mystery. Her brush with death, the misfortunes the entire expedition had suffered and Alexander's lifeless withdrawal she blamed on herself. She believed the Indians' legends of her witchery. Daily she grew more distant, and when she walked around the post, she looked constantly toward the sky as if waiting for the gods to strike.

Chubb also became introspective. He blamed a large part of the failure of the expedition on his own inability to stifle Alexander's enthusiasm. Instead, caught up in the momentum of Alexander's quick judgment, he had seconded decisions that were only almost right, that lacked the one bit of reflection to prevent a master stroke from turning into failure. Although it hurt him to see Alexander's painful struggle with despair, Chubb knew better than to approach him with false bravura. Only time and Alexander himself could heal such wounds.

Once more Alexander's journal became his salvation. He wrote sporadically at first, then so profusely and with such an abundance of detail that in two weeks he filled every page of the book Juliette had given him. Up to that point he'd recorded only the trip downriver that had brought him to the ocean. He identified the whirlpools, rapids and waterfalls that marked the disappointing waterways. At their appropriate pages in the journal, he also pressed the flowers and leaves he'd picked up in the course of the journey. He filled his days with words for his distant companion, Juliette, and eased that pain.

But Alexander wrote no words to McGill in Montreal. A report was due and another harsh winter was threatening the tiny outpost of Fort Chipewyan. Unless written soon, the messages to Montreal would have to be carried across the territory in January or February, the winter's riskiest months. When Chubb broached this matter with his partner, Alexander unequivocally replied, "I won't do it and I won't ask anyone else to do it. Not on my account, they won't."

"But there are people willing right now to make a crossing."

"Tell me, is November and December any different up here than January or February? No, and I won't ask any man to cross the territory now."

"You know what that means, *mon ami*," Chubb pressed him. "We won't be getting any word to McGill this entire winter."

"If I know that old bastard, he probably knew we failed the very minute we did. And if he doesn't know it already, he's just going to have to wait until spring. Unless you go yourself."

"I did it once before, *mon ami*," Chubb answered jokingly. "I think you were with me." Neither of them smiled.

Several weeks later, Chubb brought up the matter again. "Do you know yet what you're going to tell McGill?" he asked after they'd finished their evening meal. Alexander rose from the table and walked slowly over to the room's one window. He stared through the panes, frosted heavily by the cold. Then he turned and stood with his back to the falling snow. He didn't answer. Almost imperceptibly he shook his head no.

By then Lea had become a complete stranger to him. Speech, touch, even a look cost them more pain than any pleasure they might share. When he walked into a room, she walked out or away. If she came upon him by chance, she'd turn and walk the other way. At night she'd wait until he'd fallen asleep before crawling into bed and she'd leave it before he'd awaken.

Alexander said nothing to her. He never questioned her actions or expectations. Nor did he ever ask why she stayed with him at all. He assumed that his failure as a pathfinder accounted for her strange behavior. He'd brought ignominy to her and death to her people. To her, the tragic expedition had proved the stigma attached to her. The pale Lea was cursed by the gods and nothing he could say would convince her otherwise.

Occasionally Alexander caught Lea whispering to Tatanee. The moment she saw him approach, she would lower her head and dash off. Her continual evasions didn't mystify him. They tired him. He longed for her to leave, but couldn't bring himself to send her away, especially during the winter. That would disgrace her among her own people. It would also be unforgivable of him.

Lea, however, fooled him once again. The morning after a particularly heavy snowfall, Alexander awoke to discover that the fire was out and that stores were missing from the main house larder. He didn't have to be told that she'd left. He responded without surprise when Chubb brought the news that one of the Indians had seen Tatanee and Lea creep off at dawn. They'd built a makeshift sled, filled it with necessary supplies and dragged it along the shores of the Athabasca River.

"You're better off, *mon ami*," commented Chubb. "She was a crazy half-breed."

"I'm not convinced," Alexander answered slowly, "that shě'll stay away. Are you?"

"I hadn't thought of that. But one thing I know for sure: we'll miss Tatanee."

Chapter 17

That spring seemed warmer than any he remembered in Montreal. No matter how much he dreaded his return to this center of the New World, the city still excited him. Old-timers, greenhorns, Indians, trappers in their furs and respectable, well-dressed citizens crowded the walkways. Carriages banged into one another. Storefronts were being erected as fast as trees were coming down. There were new streets.

Alexander tried to get caught up in the excitement, but his melancholy continually oppressed him. He would have to face that old ram McGill. He would have to admit his monumental blunder. He had bungled a brilliant opportunity and he tried to believe in a second chance. As he turned with Chubb down St. Paul's he happily would have spurred his horse and headed back to Lake Athabasca at the slightest excuse.

He felt only emptier because of Juliette. He hardly could claim her with his failure. He wondered if by some trick of fate he would glimpse her riding in her fancy carriage. At the same time he yearned for such a chance encounter, he shuddered to think how he possibly could confess to her the miscalculations that had denied him all success. He'd found the backing he'd vowed to her father he would find. He'd found the faith and money of McGill. He'd found the remote outpost and a team to accompany him on his trek. He'd even found an ocean, but it was the wrong blasted one. Circumstances and his own ambition had played a grim joke on him. The Denteres had the laugh on him, especially if Marcel had managed to discover the passageway to the great Northwest.

The futility of his venture plagued him as much as Juliette's long silence hurt him. Louisa had reached Chubb and Juliette could have reached him with a message. His hurt yielded to a righteous anger. Juliette, like all the Denteres, had betrayed him.

"Mon ami," Chubb interrupted his friend's anguishing thoughts, "I cannot help but ask this. Will you see Mademoiselle Dentere this trip?"

"Absolutely not," growled Alexander, surprising Chubb with so angry a response. "Why should I see her? Has she tried to be in touch with me? Has she made inquiries of Louisa that you haven't told me about?"

"Mon ami, be reasonable. In two years I got one note, one little note from my Louisa, and that was all."

"Ah, Chubb, she's wealthy, extraordinarily wealthy, and wealthy people can do whatever they wish whenever they wish."

Again Alexander's vehemence startled Chubb. "You will forget her, then? Poof, out like a candle in the night?" Chubb tried to restore his friend's equanimity.

"Yes, Chubb. Out like a candle in the night," Alexander snarled still more angrily.

"We shall see, *mon ami*, we shall see."

Ignoring his loyal partner's remark, Alexander spurred

his horse and sped through the busy streets to Chubb's small house. Chubb followed without haste and arrived home almost a half-hour after his unsettled friend. Chubb soon forgot Alexander's strange resolve about Juliette as he and his Louisa hugged, squeezed, kissed and danced around the small rooms of their house.

Alexander slipped upstairs and left the two of them to their joyful reunion. Before he fell into a long, sound sleep, he wondered first what Juliette was doing at that very moment and then if Marcel had found the secret waterway through the mountains.

For the next several days, Alexander prowled the city. He wandered through every avenue, investigated every new building and he followed every carriage that might be hers, his beloved Juliette's. It never was. His long excursions through the city brought him not one glimpse of her, though he thought he saw her everywhere.

One evening he returned to Chubb's house with an assortment of pots and pans that he'd bought from a peddler as a gift for Louisa.

"Some gifts," sniffed Louisa. "You give women perfume, diamonds, music! Not pots and pans! Where's your sense of romance, Alexander? Where's your soft touch?"

As the three of them settled down to supper, Chubb remarked casually, "I have news for you that I found out today."

"That there's work for two old map makers?" Alexander snickered.

"They were good, those maps. Nobody wanted to see them, that's all." Chubb smiled, then added, "No, it's not news of maps, but of Marcel."

"Ah." Alexander tried desperately to seem nonchalant. "What big news did you hear?"

"That he had no better luck than we did, *mon ami*. No better luck than we."

"You mean . . ." Alexander made a squawking sound as he drew an imaginary cut across his throat with his knife.

"Nothing so bad," said Chubb, "but Reynard broke both his legs in a fall, I'm told."

"That man," commented Alexander, "has a lot of trouble with his lower extremities."

Both Chubb and Alexander burst into uncontrollable laughter that released months of tension, frustration and pent-up anger. Louisa looked at them questioningly, but they were laughing so hard that it took them almost an hour to recount the unfortunate tale of Reynard's brush with the very indignant Indian girl.

Wine continued what their laughter started. They drank away their worries and disappointments and sorrows. They drank all night and when finally they slept, they slept soundly.

They awoke with parched throats and aching heads. They both felt as if they'd been used to sweep the streets of Montreal. Still, they were happier men. Chubb decided to spend the day in bed, although his fragile constitution allowed him little other choice.

Alexander dragged himself out into the air and rode through the streets of Montreal. For reasons he himself didn't quite understand, he rode to the outskirts of the city and on to the Dentere mansion. He reined his horse and for a long while sat behind a giant chestnut tree. His anger with Juliette had also passed. He wanted now to see her, just to see her, but his hopes went unfulfilled. Not even a servant entered or left the house while he waited. When he left, he had resolved another dilemma too. He was ready now to face McGill.

*   *   *

"Where do you *think* you'd find Coombs?" Jonesy smirked at Alexander. "Setting over the accounts or the crapper as he always is."

"You've gotten a bit cheeky since the last time I saw you, Jonesy. Had an inheritance?"

"I've had the offer of a new job, I have. Next month's my last in this hellhole."

"Hellhole, is it?" Coombs called out as he entered the office and Jones rushed back to his desk. "Wait till you get a taste of MacReedy's counter on a Saturday, then you'll see what's a hellhole." To Alexander he said, "He's going to be a merchant, fancy that. Our Jonesy's going to become a retailing giant." Coombs laughed so hard his vest unbuttoned. Then fixing his eye on Alexander, he warned, "I hope you and your partner there have found employment. McGill is all for giving you a bill for wrecking his outpost."

"What are you talking about, Coombs?" asked Alexander.

"Let him tell you himself, but the outpost ain't the same according to some trappers recently come back from your neck of the woods."

"When can we see McGill?"

Coombs looked at him with a steady eye. "I'll make arrangements as soon as I can. Oh, how I wish I could be a fly on the wall during this one." Again Coombs cackled.

Two days later, with less than an hour's notice, McGill summoned Alexander to his office. Alexander had barely shut the door when McGill launched into him. "You're back here? Why are you back? Who told you to come back? I didn't. I knew you'd be impatient. Didn't I warn you against it? Everyone from your town is impatient. I know. I had an uncle there. Who's tending the fort? Our fort. Who?''

"The post is in good hands," Alexander answered with civility. He didn't want to offend his short, bald benefactor whose words came quicker than ever. "You needn't worry."

"Needn't worry!" McGill mocked him. "Needn't worry, he tells me. Well, let me tell you, laddie, that without worry I wouldn't be here and you wouldn't be there. You'd be tending a flock of dirty sheep in Balmoral, that's what." Suddenly rising up out of his seat and leaning over his desk, McGill boomed, "Now, goddamnit, you tell me who sent for you?"

At first stunned into silence, Alexander then stammered, "I thought, I, ah, thought I owed you this much, to come here to tell you in person that my first expedition failed but—"

"You owed me this much? This much?" McGill's face turned red. "You goddamn French-loving, ass-kissing bastard! You owe me this much? You don't owe me this much, laddie. You owe me everything!" In two or three quick breaths McGill tried to swallow his rage. He unbuttoned his coat and and slowly paced around the room. "So, you couldn't wait out your time? You couldn't build a business for the company and then set off?"

"McGill, we had an agreement." Alexander's voice started to rise. He wanted to shout but he couldn't allow his frustrations or McGill's needling insinuations to foil him now. He needed the old devil's support. Without it he might as well apply for Jones' vacancy. "And . . ."

"And?" McGill waited. "Cat got your tongue, laddie?"

"My expedition was not a foolhardy one. I didn't act on the spur of the moment."

"I know all the details."

"What!" Alexander was surprised. McGill was toying with him. "How could you possibly know the details?"

"Canteen with salt water. Frostbitten trappers. Cabin halfway up the river," McGill began spouting off the facts. He continued with an exhaustive list of details that only four people in the whole world knew, or so Alexander had thought. "Don't look so puzzled, laddie. It's my job to know, to know everything that uses up what goes in here." McGill pointed to his trouser pocket.

Alexander squirmed in the gaze of McGill's keen, narrowed eyes. His hat already in his hand when he'd arrived, he now stood totally on the defensive. The wily old Scotsman held all the cards. "So, you've come to tell me that you're a failure," McGill continued. "Well, join the ranks of hundreds who have sat in the very seat you're in now and told me the exact same thing."

"In that case, Hudson's Bay, I understand, can sit here too."

"What do I care of Hudson's Bay or Marcel's cock-eyed plans. The Frenchy was gone three weeks and had to turn back. Some exploration. Three weeks!"

Alexander found the opening for his proposal that McGill give him a second chance. "But still he's going out again." It might be true, but it was also a wild guess.

"So who cares. It's his Papa's money, not mine. And if you think you'll be buying more canteens full of salt water on my money, you can think again, laddie."

Alexander's stomach knotted and his throat went taut. McGill had already decided. There would be no second chance. His hopes were dwindling, but he wouldn't accept defeat, not yet. He took another wild guess. "But what did Marcel find on his trip? Dust and broken bones." He spoke steadily, confidently, and the detail about Reynard's accident gave his supposition its needed authenticity.

"The word is, laddie, that that doe-headed buffoon needs only one more thrust at the mountains and they're in. Hudson's Bay is in and over, sweetheart. And what of Northwest? We're left holding a canteen filled with salt water," scoffed McGill.

Alexander's stomach sank, but still he pressed on. "I found the wrong shore, yes. I admit it and I'm not promising the next foray will take me across. But by God, I am close, closer to it than I am to you right now. And how you can buy that hogwash about Marcel making it in one more thrust is beyond me. Three weeks! He was only out three weeks."

McGill scowled. "Is that all you have to say?"

"It's I who am supposed to be the impatient one, McGill. Hear what I have to say and then do with me as you please." McGill's scowl faded into a look of supreme boredom and Alexander improvised without caution. "The ocean's barren, McGill, but the land is not. The land is brimming with beaver and fox and marten. Everywhere, furs more abundant than any trapper, or you, could ever dream."

"Is that why your Indian wench ran off, do you think? To trap?"

McGill's knowledge of Lea surprised Alexander, but the older man's awakening interest emboldened him. "I'm sure of it," lied Alexander. "They took every trap I had for trade."

McGill stood up and patted his head. He was

interested all right. "Why didn't you tell me this earlier? Why now?"

"I told you I owed you something, and this is it. You didn't give me a chance earlier."

"I can see why you wouldn't trust the courier with this kind of information."

"Of course," Alexander replied with more ease than he'd had all day.

"But you should have come bursting in here with news like this, not crawling with your tail between your legs, you—"

"Good saints alive, man!" Alexander interrupted the vociferous McGill. "I've been here all morning and all I've heard about is your money and my failure. Well, there's more than failure here." Alexander held up one of his journals. "Here's a report that will tell you everything and you can decide if it's worth that money in your pocket or not."

"I have another question, Mackenzie, but it's to me I have to put it. Why wasn't I told about this bounty? Why wasn't I informed of these riches?"

"Did anyone tell you we found a Hudson's Bay surveying marker?"

"Certainly. You did, in a letter. Nothing unusual about that."

Alexander had forgotten the message he'd sent by courier from Fort Chipewyan, but he didn't stop to compliment the old man's memory. "Well, you're always telling me to put two and two together, so I'll tell you the answer to your question."

McGill seemed lost in thought. "What is it?" he asked absently.

"Somebody wants to be rich. Somebody you know wants to be rich all by himself."

"You go back," McGill leapt to the bait and Alexander's spirits soared. "Instantly! And by instantly I mean tomorrow. I don't need time to read your books. There's chicanery afoot, treachery and chicanery. Someone is cheating me and I want you to stop it. You will stop it. You make certain all the trappers up there are working for Northwest, and if they're not, blow them sky-high. You understand. I'll have no one, not Astor, not Lisa, not Hudson's Bay trapping these fields. Do it and . . ." Surprisingly, his voice trailed off.

Alexander's heart was pounding. He was getting his second chance. Marcel still had competition. "And?" he asked.

"And we'll make a decision as to funding your second expedition."

He had won. "When will that be?"

"When you're ready, whenever you're ready to move. But this time, Mackenzie, this time be sure. Be so damn sure or you'll not be seeing the inside of offices again. Not ever again, unless you come to point the way to the West." Then he started yelling, "But there is no expedition, no trail blazing, until the Northwest Territory is free from poachers. You must do that first. That's our bargain. Run them out. Shoot 'em if you have to. But rid me of the filthy thieves!"

He was silent then and Alexander assumed the conference was over. Excited, he almost forgot to take back his journals from McGill's desk. At the door he turned and asked, "McGill, don't you think it would be wise if you told me who these people are that have been giving you information? The poachers. Wouldn't that make my life easier?"

McGill was wearily rubbing his bald head. He

looked up, confused. "Sources? What in hell are you babbling about?"

"Your sources of information, the—"

"Tell you my sources? My sources! You must be daft, laddie. Everyone!"

He stretched out on the tiny frame bed in his upstairs room. He, Chubb and Louisa had celebrated his triumph with good food, toasts, jokes and more toasts. Alexander chuckled and congratulated himself. He'd outfoxed a fox, the fox of all foxes. With McGill's backing he'd be able to mount another expedition and with luck he'd beat Marcel across the mountains.

He'd lied, but Alexander figured he'd find the passageway through the mountains long before McGill discovered that the lands weren't as lush with fur as he'd made them out to be. Besides, the waterway to the West would be worth ten times more than the richest fur fields anywhere. On a trade like that, McGill couldn't lose.

Marcel's second attempt to cross the mountains disturbed Alexander more. He must have found something promising, or else, son or no son of a director, he'd not be going out again. No doubt, Marcel also knew that Alexander was still his major competitor, that despite his failure McGill had given him a second chance. Such news provided the grist for the gossip mill at the Beaver Club.

Alexander tried not to think of Juliette, but the thought of leaving Montreal without even seeing her tormented him. His longing for her worried his sleep and her image invaded his dreams. All the joy of his celebration, of the good wine and warm friends, failed to rouse him.

Bleary-eyed, but clear-headed enough to discuss the trip back to Lake Athabasca with Chubb, Alexander sat down at the breakfast table.

"I gave him my word, Chubb, that we would leave right away. With everyone watching us like he said, he'll know if we don't. What do you think?"

"It's incredible, *mon ami*, that everyone is watching us. What for?"

"It only means that McGill gets all kinds of information from all kinds of sources and that if we try to put one over on him, believe me, he'll know."

"I think he mostly guesses," said Louisa as she ladled out hot milk for their tea.

"He knew too much just to be guessing, Louisa."

"Does it make a difference? Have we been trying to steal from him, to take his money and run?" asked Chubb, offended by the wily McGill. "I think these are a rich man's tricks."

"The only thing I'm worried about is that he'll discover beavers aren't swimming in every wave of every river in the territory he controls. If he does," Alexander chuckled nervously, "watch out, Alexander and Chubb."

"We'll be on our way to the ocean long before that, *mon ami*."

"It'll be next year for sure. But the more time we delay, the more time we allow him to find out I lied."

"Don't worry, my friend, don't worry. This's the least of our troubles," Chubb assured him.

"Nothing's going to go wrong this time. I'm not leaving anything to chance, you'll see. I don't want someone poking around our business and running back to McGill with reports contrary to what he expects." Alexander drummed his fingers on the table.

"We'll be swimming in California long before anyone reaches Montreal with news." Again Chubb tried to allay his friend's worries, but he knew that the real cause for Alexander's jitters wasn't his lie to McGill. It was Juliette.

"There are two things I must tell you." Chubb spoke reluctantly, as he didn't want to be the one to break the news. "We must tell you," he corrected himself.

"Yes, Chubb, what are they?"

"I'm going to take Louisa with us on this trip. With your approval, of course." Chubb and his wife smiled at each other.

"I want to see how ugly these Indian girls are for myself," said Louisa, and the three of them laughed.

"Of course, it's fine with me. But what of the house? Who will take care of it for you?"

"Louisa has an ugly cousin who's getting married and will live here with her new husband. We don't have many windows so it will be hard for him to see what he's caught." Louisa smacked Chubb playfully for his jest.

"And what is your other news?" asked Alexander.

"That Louisa will tell you. I must go fetch water for the sink."

As Chubb headed for the kitchen door, Louisa rested her hands on the table, then leaned forward and looked solemnly into Alexander's eyes. She spoke gently. "Alexander, we've found out that Juliette will be married soon."

Sure he hadn't heard her correctly, Alexander asked Louisa to repeat what she'd said. She did and he tried to digest the shocking news. His breath came quickly. His insides churned. He stared at Louisa, but he saw nothing. For a long moment he could say nothing. Then, his voice cracking with sorrow, he asked, "Who?"

"Monsieur Reynard."

"Reynard!" Alexander looked at her incredulously and began to laugh. You're joking, Louisa." Alexander was laughing alone. Louisa looked more grave than before. "It's a joke all right," Alexander grieved now, "a joke on her. My poor, poor darling Juliette. What are they doing to you?" He drummed the table with his fingers again. "You're certain of this, Louisa?"

"They've announced the banns at St. Paul's."

"Then it will be soon?"

"When they return from Marcel's expedition."

"You knew of this . . ."

"Last week," said Louisa, her eyes downcast.

"We didn't want to tell you before you met with McGill," added Chubb as he set the bucket of water down on the sink.

"You knew it all this time too, Chubb?"

"*Oui, mon ami,*" he admitted reluctantly.

Alexander stood up, pushed open the back door of the small kitchen and stepped out into the morning light. Fortune had robbed him of another hope.

Chapter 18

The trip back to Lake Athabasca took a mere forty-three days. It was August. The lakes were calm and blue. Bluffs rose dramatically against serene skies. Sunsets blazed. Hazardous cliffs, treacherous passes, the menace of snow and ice that had terrorized them for two and a half months when they'd first made the journey were now a memory. So were near starvation and frostbite and countless accidents.

This time McGill had provided them with wagons, wagons filled with a fund of goods to set up a proper trading post. Although Alexander immediately set to the task of reopening the post, of finding Indians eager to work and setting up stores, he couldn't drive Juliette from his mind. She haunted his every hour. Every day the pain, the loss and hurt grew worse.

Louisa's presence at the fort intensified Alexander's melancholy. It wasn't that she looked, sounded or acted like Juliette in any way. Nor did he resent Chubb's enjoyment of the companionship of his wife. But he did envy them as he watched them walking by the lake front at sundown after a quiet dinner or listening to Chubb telling Louisa how the Indians fished and cooked and made canoes. Chubb and Louisa were daily living out the dream that he'd so long dreamt for himself and Juliette, a dream that now had become an impossibility.

Although Louisa instinctively wanted to mother and comfort Alexander, Chubb warned her that indulgence would only prolong the torment in Alexander's heart. He didn't repeat to Louisa Alexander's own sad comment on his life. "My nest is empty, Chubb. My dream of Juliette is gone and so has Lea who filled my needs. I have come back to nothing."

Alexander began walking great distances every day and at all times of day. Chubb thought it aimless wandering to get rid of the anguish inside him, to think it out and walk it off. Louisa, however, noted that Alexander strode with conviction, that he seemed to know exactly where he was going. She was closer to the truth, which they both discovered one day when they came upon Alexander sorting through a stack of yellowed leaves from old books and manuscripts.

"Are these part of your journal, *mon ami*?" inquired Chubb, for Alexander's journals had become a legend in the territory. Indians constantly came to camp to see the great white chief who marked all things down in a great leather book.

"No, Chubb, these have nothing to do with my journals." He beckoned him closer. "These are charts and maps of the stars, the planets and all the heavens."

Chubb looked at the artfully drawn maps, ornate and intricate in their design. "Not at all like our old maps, eh?" he chuckled. "Tell me, what is so important about the stars? Is that why you go out walking day after day? Except that I never see you looking up."

"No, I look down. Through this." Alexander held

up a strange brass instrument. "This is a sextant. You use it to sight stars, but you look down."

"But where did all this come from? Did you bring these charts and sextant with you from Montreal? I mean, why have you waited so long to tell—"

"I had a lot on my mind when we left. Now listen to what I have to tell you." Alexander told him how he'd never repeat the mistake that had led them to Disappointment River. Never again would he set out in one direction and end up in another. Astronomy and navigation would solve the problem. The stars would tell him exactly where they were and which way they had traveled at the end of each day. He'd been studying, practicing, learning the secrets of the sextant and navigators and stars.

"And I know something else we're going to do we didn't do last time," said Alexander as he started putting his books and instruments away.

"What is that, Alexander?" asked Chubb, still slightly amazed by the idea of the stars telling them where they were.

"We're going to ask Indians to help us, Indians who have traveled and know the land. We didn't do that last time. Another mistake I made."

"We made," Chubb corrected him.

"Thank you, Chubb, but it was my pride that kept me from asking. I'm certain Tatanee or one of that bunch who walked out on us knew paths we missed."

"They killed themselves, those people, no? Isn't that the way they do it? They keep on walking or something like that?"

"Maybe. But maybe too they knew a river right over the rocks that brought them back here in two days. We didn't ask. They didn't tell. This time, though, we're going to go looking for villages and tribes, looking for them and asking directions.''

"Fine by me, *mon ami*. And when is all this going to happen?'' Fired as always by Alexander's enthusiasm, Chubb would have left that very minute.

"Not until I figure out what I'm doing with this sextant, these charts and maps.''

Alexander and Chubb also figured out a scheme by which they could continue to delude McGill into thinking the outpost sat in the center of the lushest fur fields on the continent. Not only had they collected a gigantic supply of furs from Fort Fork after One Eye Ralston and his two henchmen had killed each other, but also they had on hand a whole cabin full of skins unaccounted for and left over from last year. They would simply load them in the wagon and send them back to Montreal, letting McGill think they'd collected them in the past three months. The ruse would buy them a full year's time, almost two counting the time it would take the wagons to return to the post. It also made obvious just how valuable a passage to the western ocean would be.

Snow was in the air when the loaded wagons headed south for Montreal. The winter provided Alexander time for learning, solitude and introspection. It passed quickly and the brief spring evaporated into summer.

By then Alexander had become more adept at navigation. He'd grasped the significance of the moons of Jupiter and the importance of calculating Greenwich time. That July a young apprentice named McDonald visited the post. A trained astronomer, he taught Alexander in great detail some of the finer points of calculation. McDonald's instruction shook Alexander's confidence. Overwhelmed by the young man's knowledge, he offered him large sums of money to stay and lead him westward. McDonald, however, refused and returned to his home in Ottawa. With more fervor than ever Alexander applied himself to his studies in order to regain the self-assurance he'd lost.

Daily, too, he checked on the progress of the band of Indians he'd hired less to attend the chores of the outpost than to build canoes. Rather than covering its skeleton with a single sheet of bark as Tatanee had done, these Indians, Alexander discovered, were using smaller pieces of bark that were sewn together and then sealed with fir or spruce gum chewed to malleability by the women.

Alexander asked every Indian who came to Fort Chipewyan if he knew the route to the great river. Every Indian did. But when he questioned each of them further, he received none of the answers he desired. He heard only the old tribal legends of born storytellers. Indeed, most of them didn't know one landmark five miles past the lake or even the terrain on the other side of the river.

His eager questions and untiring interest, which the Indians translated as flattery, encouraged the tribesmen. Young braves led old men barely able to walk to the great white chief so that they could tell him what they had heard of the big river that ran to the salty waters. Although their information was generally less accurate than Alexander's own, it always disturbed him when one of them said gravely that no river would take him to the salt water. One such old man, however, provided an additional bit of information all the others had chosen to ignore. The great river, he said, did not itself empty into the sea but it led to a river that did. With a piece of charcoal he sketched out a map on a page ripped from one of Alexander's journals. His hopes bolstered, Alexander's heart leapt. No one else corroborated the old map maker's story. Everyone warned Alexander to carry a plentiful supply of food because his route would take him to a world of barren rock where no plants grew and no game lived. One Cree taught him about pemmican, a concentrated food that would last as long as twenty summers if prepared properly. The lean meat of bison or caribou first had to be sliced thin and then dried in the warm sun. Once dried, the slices were pounded with rocks into shreds and mixed with melted fat. The shreds, each one of them filmed with fat, were then stored in rawhide bags that were carefully sewn and sealed with tallow. Pemmican, the old Cree told him, had saved many a man in a cold, barren winter.

Louisa supervised the making of enough pemmican to feed eight people for three months, although she had no idea how much that was. The Indians worked on the canoes, which were, as their white chief ordered, twice as long and twice as wide as normal. Alexander and Chubb labored around the clock to keep the trading post in running order and to prepare for the trip. Another winter passed.

As soon as the river began to thaw, they tested the new canoes. They were all dismal failures. They leaked and were much too heavy for tricky maneuvers. The crews became easily discouraged and lacked the enthusiasm of the Kutenai under the leadership of Tatanee. Alexander chastised, threatened and cajoled the crews into obedience and the builders into diligence.

Their first trip had followed but one river, the Disappointment River. This second expedition, as Alexander planned it, would take them upstream on the Peace River. When they had traveled as far west on the Peace as they could, they would look for the big river the Indians talked about. Alexander carefully guarded the charcoal map the old Cree chief had drawn for him, the map that located the tributary off the big river and into the sea of salt. He spent hours discussing his plan with Chubb. Then they settled on their crew, all men and all strong rowers. Among them were skilled hunters and two who spoke English as well as all the Athabascan tongues. This time Alexander would not ignore the Indians along the trail. He would learn from them.

"It's very different this time, *mon ami*," Chubb remarked, though he had been wanting to tell Alexander this for a long time.

"This time we'll succeed, Chubb. This time we'll get to the Pacific."

"I know it. In my heart I know we will, but I mean you, you and me. It all seems so different." Flustered, Chubb could only hint at what he wanted to say, that his friend seemed to have grown distant, more aloof to him as well as the crew, and had seemed to have lost his fire and enthusiasm.

"Of course it's different, Chubb. You have Louisa with you. Don't you think that makes a difference?" Alexander sounded jealous and petulant. He was neither, but he wouldn't show Chubb or anyone else the fire, the ambition that burned inside him so constantly. Nor would he show his constant fear that fortune would snuff out his final hope.

Chapter 19

On a frosty October morning, the expeditionary party headed westward in two canoes on the wide Peace River. They planned to travel as far upstream as possible before the cold weather set in. They would winter on the shores of the Peace and then continue west with the thaw. Thus they would have the entire summer to retreat should Alexander's strategy prove faulty. Chubb had been right when he'd said this trip was different. It was carefully planned.

Every morning Alexander checked their position with the sextant and every night he entered their location in his journals. Unimpeded by rocks and rapids, they progressed quickly upriver along the Peace. The canoes, rebuilt according to Alexander's specifications after their test and failure, were watertight and easily maneuverable.

The weather, however, turned colder much sooner than Alexander had anticipated. By the end of the month, they were looking for a suitable campsite to wait out an early winter. They found one in the middle of a magnificent birch forest. Within weeks Alexander, Chubb and the party of Indians had built cabins in the great clearing. So pleased was he that Alexander rewarded the Indian crew with gifts of rum and tobacco.

"What do you think, Chubb?" asked Alexander as they drank brandy in front of their fire one night after a dinner of venison, smoked trout and parsnips.

"It's a lot better than I would have imagined, *mon ami*."

"It's well planned. This trip will be all that the other was not. It's ridiculous to think you have to suffer in order to discover. There's only one thing that disturbs me."

"What's that? That we're going the wrong way perhaps?" Chubb joked, then parodied a message to Montreal. "Monsieur McGill, we are making wonderful progress, but unfortunately we are traveling in the wrong direction."

Alexander joined Chubb in his laughter before answering him. "I had hoped to see the local Indians, to talk to them, their hunters especially, to find out from them what lies ahead."

"But you did that, no? You got nowhere, except with one old man."

"And we learned about pemmican." Alexander paused to rephrase his statement. He felt good talking with his old friend again. He'd missed him. "Only those weren't Indians from here. They lived hundreds of miles behind us and we've not seen one new tribe on the Peace. I think that's strange."

"Maybe they're afraid of white men and have been hiding from us."

Alexander didn't believe that the case, but said, "Could be. That could be."

Alexander took advantage of the immobility the winter had forced on them by entering long and detailed accounts of their progress thus far into his journals. He also continued his study of navigation and one day found what he considered certain proof that he would indeed discover the passageway to the West. He noted several times during the snowbound months that a warm wind blew in from the direction of the Pacific and melted not only snow but also ice. From that observation he concluded that the distance between the river and the sea was so short that even though the wind passed over ice and snow in the mountains, it had no time to cool down. The warm air of the Pacific was nearer as the crow flies than he'd suspected or dreamed. Alexander was winning at last and he wasn't afraid to show his excitement to anyone.

They broke camp at the first sure signs of spring, which came none too soon for an increasingly impatient Alexander. They covered great distances each day on the strong, but readily navigable Peace River. Chubb surmised it had received its name not as a result of some Indian war, but because it was so peaceful a waterway.

As they pushed upriver they saw elk, foxes and caribou. They passed through great canyons that narrowed and deepened the river. Sheer cliffs of blue and yellow clay shot up toward the sky on both sides of the river. Beyond them the river again widened and great forests of birch, spruce and the largest poplar trees imaginable spread from its banks as far as the eye could see. Then, one night as the sky darkened, they spotted the summits of the Big Mountains on the horizon. After they had set up camp, Alexander and Chubb toasted the vista they'd sought so long and found sooner than they'd expected. Through those mountains lay their passageway.

About noon the next day they saw their first band

of Indians on a bank not a mile upriver. The Indians watched the canoes approach, but when Alexander and Chubb began waving to them, they didn't respond. Alexander asked the crew to yell to them in Athabascan languages, to tell them that his party came in friendship. The braves apparently didn't understand. Pulling arrows from their sheaths, they loaded their bows and sent a volley of arrows whizzing past the two canoes.

Both crews began rowing with all their power out of the range of the unexpected attack. Another shower of arrows streaked by them with deadly aim. Every muscle straining, the crews pulled themselves to safety as the Indians ran after them along the shore. They were preparing for a third strike when the canoes passed by banks of huge boulders that halted the Indians' pursuit and prevented their attack.

Once Alexander caught his breath, he hollered out, "Does anyone know who those braves were or why they attacked?" He hadn't expected to find hostile Indians so far north. The crews generally agreed that the Indians were Beaver, but no one could account for the attack.

They paddled on with the Beaver braves very much on their minds. When they reached a portage point, a series of turbulent rapids, the crews were reluctant to go ashore. Trees and thick underbrush lined the banks and Alexander's men justifiably feared a sneak attack. Still, they had no choice. Warily, they waded ashore, while Alexander, Chubb and two of the hunters stood guard with their rifles loaded and primed.

The portage took nearly an hour, but they encountered no difficulty and no Beaver. With relief they regrouped on the shore beyond the rapids. Then suddenly a loud whoop shattered their ears. Everyone ducked for cover. When Chubb tried to pull off a shot, his muzzle burst and the rifle flew from his hands.

No one moved. Silent, they waited. They all strained to hear a footstep, a whisper, any sound. None came. They waited longer. The forest was quiet. The river rushed on. Eventually they relaxed.

They were reloading the canoes when directly ahead of them they saw a party of six Indians appear from the woods. Certain they'd be tortured or killed, Alexander's crewmen started to wail and moan as the Indians began walking toward them.

Positive the Indians were equally afraid of them, Alexander decided on a bold move. With Chubb shadowing him in the woods and covering him with a ready rifle, Alexander walked out to meet the band of Indians. He held his arms outstretched to show that he carried no weapon while the crew shouted out words of peace to them.

The plan worked. Within ten feet of Alexander, the six Indians halted. They eyed him suspiciously as he pulled trinkets from his pockets. He offered them his gifts. Slowly and fearfully the Indians inched their way toward him. They sat down together in peace and Chubb came out of the woods to join them.

The Indians told Alexander that the river traveled a great distance. Sometimes falls and rapids, they said, made the river impassable, and because the shoreline disappeared into towering, almost perpendicular cliffs, portaging became impossible. They also told him that white men had built many houses at the mouth of the great river and that Indians with wings lived in tribes atop the cliffs. These Indians, they warned, would kill anyone who entered their sacred waters.

Alexander listened keenly to the Indians' tales,

their half-truths mixed with legend. What disturbed him were the facts, the real hazards, that had produced stories like these. What upset Chubb was their description of white men's houses at the mouth of the river, for he recalled Alexander's private fear that they would discover large cities when they passed through the Big Mountains.

The river did become unpassable. Waterfalls continually blocked their course and portage became increasingly more difficult. The banks were steep and rocky and beyond them were thick brier patches strewn with the upheaved roots of huge, fallen trees. When the lead crewman slipped and crashed through a small crevice he pulled the bow of the canoe down with him. The crewman escaped unharmed, but the canoe was badly battered. At that point, though, any canoe was of little use. The river was unnavigable and so they continued to carry the canoes laboriously, and groaning.

To lighten the portage they decided to bury some of the pemmican at an accessible spot in case they should need it on their return. They dug a deep hole for two of the ninety-pound bales and then refilled it. With brush and branches the Indians built a fire to hide all traces of their burial site. Their load somewhat lighter, but their spirits no less heavy, they plodded on four days more. The river continued to forbid them passage.

On the fifth day, shortly after spotting some unsprung traps, they heard the sound of voices not far away. They soon surprised a large band of Indians about to have a meal. When the Indians spotted Chubb and Alexander they treated them as honored guests. These Sekani Indians had heard of white men but had never seen any. They not only shared their food and offered them women, but also and most importantly aided them in their portage to the next navigable part of the river.

When the Sekani saw the condition of the battered canoe they waited on the riverbank to be sure that it would float. No sooner was it launched than it sank and the Sekani provided Alexander with a canoe of their own. It was neither as light nor as long as the canoe they'd lost. Also it leaked terribly and that flaw set off a round of new complaints from the already disgruntled crew.

Six days later the river again became impassable. Just before nightfall, Alexander asked Chubb and one of the hunters to scout the land. He, meanwhile, tried to determine their exact location with his maps and sextant. He slept uneasily for Chubb and the Indian brave hadn't returned.

They didn't return until late the next day. Though hungry and exhausted, their clothes in shreds and their skin slashed and cut, they came back excited, eager to tell their news. They were sure they had found the great river. It couldn't be reached by the waterway they were traveling, however. Its current was too treacherous. Often waterfalls and rapids obstructed passage and at some points the wild river dwindled into a mere creek. They would have to walk. Indeed, they would have to cut a path through the rough underbrush in order to walk, and they would have to carry everything, including the canoes, on their backs. But Chubb was sure that it could be done and Alexander knew that it would be done.

They began the next day. They divided the labor and worked in shifts in order to save time and backs. While some of the crew cleared a narrow path, others carried the cargo. The Sekani's heavy canoe required three rather than the customary two men to carry it and they had to be relieved every four hundred yards.

For six days they worked their way through a wilderness of briers, brush, tangled roots and mud. Then it started to rain. It was pointless to stop. They slept under improvised tents of blankets and bark. They sank thigh-deep in the mud. Drenched to the skin, scored by thorns, weary, hungry and bedraggled, the crew threatened to turn back and leave the palefaces to their own devices.

On the morning of the eighth day, the sun broke out. It did not cheer the recalcitrant crew as they trod on through the endless brush. Then the sound of rushing water reached their ears, faintly at first, but nonetheless distinct. Chubb and the hunter were right. Alexander flung his cargo to the ground. Mindless of briers, nettles and thorns, he leapt through the underbrush. His heart pounding he surveyed it, there, in front of him— the big river to the West.

What Alexander gazed at in amazement soon dawned on Chubb. Both of them overwhelmed, together they tried to explain it to the crew. The river was running in a direction opposite the Peace. It was flowing east to west rather than west to east. They had crossed a watershed. They had crossed the Continental Divide. They were on the other side of the Big Mountains. They were in the West!

Alexander and Chubb wrapped themselves in each other's arms, clinging to each other. It was a moment more glorious than any dream. They had conquered the Great Divide. Such glory is speechless, and as often as Alexander tried to record it in his journal, he could not find the words to capture that moment that in his heart would never die.

*   *   *

They had traveled less than a day on the big river when they met an endless succession of waterfalls. Just as their canoes scraped the shore a small band of Indians appeared. Without speaking a word, the Indians helped Alexander's crew pull in the canoes and unload them. They were Carrier, they told him. They too were heading for the coast and invited Alexander's party to join them, although they were traveling slowly because of the women and children. All of them, Alexander noticed, were carrying huge parcels of furs, of beaver, otter, marten, lynx and even bear as well as dressed leather. The Carrier explained that they traded with the coast Indians, who, in turn, traded with white men who sailed big boats. When the Indians added that their journey would take all of three days, Alexander did more than accept their invitation. He rejoiced.

That night they feasted. The Carrier supplied salmon and roe while Alexander supplied the rum. Everyone celebrated good fortune.

Fortune, however, had betrayed Alexander and his crew. The next morning when he awoke, Alexander looked around the campsite in disbelief and astonishment. A fool's shock soon turned to anger and he shook Chubb out of his sleep. The Carrier had left. Without leaving so much as a hoofprint in the clay, they had left. And with them they had taken Alexander's canoes, his cargo and even the clothes his crew had hung out to dry.

They were walking again. The walking was bad and the crew was worse. The slightest noise startled Alexander's jumpy men. Fearful, they crept by every boulder and bush. At night they posted not one guard, but two, for they were positive that the Carrier would come back for what they'd left behind—their lives.

They'd been walking for days before they started their descent through a forest of tall pines, blue spruce and enormous hemlocks. When they reached the valley floor, they rested in a thick wood of cedars and birch. They recognized the trees, but they felt they had entered another land. A mild, almost balmy breeze rustled through the green leaves and the air smelled sweet.

Chubb did some scouting and raced back to the tired party of men with refreshing news, the kind of news he knew they needed to hear. He'd found a stream so clean and so clear that the shape and color of every pebble lying on its bed could be seen. With a cheer the men ran to it. Some dropped to their chests to drink its cool, fresh water. Others dove into it headfirst to enjoy the first bath they'd had in weeks.

Their exhilaration and laughter quickly dwindled into cold, silent fear, for suddenly, soundlessly, they were surrounded. A stranger breed of Indians than any of them had ever seen stood ready with sharp lances aimed at their throats. They had made a disastrous mistake. Trembling, the crewmen withdrew from the water.

Once Alexander's men had scrambled back onto the bank of the stream, the Indians dropped their lances. Smiling jovially out of broad, handsome faces, they patted the backs of the frightened men. The crew then led the Indians, whose garments were made of cedar bark and whose oiled hair had been dyed red, to their white leaders.

They were the Bella Coola Indians, a tribe that lived in a valley of the same name. Though it took a long time, they managed to explain to the white men that they'd become alarmed when they discovered strangers defiling their sacred salmon waters. Furthermore, had Alexander's men not left the waters, they would have been obliged to kill them, although they would have chased the salmon from the stream for many moons.

Now, however, they were friends, and the Bella Coola wanted to share their abundance with the white strangers.

The Bella Coola guided Alexander and his men through a dense woods. After an hour they reached a great house raised on posts, which they entered by climbing up steps cut into a broad tree trunk. The Indians then placed mats before their guests and served Alexander and Chubb a whole roasted salmon each while the crew members received a half apiece.

In the morning Alexander and Chubb were given a tour of the village. They were allowed, too, to examine the salmon traps the Bella Coola had laid in the river. The Bella Coola spoke of the salmon with religious awe and they trapped them, roasted them and ate them in a manner more ritualistic than methodical. They ate no meat. Indeed, they allowed no meat at all in the village, for if the fish smelled it, they wouldn't come. When Chubb knelt down to wash off his knife in the river, the Bella Coola pulled him to his feet with alarm because they believed the salmon could not bear the smell of iron and wouldn't come to their sacred stream again.

As they walked along the bank of the river, Alexander asked, "Chubb, do you know where the crew is?"

"I've been trying to find out for the last half hour, but all I get are smiles and nods."

Alexander smiled broadly. "Well then, smile yourself, old man. Smile and let them think we're just a couple of curiosity-seekers. And point, point and talk.''

Chubb smiled and asked, ''Do you think there's trouble? They seem to be too easygoing for trouble.''

Alexander pointed to some layers of logs and gravel that the Bella Coola used for trapping and smiling he answered, ''I think we'd better be prepared for trouble, because right now these Indians have very effectively separated us from all of our men. Be prepared. And where's your rifle?''

''Back at the house.''

Still smiling, Alexander said, ''Let's go get it, then, friend.''

The two men chuckled, but when they tried to turn back, their guides smiled and shook their heads and led them further onward. They stopped before a high totem pole. Pointing to the elaborate carvings of men and beasts which were red and black and smiling, Alexander muttered to Chubb, ''I don't know, laddie, but I think these men are less interested in our seeing the village than they are in keeping us prisoner.''

At noon, their guides escorted Alexander and Chubb to the second of two canoes. Accompanied by seven braves, they followed nine others in the first canoe. Upriver, over two hours away, they arrived at a village where they were given a tumultuous reception.

As the braves led them to a large, solidly built house, Chubb thought he spotted a familiar face. ''Did you see that brave?'' he whispered through a wide grin.

''The one who just ran across our path?'' asked Alexander. ''Is he one of our crew?''

''I'm not sure.'' Chubb strained to catch another look at the familiar Indian, but he'd disappeared. ''If it was one of ours, what in hell is he doing here welcoming us?''

When they stepped inside the house, their hosts again placed mats before them and served them salmon, roe mixed with herbs and fresh fruit and an unusual delicacy, the dried inner rind of hemlock sprinkled with sweet oil. Alexander, however, was quickly losing his appetite. "Have you thought, Chubb, that those people were cheering not because we were visiting, but because we've been captured?''

They sat alone in the great house. They could hear the crowd outside. They had tried several times to leave the spacious room, but each time smiling guards had stopped them at the door. Shaking their heads, then shrugging their shoulders, the Bella Coola braves had pointed Chubb and Alexander back into the house. The two old friends paced the floor.

More than a hundred feet long and about forty-five feet wide, the room had seven hearths, which told Alexander and Chubb that seven families shared this one dwelling. Cedar panels served as partitions. Each of them bore grotesque figures, half-human and half-animal, elaborately painted, like the giant totem poles in red and black. Like the partitions, the outside walls were built of cedar planks.

At sundown they heard the sound of many voices and of people milling about. Although they couldn't understand one word that was spoken, they assumed the Bella Coola were gathering for a tribal meeting, a meeting perhaps to determine the fate of the two white chiefs. They could smell the acrid smoke of tobacco and then the Indian voices fell silent. In edgy uncertainty, Alexander and Chubb waited. They listened.

They thought they recognized the voice but couldn't

place it, when one of the Indians began a long harangue. Continually interrupted by shouts and applause, the speaker became increasingly more dramatic and intense. This speech sounded like a plea, but Alexander and Chubb could only guess for what.

After a long silence another voice, this one unfamiliar, intoned a brief pronouncement. He received no cheering or applause. "Shaman," guessed Alexander, "invoking some god."

A third voice, milder, more conciliatory than the first, entered a plea. Obviously the crowd didn't like his words, as it responded with angry sounds of dissent. Again, silence fell.

Again, Alexander and Chubb waited. With their ears pressed to the cedar wall, they sat on the floor of the long house. They heard nothing more, only smelled the pungent odors of tobacco, incense and weeds. Just at dawn, three Bella Coola chieftains shoved open the door to the long house and entered. Their clothes were simple, their hair more violently red than usual and gleaming with oil, they lined up before the two white men. Astounded, Alexander and Chubb stared at the chieftain in the middle. The familiar face they'd thought they'd spotted in the village crowd and the voice they'd thought they'd recognized the night before belonged to Tatanee.

"We thought you were of the Kutenai, Tatanee," said Alexander wasting no civility.

"There are many things you *thought*, my lord, sir, Alexander," replied Tatanee with all the sarcasm he could affect, and then charged rather than spoke to them. "You have defiled our sacred waters. Because of you the salmon will flee our rivers. For this you will die."

"Is that your decision, Tatanee?" asked Alexander, trying to think rapidly. "Because if it is, it's stupid."

The heaviest of the three chieftains addressed Tatanee, who answered him by saying, "You tell them. It's your duty." Tatanee flaunted his power and strength.

"The decision was not his alone," said the heavy chieftain at a slow, deliberate tempo. "It was the decision of the village."

"Then the village has made a stupid decision," retorted Alexander, happy that this chieftain too, spoke English.

"Why is that?" asked the chieftain.

"Because the salmon are controlled by the gods of white men, and at our bidding they will send all the salmon that swim all your rivers to the waters of eternity and you will be forever without fish. Everyone knows that." The chieftain's heavy face dropped and his dark, round eyes widened. Seeing the reaction, Alexander pressed on. "We will invoke our gods. As soon as our hearts stop beating, so will the salmon stop swimming. We can do that."

The thickset Indian was translating Alexander's words as quickly as he spoke them and the message spread from the Bella Coola gathered at the door through the entire village. Cries of alarm sounded through the cedar walls.

"It might work, *mon ami*," whispered Chubb.

"At least Tatanee will have a fight on his hands," Alexander muttered under his breath. "He's not going to win this one so easily."

Tatanee thrust out his arms to quiet the villagers. They obeyed with silence. Tatanee turned to the two white men. He paused dramatically, then spoke. "If the great white chiefs have such control over their gods, why then do they get lost? Why then can't they find the sea of salt that all red men know how to find?''

Tatanee's argument impressed the other chieftains and evoked an enthusiastic response from the crowd. Tatanee was not going to lose easily either.

"Our gods are testing us. Don't your gods do likewise? Or does Tatanee always have rain when he desires it and does the sun rise at his call? Our most powerful gods test us most powerfully. Now that we have found the sea on our own, they are most pleased and will do all our bidding. Such is the way of our gods. So be warned.'' On the last phrase Alexander thrust his finger at the face of Tatanee, a bold gesture which startled the crowd of onlookers more than the steely brave.

For a long while, no one spoke. Then the heavyset chieftain proposed that they let the village decide once and for all.

With a grand flourish the three chiefs pivoted and started to leave.

"Tatanee!'' Alexander called to him and the Indian turned to the white men with a look of utter disdain. "Do you hate us that much?''

Tatanee took two steps back into the long house and spat at both of the captives. "I despise you,'' he snarled, then left.

Alexander and Chubb listened as voices they couldn't understand debated over their fate. Tatanee spoke vehemently and often won applause, but the sides seemed to be equally drawn. The Bella Coola argued heatedly. Alexander's ploys had been good ones, but he feared that all he had won was time.

As the village meeting dragged on with long, incomprehensible harangues, Alexander started to wander through the long house. "Time," he said to Chubb, "is on our side. These oily, red-haired redskins haven't slept all night. Sooner or later they're bound to pass out and I think we should be ready with something, a plan."

"What plan, *mon ami*?"

"If I knew that, Chubb, if I knew that . . ." His voice trailed off as he began poking into containers, around the hearths, between partitions. He noticed that part of the floor in one room was badly aligned. "Come here, Chubb, let's see what we have."

Together they raised up the floorboards. To their disappointment they discovered a cache of iron and metal utensils. "This must be where they hide any iron that finds its way into the village so that it won't contaminate the river and scare away the fish."

"Too bad, *mon ami*, some gunpowder and rifles didn't find their way into town."

"Don't be too easily disheartened, my friend. Here, give me a hand with this." They lifted out a long, rusted iron bar that was a lot heavier than it looked.

"If you've set your mind to finding a rusty iron bar, *mon ami*, you've accomplished it. But what now, my quick-thinking friend?"

"I don't know, Chubb. I don't know." Alexander peered again into the cache and pulled out two arrowheads. "Let's see how we can use these."

With the arrowheads, which were not iron but copper, they began digging out peepholes in the wall, which proved to be as thin as the cedar partitions. They were soon able to see as well as hear. "*Mon Dieu*!" exclaimed Chubb as he looked out. "Half the

Indian world is out there. They mean business, *mon ami.*"

"Tatanee is getting back at us for something. He's asking the village for punishment that far exceeds the wrong we did."

"That was just the excuse he was looking for, no?"

"Exactly. Let's see what's on the other side of the house."

Again they dug out two peepholes, which allowed them to determine that the house sat on an embankment about thirty yards from the sacred river. They saw canoes, too, though certainly the Bella Coola didn't sail the sacred river. For a few seconds both their views were obstructed and they realized a guard was walking around the house.

Once they'd established the guard's routine, they returned to their first peepholes and watched as an elderly Bella Coola chief droned on. Occasionally fierce, younger chieftains tried to shout him down, but to no avail. Tatanee, after all, was asking them to take a serious and unusual measure. He was asking for the execution of the two great white chiefs.

Eventually the Bella Coola began to tire. Some slept as they sat while others sprawled out on the grass. It was the moment Alexander had been waiting for. "Before we try anything, Chubb, see if you can find any of our crew. I can't." Nor could Chubb. "They probably sent them away. It's us he wants, not our crew."

Alexander did have a plan, but they would have to time their strike exactly. Although the tribal council was drowsy, the guard was still circling the house. Once they'd gotten past the guard, their objective was to get a canoe in the river and they could only hope that no other guards were posted there.

They timed the guard's walk twice more. The third time he made his rounds, they were waiting at the door. Chubb flung it open. Startled, the guard was about to scream warning when Alexander belted him with the iron bar. Swiftly they dragged him inside and Chubb smeared some of the oil from the Bella Coola's hair on his own. Then taking the guard's lance, Chubb stole out of the house and headed toward the canoe.

The evening light was dim. Nevertheless, Chubb was certain that should he be spotted, his hasty attempt at disguise wouldn't fool a Bella Coola for more than a second. On the far side of the house he could hear the voices of the council. The braves and chieftains were beginning to rouse themselves from their brief sleep. Cautiously Chubb turned the corner of the house and silently he prayed that no guards stalked the grounds between the cedar walls and the canoes. The gods of the white men answered Chubb's prayers. Not daring even to sigh his relief, Chubb doubled back to the door to tell Alexander the good news.

Together they ran quickly for the riverbank and the canoes. They hit the soft turn and Chubb pulled a canoe into the sacred water. Alexander was holding the rusty iron bar close to his chest. A scream suddenly rent the air. The guard had come to, but it took some seconds for the drowsy Bella Coola to respond to his alarm. Confusion burst forth. By the time the first braves reached the riverbank, however, Chubb and Alexander were rowing with all their strength into the sacred salmon waters.

Soon, though, the entire Bella Coola village had raced to the banks of the sacred river. They held their lances and arrows ready to slaughter the great white chiefs who were defiling their stream, displeasing their gods and ruining their lives. But before one lance was hurled or a single arrow shot, Alexander held the long, rusty iron bar aloft. Had they made their escape minutes later, darkness would have hidden their most powerful weapon. The Indians froze as Alexander threatened to drop the bar into the waters where the salmon swam.

The canoe rode with the current and the two great white chiefs headed for home.

Chapter 20

The Beaver Club was practically deserted. Alexander took a table on the other side of the spacious dining room from two old trappers already in their cups. The waiters were using the morning lull in business to re-stock the bins behind the long, mahogany bar. Despite the hour, Alexander had expected more patrons and livelier trade. Perhaps the fashionable club had lost its reputation among the elite for barons of Montreal, but Alexander didn't much care. It was serving his purposes. He was using his new membership as a lure to hook Coombs into a private interview.

Although Coombs had been working for years for one of the most powerful companies in all of North America, he'd never set foot inside the exclusive Beaver Club. Because he hadn't spent any time in the wilds, he was ineligible for membership, and McGill, not out of thoughtlessness but sheer perversity, had not once invited him. Mackenzie's offer had been too tempting for Coombs to refuse, even with the risk of running into McGill. McGill had forbidden any employee at Northwest to talk with the Scots explorer or to admit him into the company offices. As it turned out though,

Coombs didn't have to worry about the old man's wrath. With no misgivings he mounted the steps of the Beaver Club. McGill wouldn't be there that day. Nor would anyone else, as a matter of fact.

Alexander waited impatiently for McGill's crotchety secretary. He'd been back in Montreal for three weeks. For three weeks he'd been trying to get past a stony, silent Coombs into the office of his erstwhile benefactor. Finally Coombs appeared at the door to the dining room. The waiters detained him with all kinds of questions. For a few minutes Alexander enjoyed watching the secretary's discomfort, then called out and waved at the waiter to allow Coombs to enter. He greeted Coombs cordially, but didn't stand to welcome him. With a flick of his hand toward a chair, Alexander invited him to sit.

"So this is what it's like, eh?" Coombs blew on his red, chapped hands and tried to catch his breath which he'd lost running up two flights of stairs. He craned and twisted his neck. His eyes darted eagerly over the room. "Not much," he commented. "Not much is all I can say."

"You have to see it with all the tables filled and the beautiful ladies running half naked between them in order to truly appreciate it." Alexander whetted Coombs' secret appetites.

"Well, that won't be today, will it?" rasped Coombs. Then in a mutter he added, "Damn pity."

"Not now, not at this hour, I don't think," laughed Alexander.

Coombs ordered black tea and brandy. After he'd downed each in a single gulp, he leaned back and asked, "Now, what do you think I can do for you?"

"First off, tell me straight out where I stand with McGill."

"Tell you where you stand, laddie?" Coombs scoffed. "In McGill's eyes, you're standing just left of and definitely lower than Satan himself."

"Are you telling me, Coombs, I'm finished?" Alexander asked.

"When the word first came you'd made the crossing, the whoops and hollering were so loud they were likely to wake the dead." Relaxed now, sure of himself and appreciative of his host, Coombs leaned back in his chair and rested his head above the wainscoting.

"Who told him? Who told McGill? Who brought the news?" asked Alexander, hungry for every detail.

"Who else? Trappers. He has them up and down every trickle of water in the territory and they're quick to tell him who spit where and how far. They'd gotten the news to the old bastard while you were still lollygagging in the warmth of the western ocean. Some of your crew came back with word too." Coombs spoke easily, without sarcasm or hidden motives. He liked this Scotsman who'd invited him to the Beaver Club. "You think a man could get a refill in such a fancy place like this?" Coombs tapped his empty glass and Alexander immediately signaled for a waiter.

"So, McGill was happy when he learned I crossed the mountains? And how about the town? How did Montreal take the news?"

"You really mean to ask me how the Frenchman what's-his-name and his family took it, don't you, son?" Coombs chuckled at his insight. "Like everyone else who had a set of ears and a pocket of money invested in fur. You were celebrated and toasted everywhere for one whole day. One whole day your fame lasted. But only one.''

''Then what happened?''

''They started bragging, your own local Indians did. They started giving out the details of that north-west passage you'd discovered. If they'd kept mum, you could've walked into any office in town and got paid a king's ransom for what you knew. But the cat was out and when old McGill found out the trials and troubles you had crossing, he felt he'd been played for a fool. He cursed you harder than he'd cheered you the day before, and if you'd walked in then, he would have strung you up by the lamp cord.''

''And that's exactly what I don't understand, Coombs. That's what I can't get through this thick Scots head of mine. I found a passage to the western ocean. It's there for all to use. How in all of heaven and hell did I fail McGill and the Northwest Company?'' Alexander was shouting across the table.

Coombs pressed himself back against the wall. ''Slow down, Mackenzie. Slow down and use that head. Pretend you're sitting here and McGill and his company is out there. How long is it going to take you to reach them?'' Coombs cleared a spot on the table to make room for his second tea and brandy. ''How long did it take you to make the crossing?''

''Seventy-three days.''

''Seventy-three days! And how many of those days did you travel on water? Just guess, you don't have to be exact.''

''I can be exact, Coombs. Thirty-two, precisely. Now what are you driving at, man?''

''The plain and simple fact that you couldn't very easily transport forty or fifty tons of fur pelts over that route to the western sea. Think about it. Could you have taken thirty tons of fur with you on that trip? The answer is obvious. It's no.''

Both men sat silent. Then, feeling compelled to speak, Coombs continued in a softer voice. ''Transportation is McGill's key interest. He wants to get furs out of the wilderness and into the city as quickly and cheaply as possible. A northwest passage is good only if it works to that advantage. Yours doesn't. Now do you understand?''

''Great God Jehovah and all the saints, Coombs! That's not what I went out there to do. Transportation be damned! Discovery was my interest. I wanted to find out if someone could cross the mountains to the West. Until now nobody knew that it could be done. Nobody knew—''

Coombs held up his hands. ''Now take it easy, Mackenzie. Don't be having conniption fits with me and remember all I know is what the old buzzard tells me. And all I know is that you were to find a waterway—a *waterway*—that was wide enough and deep enough to take goods and trappers to the western sea.''

''You should know too, Coombs, you take one step at a time on a venture like this. First you find out if the bloody sea exists. You find the damned passes next, and by and by you find the quicker, shorter ways. Remember that it took us just over a month to get back. One month! That's less than half the time it took for the trip out.''

''You needn't convince me, laddie,'' lied Coombs in an attempt to calm Alexander. ''I think you did marvelously, but the old man thinks the expedition a waste of money, a folly, and himself a fool for believing the biggest fool of all—you.''

"What did he expect me to do? Dig him a river while I was at it?"

"Don't be bitter, laddie. Don't go sour on the world. You had more opportunity than most." Coombs looked into his empty teacup, then prepared to leave. "I thank you for the invite, but now I got to get back to the books or the old man will have my skin."

"Hold on, Coombs, hold on. Have another round. I've got more to ask."

"There's nothing more to tell. I've told you all I know and that's the gospel truth. It's a closed case Mackenzie. The company is no longer interested in your services, I'm sorry to say. You'd best look elsewhere."

To gain a few minutes, Alexander reached out and held Coombs' frail, bony forearm. With his other hand he motioned to the waiter for another round of drinks. He felt devastated. The bitter taste of bile stung his throat. He couldn't understand how McGill could dismiss an achievement like that or how Coombs could sit there and tell him not to go sour on the world after the hardships he'd suffered to make a path. Somehow they failed to realize the significance of his discovery or refused to acknowledge it. They owed him at least some answers to the questions that had been tormenting him since his return to Montreal.

He ached to hear about Marcel, Papa Dentere and, most of all, about Juliette, Juliette lost to him and married to Marcel's odious partner, Reynard. Alexander's stomach soured, as did he, indeed, on the world.

The waiter served Coombs his third round of drinks. McGill's secretary sniffed at the brandy, sipped at the tea. He seemed to have lost his taste for drink as well as for conversation. Alexander would have to pry any further news or gossip out of him, would have to reveal the obsessions that plagued his soul to this stranger who sat across the table from him in the empty Beaver Club.

Alexander swallowed his pride and asked, "What of Hudson's Bay's exploration, the one Marcel was heading? What became of that?"

"A failure," Coombs answered without hesitation. Alexander's heart leapt. "Like you, he spent half a year in the wilderness and came up with nothing. Nothing except a great lake of salt water, that is. Who would have believed a lake would hold salt water?" Coombs mused, "Kind of defies nature, and so big a lake too."

"A lake of salt water?" Alexander was no less astonished than anyone else when they first heard of it. "They were sure it was a lake?"

Coombs nodded. "They walked around it, all around it, Marcel and his gelding partner. You must be the only person in Montreal who's not heard about it."

Alexander had heard little in the past three weeks, as he explained to Coombs. A fire had gutted Chubb's house in their absence, and when he hadn't been trying to see McGill, he'd been helping Chubb and Louisa restore their home. Chubb swore that the fire had been set by Louisa's cousin's husband who could no longer bear his new wife's ugliness.

"Then you don't know the big news!" exclaimed Coombs. "The very big news."

"Someone's crossed?"

"Can you think of nothing else? That's not what most people have on their minds, you know. The news is, Dentere has died. Just like that." Coombs snapped his rawboned fingers. "His old pumper stopped."

"Papa Louis is dead?" Alexander couldn't digest the fact. "When?" Bewildered, he shook his head. He'd lost the first man, the only man who'd truly believed in him, had faith in him. Grief routed any anger he still felt toward Papa Louis.

"They're burying him today. Right now, I think. Why do you think the place is so empty?" Coombs gestured with a sweep of his arm at the room. "Everybody who's anybody is at the funeral."

The morning seemed more bitterly cold than it had the hour before when, full of resolve, Alexander had walked up to the heavy oak doors of the Beaver Club. He searched the pockets of his greatcoat for his gloves. In vain he searched, then frantically, as if a lost pair of gloves was the source of his overwhelming grief. In a blind rush he'd run down the empty corridor, down the wide marble steps of the club. He'd left Coombs at the table. He couldn't remember paying the bill. And Papa Louis was dead. He headed down the wintry city street. Abruptly he stopped, turned, collided with a huge woman bundled in woolen cloth who offered him a glare and a curse. Alexander rushed on.

He had to get to the cemetery. His mentor was dead, and now he would never be able to right the wrongs Papa Louis had accused him of that catastrophic Christmas night, never be able to stand triumphantly in front of the man whose initial faith in him had helped him find the passage to the West. Alexander stormed down another block before he realized he couldn't possibly get to Holy Rosary Cemetery in time without a carriage. When he saw an empty wagon and team of horses tied off at a nearby post, he offered the driver a week's wages to drive him to the Catholic burial grounds.

He couldn't believe he hadn't heard of Papa Louis' death. Not a whisper of it had reached him or Chubb or Louisa or anyone in their crowded city precinct so far removed from the world of the Denteres and Montreal's elite society. Yet they were never distant from his mind. Marcel's name still aroused his anger and the very thought of Juliette produced heartbreak, misery and betrayal. The wagon pulled into the long, curving driveway of the Cemetery of the Holy Rosary.

In the distance Alexander could see the solemn crowd of mourners silhouetted in black against the pale, slate-blue sky as they stood silent in a stark white field of snow. He shivered in the open wagon as it bumped and rattled up the drive. Alarmed that he might disturb the burial rites, Alexander stopped the driver, got down off the wagon and asked him to depart as quietly as he could. Then he walked across the dry, crunchy snow.

The mourners were gathered near the Chartrel, the long, unadorned building that would hold the casket until the ground thawed enough for the grave to be dug. They bowed their heads as the monsignor of the parish led them in prayer. Alexander could hear his deep, moving voice as he approached. Then he heard the weeping. Alexander halted outside the ring of mourners. He pulled his greatcoat more tightly around him. His personal grief chilled him more than the cold.

Mariou saw him first. She raised her eyebrows and stared long at him, but she seemed neither surprised nor upset that he was there. Alexander didn't meet the steady gaze of the maid. Embarrassed and uncomfortable, indeed as intimidated by these French people as he had been the day he first arrived on the docks of St. Paul's Street, he lowered his eyes. When he glimpsed up, he saw Mariou nudge Joseph whose jaw dropped as he too fixed his eyes on the troubled Alexander.

The prayer ended. The congregation responded its "Amen" and Alexander studied the snow at his feet. The mourners began to shuffle past him. He couldn't look up. Then he had to. In front of him stood Mama Dentere, Marcel and an awe-struck Juliette.

She was more lovely than any memory of her. The black shawl that covered her head and delicate shoulders accented her flawless white skin. Though grief had paled her, the wintry chill had given her complexion a soft, pink glow. She was crying. The last time he'd seen her, she'd been crying, but then they'd been tears of passion, not of grief.

Alexander's confusion paralyzed him. He couldn't move the few yards to the family that once had been his. He stood frozen to the wintry ground and watched the mourners pass by Papa Louis' coffin, a casket of polished oak and brass topped with boughs of pine, where they made the sign of the cross or murmured some last prayer as they sprinkled the coffin with holy water before proceeding to the family to pay their respects. He watched, and when he no longer could bear his own indecision or the inquisitive glances of the mourners as they walked slowly past him, he too approached the coffin of Papa Dentere.

Remorse conquered every other emotion in him when Alexander dipped his fingers into the holy water. He gasped for breath and for control and a painful sob escaped him. His throat ached with sobs as he sprinkled the water over the coffin. Then hot tears blurred his vision, streamed down his face, and he wept for a man he loved.

Distraught, he turned away from the coffin and tried to find words to speak to Mama Dentere.

"Mama," he whispered hoarsely, "I cannot begin to tell you how much . . ." Unable to utter his sentiment, he clasped her hands tightly.

"Mama?" She looked at him kindly. "You still call me that? After all this time?" Their eyes met and they shared each other's long sorrow. "He loved you more than you know. He knew what you accomplished. He was proud."

Alexander buried his face in her hands and kissed them gently before turning to Marcel. "Marcel," he said stiffly, "I have . . . I'm sorry for your loss."

"Thank you for coming today, monsieur," muttered Alexander's ashen-faced rival.

To Juliette he could say nothing. At a total loss he stood before her, then took both her hands in his. He longed to embrace her, to console her. Hesitant, he bent forward and kissed her cheek. She trembled and still neither spoke. Reluctantly Alexander let go of her hands. He stepped back. He yearned for a word from her, then turned to go.

"Alexander," she halted him with a tremulous whisper. "Please, I must see you. Please meet me if you have any feelings left for me at all. Meet me tomorrow at the stables. Like always."

Like always. With that simple phrase she'd melted their years of separation into a mere yesterday. And in her eyes, brimming with new tears, Alexander read an urgent plea. He fought the excitement it aroused in him. "Of course, Juliette," he replied softly. "Of course, I'll be there if you wish."

As Alexander turned to leave, Marcel glared scornfully at him. Marcel's hatred worried him less than the final ordeal he had to face. Reynard, Juliette's husband, had not been standing with the family during the funeral ceremony. Alexander dreaded the humiliation he would feel, the nausea and the wretched sense of loss when he encountered his rival in love, this unlikely man who'd won Juliette. Alexander, however, was spared. He didn't even catch a glimpse of the gelding Reynard.

In a grove of cedar trees capped with snow, Alexander stopped to watch the funeral procession depart. Once the last of the mourners had paid their respects, the family was led to a magnificent carriage draped in black and pulled by a team of matched black mares. Slowly the carriage descended the drive. The snow muted the sound of the horses' hooves.

Silence and sadness again overwhelmed Alexander. His heart heavy, he walked back to Papa Louis' coffin. He said a final, private good-bye, then stepped back as the caretakers eased the coffin off the platform onto the sled that would carry it to the Chartrel. It was time to start his long walk homeward.

Someone tapped his shoulder. "Monsieur Alexander." It was Mariou, with Joseph. "You've come back to us." Because of her strange inflection, Alexander couldn't tell if she'd asked a question or made a statement.

"It's too bad it had to be on so sad a day," said Joseph.

"I only heard this morning," Alexander apologized.

"But you've been in Montreal for several weeks now!" Mariou exclaimed.

In no mood to elaborate, Alexander merely said, "I never heard. I never heard a thing. How did it happen?"

Suddenly, they told him, so suddenly no one could quite believe it had happened. They were preparing for a grand celebration for Marcel's birthday. As usual, Papa came back into the kitchen to taste all the food. One moment he was laughing and joking with Mariou, and the next he was lying on the kitchen floor. "Incredible," lamented Mariou. "His wonderful heart simply stopped."

When they reached a small, covered carriage, the three of them climbed inside to protect themselves from the cold.

"You knew I was back?" asked Alexander.

"We know everything about you. Mademoiselle insists," Joseph blurted.

"Joseph, you talk too much," admonished Mariou.

"Mademoiselle?" Alexander's heart skipped a beat. "Juliette you mean. But what has she to do with me?" Alexander fished for information. "She's a married woman."

"Married! But no, Monsieur Alexander," said Mariou plaintively. "No, she's not married. Is this what you've thought? Is this why you stayed away so long, why you didn't visit the last time you were in the city?"

"Juliette was to be married, but . . ." Joseph hesitated.

"But Papa stopped that," continued Mariou.

"No one told me this!"

"When Papa discovered Monsieur Reynard's eh, uh . . ." Mariou stammered, "his, ah, problem, he screamed for a whole week."

"More like a month," commented Joseph. "This is what killed him."

"Don't be silly, Joseph. It was so long ago." Turning to Alexander, she added, "He almost did to Marcel what he did to you."

"He banished him too?"

"Yes, but you took Papa so seriously, so true to his word . . ."

"Are you telling me I shouldn't have?"

"You knew him as well as anyone. He was always screaming. His anger came quick, but he didn't stay angry very long."

Alexander flushed. Again his own pride and stupidity had denied him an invaluable opportunity. His remorse over his lost mentor deepened. "Then Juliette is . . ."

"More in love with you than ever," Mariou finished the sentence for him. "This I know. And you? I saw you with her today. Surely your Indian can no longer mean so much to you, not so much as Juliette." Mariou's assumption, for all its truth, embarrassed Alexander. His life was an open book and it seemed everyone was reading it. "Don't do anything else silly, Monsieur Alexander," Mariou pressed him. "And you'll call on her? Please."

"She asked me to meet her tomorrow at the stables."

"And will you?" she asked hopefully.

"Yes, Mariou. Yes, I will."

For the twentieth time, Alexander paced the long courtyard in front of the Dentere stables. The snow was falling steadily. The relentless cold finally drove him inside the barn where he warmed himself at the fire barrel. He was getting soft, he told himself, as he recalled days, sometimes weeks, that he and Chubb had been deprived the comfort of a fire in the northwest wilderness. It felt good nonetheless and thoughts of Juliette warmed him.

He was stepping back into the courtyard for another round of pacing, when, suddenly, Juliette was no longer a thought. She was there, in his arms, and he was kissing her tender lips and drowning in the fragrance of her hair. "Juliette," he murmured. "My Juliette."

"Alexander, Alexander," she whispered her happiness and clung to him to dispel any disbelief in her wishes and dreams.

They separated unwillingly. Then with her hand in his they started slowly down their familiar paths. The snow blew round them, but nothing could chill the warmth they found in each other.

"I thought I had lost you, Juliette. I thought I had lost you forever."

"That could never be. Never could anyone take me away from you."

"You waited for me? You waited for today?"

"I always knew today would happen. I prayed, Alexander, not to make it happen, but for the patience I needed until it happened."

All the long months of anguish, false hope, despair and shattered dreams faded into a forgotten moment as they walked together in the snow. They talked of their lost years and they built new dreams, but mostly they rediscovered and shared their love.

"I have very little to offer you, my Juliette. I've returned to you a failure."

"A failure! In whose eyes? Not in Marcel's and certainly not in Papa's when he heard of your exploits.

How proud he was of you, Alexander! He pretended not to be, but I could tell. I knew. And you know what? He knew that I knew. Oh, I shall miss him.'' Juliette began to cry.

He held her tightly in his arms. This time Alexander could console and comfort her. ''I shall help you remember only the happy hours, my love.''

''I know, Alexander. I know. You are my strength.''

For a long while they walked in silence. Then Alexander told her, ''We must face the truth, my love. There's nothing left for me in Montreal. No one here will hire me for my work. No one.''

''That's because they don't know it as I do, as you do. They know only hearsay and rumor, the reports of some Indians who cannot even speak the language clearly. When they know what you've accomplished, what you've found, they'll listen to you. They'll seek you out.''

''How can I do this, my love? It's not in my power, it's impossible.''

''No, it's not.'' She looked at him with a smile that seemed to be hiding a wonderful and mysterious solution. ''You're forgetting your journals. Your marvelous, exciting journals. On every page I feel that I'm with you and that I'm going with you, freezing with you, discovering and seeing new worlds with you. When I read your words, I feel that I too am finding the paths that will open the great Northwest. I've tasted salt water and bathed in the Pacific.''

''But what would I do with them?'' asked Alexander in a small voice.

''Print them.''

''Print them? To sell? No,'' he objected, ''they

were written for you. My thoughts were of you when I wrote them.''

"They should be read by everyone. They could be, were they rewritten and put in another kind of order. We could work on them together.''

"That would take a lifetime, my Juliette,'' he said softly.

"I think that would be wonderful, Alexander. Wonderful.''

Their lifetime before them, they walked together back to the house.

Epilogue

It's been almost two hundred years since Alexander Mackenzie first sailed up the Slave River in search of a waterway to the Pacific Ocean. In that time he has become a legend.

His accomplishments greatly disappointed his early supporters as well as Alexander Mackenzie himself. When he returned to Montreal after his second attempt to find the Northwest Passage, he was close to despair. Time healed his wounded spirit and restored the courage of this man who found a waterway to the Pacific Ocean and the West. Time, too, has all but erased the names of his bitter rivals and inconstant financiers, while his own is now inscribed indelibly on every map of North America.

He called it the Disappointment River, but we know it today as the Mackenzie River. The land where he almost froze to death is named the Mackenzie Territory. There is also a Mackenzie Range and a Mackenzie Delta. Alexander Mackenzie has achieved the immortality of which he first dreamed, then fought against all odds to find.

But more important than any geographical names

are the spiritual courage and physical fortitude that Alexander Mackenzie has come to represent. These qualities enabled him to mark the first route across the North American continent. He was the first white man to cross the Rocky Mountains and the first to cross the Continental Divide.

Fame eluded him until he published his journals in 1801 under the title *Voyages From Montreal*. This book so greatly impressed Thomas Jefferson, that when he commissioned Lewis and Clark to blaze a trail across the American frontier, he made sure they had both read Mackenzie's remarkable book. Lewis and Clark did better than that. They carried a copy of it with them in their legendary expedition west.